What Cat Lost

A novel

One night can change your life forever

W • N • P

Write Now Press

CHELSEA WILSON THAYER

Contact the author:
www.chelseawilsonthayer.com

Editing by Victoria Gracia'a
Book cover and interior design and typesetting by Lisa Von De Linde of LisaVdesigns
Cover photo credit: Dewberry Photos and Design
Author headshot credit: Sarah Stover

ISBN: ISBN: 978-1-7355117-0-2
ebook ISBN: 978-1-7355117-1-9

Published by Write Now Press, LLC

Printed in the United States of America

First Edition, 2020

For Bryan,
my first and forever love.

She made broken look beautiful

and strong look invincible.

She walked with the Universe

on her shoulders and made it

look like a pair of wings.

—ARIANA DANCU

PROLOGUE

CATHLEEN RHODES STARED NUMBLY OUT THE WINDOW FROM HER FIRST-class seat on Delta flight 1705. Outside, the rain fell in torrents. Around her, passengers grumbled and groaned over the news that their flight would remain grounded at least another half hour; yet none of it could make her feel worse than she already did. She reached automatically into her bag to fish out her iPhone and escape into some music before remembering that it had been unceremoniously usurped by her parents, moments before they had practically thrown her out of their town car when they reached LaGuardia. Her iPhone, her Louis Vuitton, her social status, her life as she knew it had all been ripped away before what was supposed to be the best year of her life. Senior year at Spence in the most elite social circle on the Upper East Side. Perfection. How had it turned to ruin so quickly? Three months ago, she was on top of the world. Three months ago, she was considered the ideal daughter, the honor student, the Ivy League shoe-in. Three months ago, it all changed. Landon was gone. Cat knew that night had been the catalyst for the nightmare she had been living as of late. If only she could escape, somehow. If only she could leap from the plane just as it started to climb. She chuckled, drawing a sideways glance from the polished businessman who sat beside her. She wasn't brave enough to choose death (or cowardly enough, depending on how you looked at it.) She'd found that out the hard way, several weeks prior. Instead, she decided to let some much-needed sleep take its toll. Closing her eyes, she leaned against the cool window. She couldn't help but think of Landon. She couldn't help but wonder if one small decision would have changed where she was today, where she was going ... everything.

CHAPTER ONE

MOST PEOPLE YOU ASK CAN TELL YOU THE MOMENT THEY MET THE person who was to become their best friend. They can recall where they were, what they were doing, and perhaps the more fashion savvy can even remember what they were wearing. Cathleen could tell you everything about the moment she met Landon Alexander Jennings III.

Four years old and trembling with anger from head to toe, Cathleen blinked rapidly to keep the tears from spilling over. Her hands were balled into fists straight by her sides, and her teeth were clenched as she watched her beloved Samantha doll being spun by her ponytail over the big boy's head like a helicopter. Cathleen had every American Girl doll, but Samantha was her favorite.

"Whoo, whoo, whoo! Prepare for blastoff," cried the young terrorist with glee. His face was plump and painted with a smirk only The Joker could rival while his eyes narrowed menacingly.

"Give. Her. Back," her voice threatened, though barely audible over the playground noise.

She came to Hippo playground nearly every day, and nearly every day she had managed to avoid him. Nearly every day, except today, of course.

Poopy Paul they called him behind his back. He was always there, as he only lived a few blocks north. He ran the place amongst the pre-k's. Never supervised, his older brother always brought him along, and then darted off to play with the 6th graders on the other side.

He began spinning wildly around the sandbox, kicking wet sand onto Cathleen's red toggle coat, navy wool tights, and brown leather Mary Janes. She was the spitting image of the Ralph Lauren Children's store on Madison Avenue, minus the fact that she was now covered in sand. She watched as Paul, howling with delight, sent Samantha flying into the air.

"No!" she shrieked, as she watched Samantha tumble towards the ground. Suddenly, as if out of nowhere, a hand caught her by the leg.

The boy was small, nowhere near the size of Poopy Paul, yet he had a confidence that seemed to radiate right out of him. His navy blazer was unbuttoned, and his tie loosened, as to enjoy some well-earned after-church frivolity; and, his honey blond locks curled haphazardly around his head as if to create a little golden halo. One would think he could have been a pint-sized angel if it weren't for the mischievous twinkle in his eye.

"I didn't know Poopy Paul played with dolls," his voice was unnaturally calm for a little David who was facing Goliath.

"It's not mine doofus! It's hers," Paul's fat little finger poked Cathleen in the chest.

Scared to look up, she focused all her attention on the Nike symbol on the side of Paul's worn out sneakers.

"Well then, maybe you should apologize and give it back to her," the air in his voice sounded as though he may as well be talking to a dog rather than a boy easily twice his size.

Paul's jaw clenched, "Why should I do that?"

"You do it, or I'll make you," her savior retorted.

Then, the young hero struck an odd karate-like position. He began to swing his arms and kick his legs, all the while emitting a roar that sounded like an odd combination of Tarzan and a bear. Cathleen bit her lip to hold in her laughter, though she supposed he would look kind of scary if it was directed at her. Paul began to back up. The boy didn't relent, he advanced on Paul making his noises even louder and his motions even more pronounced. He continued until Paul, tripping backwards over the edge of the sandbox, scampered to his feet and took off.

When Paul was assumedly a safe distance away from his assailant, he did an about-face and called, "You'll be sorry! I'm going to get my big brother and then you'll be very sorry!"

Having watched the whole ordeal as still as a statue, Cathleen let out her breath. She hadn't even realized she'd been holding it in for so long. She watched her attacker retreat and turned to thank her mysterious new friend. The sandbox was empty. He seemed to have vanished as quickly as he had appeared. A cry caught in her throat when she realized with terror that dear Samantha had vanished along with him.

"Hey! Over here!" She heard a cry, and turning, spotted them under the jungle gym.

Daintily, she skipped over to him, climbed through the bars, and seated herself cross-legged in front of him before holding out her arms for Samantha.

"Can I have her back now?" she blurted out. She hadn't meant for it to come out in such an ungrateful tone.

Frowning slightly, he handed her over. Taking the doll, Cathleen turned her over in her hands inspecting her for injury. She squeezed the doll tightly in her arms as though to make up for the rough treatment she'd endured.

"Thank you," she said at last. "Thank you soooooo much for saving Samantha."

"Samantha?" He inquired.

"Yes, that's her name," Cathleen's voice had gotten a bit haughty again.

"Okay," her rescuer replied. "But, what's *your* name?"

"Cathleen Rhodes," she said with a warm smile and extended her hand. "Pleased to meet you."

"I'm Landon. Landon Alexander Jennings III," he shook her hand with such vigor her little head wobbled.

"Oh! That sounds like an important name," Cathleen nodded, impressed.

"My dad says it will be someday," Landon replied, knowingly.

"What does that mean?" Cathleen tilted her head to the side with childish curiosity.

"I have no idea," Landon shrugged. Then, they began to giggle like old friends over an inside joke they'd shared for ages.

Any adult watching them would have been highly amused at the formality with which they addressed each other. Children who are reared with high society expectations grow accustomed to interacting with adults at such a young age that they often forget how to behave as children. Perhaps that is why Cathleen always found it somewhat difficult to play with the other children on the playground, until now. Landon was her match, her equal, and her new best friend.

"Do you think he'll come back with his brother?" Cathleen leaned forward with a whisper, casting a quick glance around the playground.

"Not if he knows what's good for him," Landon teased as he began to karate chop once more.

Cathleen erupted in a fit of giggles.

"But we should get to the lookout tower just in case he does," Landon added seriously.

"The lookout tower?" Cathleen questioned.

"Yeah. The top of the monkey bars, Cat." He took off running, with Cathleen scurrying to catch up.

"What did you call me?" Cathleen laughed as she hurried to catch him.

She reached the monkey bars as Landon seated himself on the top rung.

"I'm going to call you Cat. It's going to be what I call you starting — now," he announced decidedly.

"Cat. Cat," she let the word resonate in her mouth. It felt new. It fit her perfectly. "I think I like that." She nodded definitively. "Yes, you can call me Cat," smiling from ear to ear, she reached out her small hand as he extended his to pull her up.

She hesitated.

"What's wrong?" he asked.

"I'm not allowed to climb on top of the monkey bars. My mother says they're too high," Cat added sadly.

"How old are you?" Landon questioned.

"Four and a half," Cat replied.

"Well, I just turned five last month, so I'll protect you," Landon urged with certainty in his voice.

"Alright," Cat took his hand and after a moment's hesitation, she allowed him to help her climb through the top rung until they were both seated on top of the monkey bars.

Cat took a second to reposition her tortoise shell headband that held her windswept, caramel waves neatly in place as she looked around. She could see the entire playground from up here; and she noted, with some relief, that Poopy Paul was nowhere to be seen. She cupped her hands over her eyes and gazed around until she found her nanny, Corey, pushing her two-year old sister, Lilienne, on the swings. She was talking on her cell phone as she usually was. She had taken no notice of what had recently transpired and was showing no interest now, even though Cat was breaking one of the most important playground rules (according to her mother): no climbing on top of the monkey bars.

Well, ha, thought Cat sneakily. No one could stop her now. Landon stood up and walked carefully across the monkey bars, balancing each foot on the bar before stepping to the next one. Cat stood up to follow suit. She must have stood too quickly though, because in the same instant that she stood, she also found herself falling to the ground. Reaching both hands above her to break the fall, she heard a sickening "crack" and felt a severe pain shoot through her left arm as it cushioned her fall. Cat closed her eyes for a minute, maybe two, maybe five, she wasn't sure; but when she opened her eyes, she was staring into Landon's and she knew everything would be alright.

"It's a good thing you're a cat. It means you have nine lives," he smiled and brushed her hair out of her eyes as other faces crowded into her view, "I think you have eight left now."

Landon's nanny, a big lady with a warm Jamaican accent, went to get some ice for her arm. Corey was talking with her parents on the phone, who were sending a car to pick them up and take her to the ER for x-rays. Lili held Samantha for her and Landon held her right hand and patted it reassuringly. It was the first time in her life Cat would have the excuse, "Well, Landon did it first," but it wouldn't be the last.

Over the next 13 years, their friendship would grow from being playground pals with occasional playdates, to inseparable friends--best friends. Landon would use the line about her nine lives on several other occasions. Once, when they were eight, Landon decided it would be a good idea to send his mother's Pomeranian, Moose, down the laundry chute with a

Barbie parachute on. Luckily, Moose was fine, thanks to the housekeeper who had called in sick, leaving piles of laundry yet to be washed at the bottom of the shoot. Unfortunately, Cat had slipped on the entry hall rug while chasing Landon out the door in their escape and had received a concussion. Then, there was the time they decided to ride their scooters from Hippo Park down to Chelsea Piers to the skating rink one winter. Cat's parents grounded her for a month for that little stunt. Though she had insisted, as always, it was at Landon's bidding. They had entered kindergarten at Cathedral together the fall after their initial meeting, and even though they had parted ways their freshman year of high school, they still met for breakfast each morning at Eli's and did homework together in the evenings. When Cat entered Ninth grade at Spence and Landon at Allen-Stevenson, their parents thought they might fall out of touch, making their lives a little less fraught with worry about what shenanigans the two might get into. If only that had been the case.

CHAPTER TWO

CAT BLINKED AS THE LIGHTS OF THE CITY TWINKLED BELOW, THE SKY was a dull gray on the eastern horizon. She hadn't even realized her eyes had been open. She blinked hard in an effort to break the trance. Her eyelids were so dry they moved as though they were painfully glued open. I shouldn't even be awake yet, she thought with chagrin. They had finally taken off, though she had been completely unaware. She had hoped that she would be able to sleep and forget the many problems that vexed her, but her thoughts seemed to turn to Landon. Memories. Happy memories, but sad in light of what had happened. With a sigh, she reached into her bag for the book her mother had handed her at the airport.

"Your summer reading for Watauga High," she had said sourly. "You had better get started on the plane since you begin classes next month."

Certainly, reading would turn her mind elsewhere. Cat stared at the cover of the book. Public school. She had never attended one, nor did she want to. Jack London's "Call of the Wild" looked blankly up at her. The snowy scene painted across the cover only served as another portal to take her mind elsewhere: back to Landon. It reminded her of the last "life" she lost with Landon. It had been this past January. Only six months ago. She squeezed her eyes shut. Tears wouldn't come, but the memories persisted.

Cat grabbed her Burberry jacket from the coat rack in the foyer.

"Maria," she called up the winding staircase.

The young housekeeper's head appeared above the railing.

"Yes, Miss Cathleen?" her heavy Puerto Rican accent marred with disdain over having to address this privileged teenager as Miss.

"I'm stepping out to meet Landon. Please let my parents know. They should be getting back from Nice Matin in half an hour or so. Thank you! I won't be long," she called behind her, letting the door slam before she added, "I think."

Buttoning her coat as she skipped down the steps of their townhouse on 84th between Columbus and Central Park West, she glanced at the text she had received from Landon not even five minutes before, "Water fountain — 10 min." She was accustomed to receiving texts from him, requests to meet to discuss the latest bits of gossip (Cathleen mainly), or to divulge the specifics of the latest prank that was pulled (always Landon). But rarely did these requests happen later at night, especially on a night when she had been with him until two hours ago.

He had proofread her report on *Anna Karenina*, and as he always did, he left her paper bleeding red when he finished. Cat was great when it came to writing content, but terrible when it came to being grammatically correct. Time and time again, Landon had badgered her over learning how to write properly, minus the comma splices and extra semicolons that always came with her work. And, time and time again, she reminded him that she had no need of being grammatically correct when she had him.

That had only been at eight o'clock. She shuddered away the

thought that something terrible had happened. What could possibly have gone wrong in the two hours since she had left? Mentally, she reviewed their time together: no new news, all was well at school, and his parents would be pleased to know he was now passing physics (thanks to Landon's superior negotiation skills).

He could sweet talk his way out of anything. He could walk nude through Times Square and not be charged with indecent exposure; he was so smooth. Cat had witnessed such skills on numerous occasions. She could be stammering and making a fool of herself until Landon would swoop in and save the day. No, nothing had been awry.

As she left his house, she had noted his mother had made his favorite meal: stuffed pork roast with fig gravy, roasted asparagus, garlic rolls, and cherries jubilee for dessert. This was of course a rarity, since his mother seldom cooked their meals. His father would soon be home for a family meal, Landon had happily confirmed — they had so few of them. Mr. Jennings returned from his recent business trip to Tokyo just as she was leaving. Landon looked so happy, as he saw her to the door and reminded her of their morning breakfast plans. As if she could forget, they'd been going to Eli's every morning for breakfast since they started Ninth grade. She always got her usual: egg white omelet, wheat toast (no butter), and o.j.. Landon got something different every time. After breakfast, they would ride together across 79th to the Upper East Side, where their car would drop her off at Spence before taking Landon down to Allen-Stevenson.

Maybe he wanted to meet to tell her, after all this time, that he'd rather eat somewhere else, Cat thought sarcastically.

"No time for jokes, Cat," she said aloud.

No, something was most certainly wrong. He had wanted to meet at the water fountain. He didn't need to specify which water fountain he meant. They always met at the one on the southwest side of the reservoir when Landon wanted to walk and talk. They only walked and talked when one of them had something particularly serious to discuss.

The snow crunched under her feet as she walked up the road. She reached the gravel path that broke off to the right and led to the reservoir. An icy gust of wind blew her hair across her face and she reached automatically for the elastic band she kept ready around her wrist to pull it into a messy bun. The wind swirled around her again biting through her coat.

Why on earth didn't I grab my winter coat? Or a scarf at the very least, she wondered, inwardly cursing herself at her own thoughtlessness. It had to be 20 degrees by now, maybe less. She pulled her cashmere gloves out of her Louis and pulled them on, thankful she always had a pair on hand. A true New Yorker, always prepared against the elements.

He was standing with his back to her when she walked up, hands in the pockets of his army green wool military-style jacket. He smartly had his scarf wrapped tightly around him and a gray knit skullcap pulled down over his ears, hiding his always-messy golden curls.

She stopped a few feet away from him. She didn't call his name. She didn't clear her throat or do any of the usual things one does to announce themselves. She knew that he knew she was there.

He turned, revealing red eyes, tight firm lips, and a lump in his throat. He'd been crying.

In all the years she had known him, Cat had only seen Landon cry once. It was when they were seven, and he had forced her to rent *Godzilla vs. Mothra* at Blockbuster when she had begged him to watch *Beauty and the Beast* for the 10,000th time. At the end of the movie, when Mothra died, the utterly devastated Landon had broken down in sobs. They joked about it often, but it had remained, until this moment, the only time she'd seen him cry.

She needn't run to him. He wouldn't want to be coddled. She simply stepped to his side, took his hand, and they began to walk. She looked so petite beside his lanky 6' 4" frame, even though she was 5' 6" herself. She held his hand tightly as they walked together.

Cat didn't mind the darkness. The lights of the city and the street lamps around the reservoir provided ample light.

They walked.

Once around the reservoir.

Twice.

They were beginning to walk around a third time when he finally spoke. It was a good thing too, seeing as how the panic and worry was about to rip Cat to pieces on the inside.

"Divorce," he said quietly.

Cat stared at him. So many parents they knew had gotten divorced. It never seemed like a big deal. Now, it seemed like a catastrophe.

"Lan-," she began.

"He's screwing his secretary," he practically shouted, "SCREW-ING his secretary!" he repeated at the top of his lungs to emphasize his anger. The pigeons heard him loud and clear as they flew from their cozy perches in the branches above and from the nearby stone building at the south end of the reservoir where they stood.

He sat quickly on the stone bench adjacent to the building and buried his head in his hands. Cat trembled, either from the cold or the sight of her best friend in agony, she wasn't sure.

The temperature was dropping fast, and with as much trouble as she and Landon had gotten into in the past, they had never been in Central Park so late before on their own. Her teeth started to chatter as she sat beside him and laid her head on his shoulder. Landon sat upright; unwinding the scarf from his neck, he wrapped it around hers.

"Leave it to you to come out at night in the middle of January in nothing but James Jeans and a Burberry coat," and with that, he kissed her forehead in a brotherly fashion and gave a sad smile.

Cat pursed her lips and crinkled her nose at him, "Thanks."

Now that she thought about it, sitting down on a cold stone bench was not very bright — her backside had gone numb in a matter of minutes. They sat there in silence, hand in hand.

Anyone who saw them would have pegged them as young lovers. The lights, the mist on the water, the snow piled to the side--it would have provided the perfect romantic backdrop. But it wasn't like that between them. Never had been, never would be. He was her protector and she was his guiding light.

The thought of talking to Landon about romance, or worse, about what they had done with the opposite sex made her uneasy. It would be like talking to a brother. Uncomfortable. She knew he was more experienced than her in that area, but she had no desire to know the details. Of course, other than a few kisses in truth or dare, she didn't have much to tell.

They sat that way, hand in hand, until she heard a distant church bell tolling the midnight hour. The knowledge that she would be grounded the second she walked in the door didn't put her in any hurry to get up. If it wasn't for the fact that she was freezing her butt off, she would have been content to sit with him all night. Instead, she focused on the visible breath she created from each exhale. Tears were steady on Landon's cheeks and she fought the urge to wipe them away with her sleeve. What if they froze? Could tears do that? Oh, the thoughts that creep into our minds when it's 25 degrees on a stone bench in Central Park.

Landon turned to look at her, bringing her mind back to the moment. He wiped his eyes and stood up, pulling her up firmly and draping his arm easily over her shoulders.

"I guess you'll only have three lives left after your parents get through with you tonight," he said with a wink.

"Two, Landon. Two lives left," Cat responded resolutely.

"Two? Damn. I guess that means we'll have to start being careful."

She could hear his voice echoing in her head as the memory faded away. She was still staring at the cover of the book. If the memory was gone, then why was she suddenly so cold? Seriously, freezing cold. She snapped back to reality to realize the man beside her had just inadvertently tossed the ice in his cup into her lap. He was already stringing together a handful of apologies and brushing the ice off of her with his napkin before she reacted. Taking the napkin from him with a polite smile, she began to dry the water off of her pants.

"It's fine. Don't worry about it," she mumbled.

"Oh, I see you go to Spence," the man remarked, obviously trying to be overly pleasant towards her after the ice accident.

"Your class ring," he added, after Cat gave him what must have been a look of sheer confusion.

"Oh, hmm," Cat replied, glancing at her ring and then turning her attention back to cleaning up her pants, though there was no more she could do.

"Fantastic school," the man continued, "My daughter went there. You probably wouldn't know her, she graduated six years ago. Abigail Wyatt."

Cat shrugged her shoulders and shook her head. She had heard the name, but didn't want this conversation to last any longer than it had to. She wasn't in the mood for any small talk at the moment, particularly any that involved Spence.

"She's at Harvard Law now," he continued proudly, "Of course, you'll be able to get in anywhere with a diploma from Spence."

He shot her a winning smile as though this news was new to her or should make her feel better. It only made her nauseous.

"So I hear," she replied, trying with all her might to keep her voice from shaking, as she turned her attention to her novel, pretending to be completely engrossed.

This stranger's comment would serve as the first reminder that she was no longer a part of her old world. That somewhere in the last few months, her life had changed its course. Perhaps only for a little while, perhaps forever.

CHAPTER THREE

"MISS, EXCUSE ME, MISS," THE FLIGHT ATTENDANT LEANED IN TO Cat, waking her from a deep, dreamless sleep. "You need to raise your seat up now. We'll be landing soon."

The morning sun shone all too brightly as Cat opened the window shade and moved her seat into the upright position. Rubbing her eyes with her cardigan, she noticed the book in her lap was still open to page two. She had read and reread the first two pages probably a dozen times and still wouldn't be able to tell anyone what it said.

"The time in Charlotte is 8:35 am, and it is currently 67 degrees, a high of 84 today and sunny. Looks like a perfect day," the voice of the captain said brightly, as they began their descent into Charlotte-Douglas International Airport.

"Perfect," she muttered sarcastically under her breath.

Is there ever the "perfect" day to move from Eden into exile? She had a bitter taste in her mouth. Even though her recent living situation with her parents was a self-proclaimed hell as of late, she could only imagine that this relocation would just be a new level of purgatory.

The plane took a sharp turn down and to the right, momentarily positioning itself over Lake Norman and giving Cat a view of people in boats and watercrafts, out early to enjoy the beginning of a beautiful weekend. Little white lines shone dazzlingly off the lake where speedboats and jet skis had already begun to weave their way across the water. Cat could only spot a couple of them, but she knew by lunchtime the waters would be teeming.

The sky was a cheerful robin's egg blue — clear, fresh, and full of promise. It made Cat positively nauseous under the circumstances. The scene could not have been more different than when she sat on the runway at 6:10 that morning. If only the storm in her life could be transformed as quickly as the weather. Angrily, she pulled the shade back down, blocking the view from the ice-spiller beside her who had been craning his neck to get a view of the lake. A momentary pang of guilt clutched around her heart. She closed her eyes and refused to feel sorry for anyone; well, anyone other than herself.

Smoothly, the plane glided onto the runway, approached the gate, and came to a halt. There was no denying it now. She was in North Carolina. Her grandmother would be waiting at baggage claim to take her to her new home in Boone. Her knees didn't allow her to move. She sat there fiddling with her belongings, much longer than necessary, until she was the only passenger left on board. Her eyes began to burn as she pushed herself up.

No, don't cry, her mind willed; you will not be a cry baby, Cat. Don't you dare let go now.

She had held her composure this long. She knew once she started, it would be impossible to stop. Not to mention how embarrassing it would be to fall to pieces in the middle of the airport.

Her legs felt like lead as she dragged them forward, off the plane, and towards baggage claim. One quick stop at the restroom before her reunion with Mimi she decided quickly, as she passed the door — anything to postpone the inevitable.

Entering, she was caught off guard by her reflection in the mirror. She nearly didn't recognize herself. Walking towards her reflection, she touched her own face — it felt like some scene from a movie when the character simply can't believe what they're seeing. Only, Cat could completely believe it.

"Ugh," she groaned audibly as she tried to vigorously rub some color into her pallid cheeks.

Her unkempt waves had come half-way down during the flight. She pulled her hair down and expertly whipped it up once more into a fashionably messy bun. She unwrapped her thin cashmere cardigan from over her shoulders and peeled it off to splash some water on her bare arms. Then, she bent over the sink to rinse her face. Drying it with a paper towel, she stepped back for inspection. No makeup — though her clear complexion didn't make it necessary. She could live without that. The dark circles under her eyes bore witness to the many sleepless nights she had been experiencing lately. Her gray tank hung loosely off her shoulders. Only now did she notice how terribly thin she'd allowed herself to become in the last few months. Echoing somewhere in the distant corner of her mind, she heard the shrill voice of her mother. Those premonitions about letting what had happened to Landon affect her eating habits invaded her thoughts. Evasively, she covered herself back up with the cardigan. The skinny jeans and Tory Burch flats finished the look she had had minutes to throw together this morning. If only she'd been granted the time to shower. She still smelled like the Greenwich Avenue dive bar she'd been dragged out of at three a.m. by her father. How utterly embarrassing! Touching a dangling curl to her nose, she inhaled the scent of cigarette smoke and wrinkled her nose.

Convinced there was nothing more to be done, she finished up in the restroom before resuming her march toward fate: Mimi.

Her mom's mother, Martha Wilson, or Mimi as she was known

by her two granddaughters, was a farmer through and through. She still ran the family Christmas tree farm on her own, even though Pop had passed away four years prior. Only 65 years old, she looked young for her age, despite the lines on her face from years of hard work in the sun. She had been 18 when she had Cat's mother, only a year older than Cat was now. Cat couldn't even begin to imagine having a child so young. They saw her for Thanksgiving each year, but rarely on any other occasion. Mimi's relationship with her daughter had been strained since Darcie's move to New York City. After she chose to remain in New York City and raise her daughters there, the strain gave way to an almost complete but not eternal dissolving of their relationship. It had begun to mend over the last few years.

Cat scanned the crowd for her as she descended the escalator into baggage claim. She saw happy reunions happening all around her, she wondered how she would be received. She loved Mimi, of course, but they had never spent more than a few days together at a time. Living with her for a year was sure to be interesting. She hadn't seen her in nearly two years since she had gone with Landon's family on their Thanksgiving ski trip to Banff the year before. Finally, she spotted her standing towards the back; raising her hand halfway, she gave a small wave and tried her best to smile. Her greeting was reciprocated with more enthusiasm, as Mimi hurried forward with arms open wide.

"I already have your bag, Catie-bug," she informed, "Now, let me look at you." She pushed away from her embrace, and examined Cat's haphazard appearance.

Mimi, Pop, and Lili had been the only people to ever call her Catie. She had liked it as a child, but now it sounded just that — childish.

Mimi clucked her tongue as she looked Cat over, making her

feel entirely self-conscious. Her eyes scanned Cat's waif-like figure, but stopped when they met her eyes. It's as though she could see the weight of Cat's sorrow in them. She brushed a strand of hair from her granddaughter's face and put her arm around her thin shoulders.

"Let's get you home," she said finally.

"Mimi," Cat wasn't sure what to say. Should she tell her she had no desire whatsoever to live in the mountains, go to public school, or help out on the farm? How much had her mother told Mimi, she wondered? Did she know about Landon? Cat hadn't thought to ask her mother any of these questions when she had told her this morning that they were sending her to North Carolina. No, after hearing *that* news, Cat had a few other thoughts to express to her parents.

"Thank you for coming to get me," she concluded. Politeness was the best route she decided. Mimi would probably reveal what she knew in due time.

"Of course," she smiled, leading her outside towards the terminal parking lot.

"I don't know what mom told you," Cat began, she needed to face some facts rather than pretend that she was only here on vacation, or of her own free will.

"Catie," her grandmother's tone turned suddenly serious, "I don't know what's been going on in New York City. I only know that the things your mother said you'd gotten into don't sound a bit like the Catie I know. She told me what happened ... about your friend."

"Landon," Cat interrupted.

"Yes, Landon," Mimi continued, "I'm sorry. It's terrible what happened, Catie. It's just awful. This time away will be good for you. You need to find yourself again, sugar. Sometimes, when tragedy happens, we let it take over our lives and we get lost along the way."

Cat was beginning to feel queasy. For someone she had spent so little time with, how on earth could Mimi see her so clearly?

"Your mother said you've been acting out," Mimi went on, "No, no. I told her you were just reacting." She lifted her suitcase with surprising strength and tossed it into the back of the farm truck. The suitcase slammed against an assortment of tools, rusty chains, scraps of metal, and whatever else already cluttered the bed of the pick-up.

"Holy shit … good thing there's nothing breakable in there," Cat muttered under her breath.

"What's that?"

"Remind me not to cross you, Mimi … seriously, do you lift?" Cat attempted a lighthearted joke. No one was fooled.

Mimi's raised eyebrow spoke volumes as she reached to unlock the passenger's side door. Catie wasn't sure how to respond to this psychoanalysis, or if she was even expected to. Instead, she remained silent but attentive as she climbed into the old Dodge Ram pickup. Her grandmother had Christmas tree tagging ribbon strewn across the dashboard and the pine needles of Frasier Firs littered the floorboards. It smelled of Christmas and pine sap. Cat knew enough about the Christmas tree business to know that each color of ribbon denoted a specific height range for the trees; so, when it came time to cut, it was easy to see exactly how many 6'–7' trees they had, and so on. But other than that, Cat was clueless. She wondered again how much she would be expected to help on the farm.

Oh, please God, please, don't make me work in Christmas trees. Isn't this exile punishment enough?

"I feel like I need to say this," Mimi's voice focused Cat's attention once more, "The things you were getting away with in New York won't cut it here. Not that you'll have time for any of that tomfoolery. Now, I'm not trying to be hard on you, Catie, but your parents specifically expressed that I am to keep you busy. So, between school and helping me on the farm, I think you'll have enough to keep your mind off of ... things."

"Mimi, I don't know how much help I'll be," Cat tried this approach, "I don't know anything, at ALL, about Christmas trees."

"You'll learn," Mimi patted her hand. Though her response was short and sweet, the tone in her voice told Cat that there was no room for discussion on the matter. She would be helping on the farm, like it or not.

Cat leaned her head against the window as the truck merged onto 321 North. Maybe she would rest her eyes for a minute or two. She let the heat of the sun warm her cheeks. Maybe Mimi was right, maybe working on a farm would keep her mind off of Landon. Maybe, just maybe.

Cat stood outside of Allen-Stevenson, shifting her feet from one foot to the other. He should be getting out any minute now. And when he did, he would have nowhere to run to, he would have to face her. Landon hadn't returned Cat's calls or text messages in over a week, and when he stood her up for their dinner date last night, it had been the last straw.

It had been three months since he'd given her the news of his parent's divorce, and they'd seen each other less and less. At first, Cat chalked it all up to him needing some alone time to deal with things. But lately she'd begun to suspect something a little more sinister going on in her best friend's life. A week and a half ago she had finally confronted him about her suspicions. Since that night, they hadn't spoken.

They'd ordered pizza at Patsy's on the Upper East Side, the food had arrived, and they were each eating in silence — a phenomenon that had been occurring all too often lately. Landon's cell phone beeped. Cat watched him glance at the text, delete it, and continue with his food. Mysterious texts were coming more and more these days, with little or no explanation from Landon. She thought at first perhaps it was a girl; however, he'd laugh off that idea. She was pretty certain about what it was now, and was just deciding how best to broach the subject when Landon spoke.

"I just remembered," he began nonchalantly, "I have a paper to finish by tomorrow, so I don't think I'll be able to catch a movie after this."

"Hmm," Cat replied with a mouthful of vegetarian pizza, "That's alright," she lied. "We're still on for dinner next Saturday, right? You're still my date for my International Baccalaureate dinner," she reminded him.

"Oh, yeah," he reassured her. Though his tone told her he had completely forgotten.

He quickly jotted it into his Blackberry calendar and the rest of dinner continued as normal.

Cat knew what she had to do. She knew the text he'd received was the reason he wasn't coming to the movie with her, and not some suddenly remembered term paper. She decided, in that moment, that she wasn't going to ask him about her suspicions. No, that would only force him into another lie. She would follow him, and when she saw it for herself, she would confront him. He couldn't lie to her then.

Never in her life had Landon kept something from her. They

shared practically everything with each other. This secret he was keeping was surely something Cat would disapprove of. That wasn't a good sign.

She let him walk her to the theater afterwards. He gave her a quick hug goodbye, and she slipped inside under the pretense of purchasing her ticket. She waited for just a moment before she peered back out the door. When he rounded the corner, she was after him. She had no idea how to follow someone; she had never done it before, let alone to have to follow her best friend. How far behind him should she keep? Should she stay close to the side or try to hide behind the trees that lined the street? She decided walking like a normal human being would be best. Trying to appear all spy-like and slink in the shadows would inevitably make her more conspicuous. She wasn't very good at being covert.

When he started down the stairs to get on the 6 train, she frowned. This was going to be more difficult than she thought. In an instant, she made up her mind; this was her best friend and no matter what he had gotten himself into, he clearly needed her help to get him out of it. She skipped down the stairs and went through the turnstile, all the while hoping he wouldn't look back over his shoulder and see her.

She knew she couldn't get into the same subway car, but she needed to be in the car beside him to see where he got off. This was harder than she thought. She stood behind the metal beam about 20 feet away, hoping that he didn't already know she was there. When the train approached, she waited for him to get on first, then she slipped into the next car just before the door closed.

She exhaled with relief. So far, her mission was a success. But where was he going? The train made its way downtown, past midtown, past the village, past Spring Street. At Delancey, she saw him step off; she hesitated a second, then stepped off to follow.

The lower East side was once considered a generally gritty neighborhood, but it had become very hip in the restaurant scene in the last ten years. Cat knew her parents frequented Stanton Social with friends, or 'inoteca on their dates nights, but she had never spent much time down here herself.

She followed him further and further through a maze of small side streets until they were well away from any trendy restaurants or nightclubs. They were somewhere they truly didn't belong and a sixteen-year-old with any sense would stay clear of. Trash littered the sidewalk and Cat cautiously stepped through it. Her left sandal slipped on some brown sludge leaking from a torn trash bag. The smell of old garbage made her queasy; if any of the mess got onto her feet, she feared she might puke. She had taken so much time to carefully step through the refuse that she had fallen further behind Landon. She would have to pick up the pace so as not to lose sight of him. She saw him round a corner to what appeared to be another smaller alleyway. As she crept up to the corner to cautiously peek her head around, she felt a large hand on her shoulder. Unable to stop herself, she shrieked and looked up to see two intimidating men staring at her far too intently to have been thinking any benevolent thoughts.

"Hey, Mami," came the Puerto Rican accent of the one who still had a firm grip on her shoulder, "You look lost. I think we can help you find your way, no?"

The looks that passed between them terrified Cat far more than the words they spoke. She wished with all her might she was wearing something more than the short sundress she had on. She pulled her cardigan together across her chest.

"Yeah, honey, why don't you let us help you out? I could take you places you have never been before," the other added, his

Jersey brogue barely discernible under his slurred speech.

The first, with his hand still firmly planted on her shoulder, pushed her against the wall. She opened her mouth to scream but no sound came. A million thoughts ran through her head at once. She remembered the things to do if ever attacked: scream "fire," kick them in the groin, hit the base of your palm against their nose as hard as possible, or gouge their eyes. Mentally, she ran over the list, but remained thoroughly frozen in fear. She knew it had only been a few seconds since they had advanced on her, but it seemed like forever.

"Nice dress," the Jersey voice added. He was close, too close. She could smell the alcohol on his breath. His hand touched the hem of her dress; she felt his filthy fingers move to her thigh. She closed her eyes, her hands in fists, immobile by her sides.

"Please," she was able to get out through her clenched teeth.

"Mami, it's all good," the other smiled, advancing.

"She's with me," it was the voice of her savior that made the men release her from their grasp.

Cat's eyes flickered open, but she could not make them meet Landon's. She was afraid of what she might see there.

"Sure man, sure. You get what you came for? Frosty makes a good deal, right?" The second man slurred his words together at the end, "You get a taste bag?"

Landon nodded, not looking at Cat.

"We didn't know she was with you. Sorry, Mami," he added, "I don't harass customers."

Her assailants backed away and continued up the alley and disappeared behind the door Landon had just come out of. Her heart was pounding so loudly she was certain Landon could hear. Is this what a heart attack feels like? She rubbed her left arm just to be sure there weren't any shooting pains. Physically, she seemed to be alright. But she couldn't stop shaking. They stood in silence; neither one able to meet the other's eyes, both ashamed of what they had done.

Landon finally broke the stillness by placing both hands firmly on her shaking shoulders, "Let's get out of here."

Cat nodded. She was still trembling as he led her out of the alley, down a few side streets, until they reached a main avenue.

There was only silence and the reassuring, super-glue grip on her hand until they were safely in a cab and headed uptown.

"Did they … hurt you?" Landon's voice quietly inquired. It was full of remorse.

"No, I'm fine," came Cat's terse reply.

"Cat, I'm sorry," she knew he wasn't just apologizing for what happened with the men.

"Why, Landon? Why in the hell are you doing this to yourself?" she began to cry.

His arms wrapped around her automatically. The cabby's eyes flickered back at them in the rearview mirror for a brief second, it went unnoticed.

"You scared the shit out of me back there, Cat. You shouldn't have followed me. Don't you know what could've happened to you if I hadn't come out when I did?"

She sobbed harder.

"I don't do this often, I swear," he attempted to assure her. "It's just, everything that's happened with my parents, I need to escape every now and then, you know. Take the edge off a bit. I know that's no excuse."

"Damn right, that's no excuse!" she cut him off. Her hand slapped across his cheek before she even realized what it had done. They both sat stunned for a moment. Cat grabbed the hand that had lashed out and held it tightly as though it didn't belong to her. How could she hurt the person she cared about most? What had come over her?

"I — I," Landon stammered, making her feel 10,000 times worse than she already did. "I just tried it the first time a few months ago at one of Samuel's parties. I really hardly ever do it. This is for his party in a couple of weeks, it's not all for me," he said defensively, holding up the bag of coke. The cabby cleared his throat. Landon glanced at the cabby and quickly hid it back in his backpack.

"This is not you, Landon. This 'method' of escaping. It's stupid. And you're not stupid."

His eyes avoided hers. Cat grabbed his face with both of her hands, rubbing the red lines that remained, and stared into the eyes she knew as well as her own.

"Stop, I'm begging you. Stop."

The cab approached Cat's townhouse.

"I will, Cat. I'm sorry. I really will," his voice sounded sincere.

She nodded and leaned over to kiss him on the forehead as she got out of the car.

That had been the last time she'd heard from him. But at least now she knew the truth. At least now she knew what he'd been hiding the last few months. Time to find out if he's kept his word. The fact that he hadn't called her back or attended her dinner with her as promised had her severely worried.

The boys started filing out of the building, ties were coming undone left and right, as blue blazers were thrown over their shoulders. Any moment now she would see him. She stood on her tiptoes unnecessarily; with his height, she would easily be able to see him above the rest.

He froze for just a second when he saw her, before continuing towards her sheepishly.

"You skipped class," he said knowingly.

"Yep," she confirmed, "Otherwise, how was I going to be here right when you got out? Why weren't you at my dinner last night? You promised."

"Oh, shit. Look, Cat. I'm sorry," the honk of a horn interrupted them, and they both turned to see Landon's mother in the passenger seat of the town car waiting for him.

"What?" Cat began.

"Grounded," he replied, "From everything. No phone. Nothing. That's why I haven't called or emailed. She wouldn't even let me call you to cancel last night. The maid found the coke in my drawer and took it to her. She has been acting as my escort to and from school. I even flushed it to prove to her that it's not a big deal to me. I'm done."

Cat exhaled, "Well, since that's the reason for your absence I have to say I'm relieved."

"You're happy I'm grounded?"

"No, I'm happy you've come to your senses."

The horned blared absurdly once more.

"Hop in, Cat. We'll take you home," he escorted her to the black town car, "I still can't believe you skipped class to corner me."

He held the door open for her.

"I have to say Landon, I'm glad I did."

"Yeah, me too."

And with that, he slid into the seat beside her.

The horn honked, taking Cat swiftly from her memories, from NYC, and returning her to where she sat in an old gray Dodge Ram with a red farm truck license on the back. She looked around. Mimi pushed the accelerator to the floor to give the old truck enough speed to pass the tourists in front of them.

"Flor-idiots," she murmured. The term was not a polite one. Though, it was one often used by the locals to describe the summer tourists, many from Florida, who come up to escape the heat in exchange for cool mountain breezes and beautiful scenery. She had heard her grandma say it several times over the years. Cat didn't blame them; it was gorgeous here.

They began to climb the mountain that bordered Catawba County and Watauga County. The view was incredible. You could see miles and miles of hazy blue mountains giving way to rolling hills far in the distance. There was a time Cat thought of this place as the most beautiful in the world. Now, having traveled quite a bit, she knew for a fact there was no place lovelier than this. But, under the circumstances, she couldn't allow herself to enjoy it. She refused, turning her back from the window and the views, and instead, began to count dead stink bugs on the floor board. That was what she deserved now anyways — a stink bug counting existence.

They crossed through the quaint resort town of Blowing Rock; tourists walked from shop to shop, many enjoying an ice cream cone from Kilwins. It was a day worthy of ice cream and soaking in the sun. Maybe even a double scoop kind of day. The beauty of it only seemed to make Cat's suffering more pronounced. Here she was, being allowed to live on this gorgeous day, while Landon was ... no, she wouldn't think that. Tears started to burn behind her eyes. She pulled out her sunglasses and put them on. At least part of her could hide behind them.

"We'll be home in about thirty minutes," her grandmother said happily, drumming the steering wheel like some maniac drummer in a rock band, "Wooo wee! It's so darn pretty outside.

You can't ask for better weather than this."

She reached across Cat, while endeavoring to steer, and started rolling down the window.

"Mimi!" Cat yelped, certain this could only end by her running over a pedestrian — likely a small, adorable child, licking a double scoop of ice cream.

"I got it! Let me roll it down," Cat pushed Mimi's attention back to the road and vigorously rolled down the window. The July breeze swept into the truck. It was blissful. Ugh.

"I thought I would take you to dinner tonight. Would you like that, Catie?"

"Fine," Cat replied with as much enthusiasm as she could muster.

"There's Mellow Mushroom. I know how you like their pizza," Mimi judged her response, "Or there's always Outback, if you're in the mood for steak. Or there's a little vegetarian place called Angelica's you might like."

"That's fine. Anywhere is fine, Mimi," Cat cut in, before Mimi had time to suggest another place. Cat couldn't care less where they ate, and she doubted that Mimi really cared, either. She knew it was her way of showing her love and concern. And for her sake, Cat would pretend that it made a difference.

The old truck weaved through the curvy mountain roads. Cat realized, as her stomach lurched, that she had forgotten to take any Dramamine. Her mother always had some on hand when they came for visits. She was about to ask Mimi to pull over when the truck slowed and pulled onto the gravel drive. She leaned her head slightly out the window and let the breeze hit her squarely in the face. She drank in the coolness, letting it settle the rising waves of nausea.

She could see the white farmhouse in the distance. White

clapboard siding, two stories, stone chimneys protruding from either side, and a big wraparound porch with a porch swing. It could be a farmhouse in a picture book. She sighed a sigh of relief. It was in the moment that she let her guard down that the nausea she had been keeping at bay overcame her.

"Sto-," she began, as she vomited all over the dashboard and herself.

"Good gracious, Catie," her grandmother pulled the truck to a halt, about 100 feet or so from the house. "You should have told me you were feeling sick," reaching across Cat, she pulled napkins from the glove compartment and began wiping at her mess.

Mortified, Cat took the napkins from her and began wiping. "Mimi, I'm so sorry. I didn't think I was going to be sick. I — I'm so sorry. Let me clean it up. Really."

She kept shrugging off Mimi's attempts to assist her. Throwing up everywhere was bad enough; but having someone else clean it up would only make it worse.

"Let's get your stuff inside. You can wash up, and then you can clean the truck out," Mimi decided, getting out of the truck and grabbing Cat's bag from the back.

Annoyed with herself, Cat opened the door and hopped out. She was just brushing a few remaining chunks of vomit from her jeans when she looked up and saw him. The sun was behind him creating a perfect silhouette so she couldn't see his face. But she knew those curls, and the confident stride. Landon. And that was her last thought before she passed out cold on the grass, still wet with morning dew.

CHAPTER FOUR

CAT STOOD IN THE FRONT OF HER FULL-LENGTH MIRROR; THIS WAS maybe the seventh outfit she'd tried on so far. Examining herself carefully, she finally nodded. Yes, this one was perfect for the party. It was cut just right to be sexy while remaining classy at the same time. It was a navy halter dress she had gotten recently at BCBG Max Azria. The high ruffles around the collar offset the lower-than-she-would-usually-wear neckline. Its pleated skirt was crisp, polished, and cut well above the knee. It was perfect for her debut as one of the most popular rising seniors at Spence next year. And this party would be just the place to make her new title known. She was one of the Spence Seven. Before graduating each year, the Spence Seven, or the seven most popular girls in the senior class, carefully choose seven juniors to bestow the much-coveted title upon. Junior girls grew anxious in the spring, all wondering if they would become part of the Spence Seven. Cat hadn't even thought about it. Her thoughts had been consumed with Landon when she heard the news that she had been one of "the chosen ones". She had always thought it would be fabulous to be one of the queen bees and control the social calendar at her school, but who wouldn't? However, she had never made it a priority. Maybe that's why she'd received the honor. She had remained cool and collected, while other girls had fallen over themselves, running errands and doing deeds for the current elite. Cat turned once more in the mirror before grabbing her Louis and heading out the door. Her iPhone beeped.

It was a text from Landon. "RU ready? B there N 5."

She smiled, "CU soon," and sent her text as she hopped joyfully down the stairs.

Lili was at the bottom, pleading with her mother to attend the party as well.

"Mom," Lili's voice whined, "This is THE party! It's Samuel's last one of the school year and everyone who's anyone is going."

"Lili, you know Samuel Alden would NEVER let a freshman into his party. He doesn't even invite sophomores," Cat's voice reasoned with her.

"See Lili, listen to Cat," her mother said, patting a furious Lili on the head, as she ducked away, "You have finals to study for anyway."

"So does Cat!" Lili shrieked.

"But Cat was invited and her father and I are allowing her to go," the finality in her mother's tone sent a sulking Lili up the stairs, but not before shooting an icy glare at her sister.

"Have fun," Lili barked, stomping up the stairs.

Cat's mother sighed.

"You look lovely, Cathleen," she smiled, "Just don't let your father see you in that dress. He'll say it's too grown up for you."

"But you bought it for me," Cat reminded her.

"I know," her mom laughed, "It would get me in trouble, too!"

Cat saw Landon's black car pull up outside, and turned to give her mother a quick hug goodbye.

"I'll be home by midnight," she said turning towards the door.

"Oh, you can stay out later tonight, I guess," her mother said with a sly smile.

"Seriously?!" Cat spun on the spot and stared at her mother

in disbelief. They hardly ever let her stay out past curfew.

"You've worked hard this year, sweetie. You deserve a night to let loose a little bit — a LITTLE bit," her mother held the door open for her, "Have fun!"

"Love you!" Cat gave her a kiss on the cheek and practically danced to the car where Landon was waiting.

She was all smiles when she slid into the back seat beside him.

"Let me guess," Landon studied her face curiously, "You aced your Chem. final?"

"Yes, but that's not why I'm smiling."

"What then?"

"No curfew tonight!" Cat squealed with excitement.

"Geez, Cat. Only dogs can hear you at that pitch," he held the ear that was closest to her.

"Haha," she responded.

"Guess what?" Landon urged her.

Her eyebrows drew together in thought, "What?"

"No curfew for me, either!" he imitated her high pitch squeal.

Cat ignored the fact that he was making fun of her and threw her arms around him.

"Ahhh! Rock on! I thought you were still grounded," Cat exclaimed.

"Well, I was. Mom is making an exception for tonight. End of the year party and all that. Before I left, she told me that I'd served my time and I could stay out as late as I wanted."

"No way!"

"Yeah well, I told her you would be with me the whole night. I think she trusts that you'll keep me out of trouble," he said with a wink.

"Well, she's right. You know what I would do to you if you ever touched that stuff again," Cat informed.

"What?"

Cat began a wild karate chop and scream that sent them both doubling over in laughter and elicited some curious looks from Landon's driver. Landon karate chopped back with tickling fingers at Cat's mid-section.

"Stop, stop, stop," Cat laughed with tears streaming down her face, "You're going to make me pee!"

Landon carried on an exaggerated imitation of Cat's karate moves, until the town car finally came to a halt in front of one of the most massive and ornate townhouses on the Upper East Side.

The home of Samuel Alden could make any aspiring socialite green with envy. His father was Vice President of Goldman Sachs and his mother the president of Junior League, which meant Samuel was often left unattended, while his parents worked and served on their various committees. The pampered lifestyle of one of Manhattan's young elite served Samuel well; and, he always threw the most lavish of parties to show it off. He attended Dalton but knew Landon from summer camps together in Maine as tweens. This party would be the who's who among prep school princes and Park Avenue princesses.

Landon helped Cat remove the mascara that had run down her cheeks.

"I think you've got it all, Cat," Landon commented as she scrutinized her appearance in her compact mirror.

"Cat, seriously. You look really good. Great even," he hurried her along, opening the door and extending his hand to help her out.

"Are you sure?" she tilted her head to the side. He knew she was fishing for compliments, but he told her again anyway.

"You look great. If I liked you that way, I'd even say you were hot," he winked.

"Aww, thanks," she grinned, "But don't say I'm hot. That would just be weird."

He laughed and led her up the stone steps to the door. He turned the doorknob as he said, "Here's to your first party in the Spence Seven."

"How did you-?" she began.

"Word travels fast," he swung the door open to reveal an immense foyer with a winding staircase leading to the floors above.

Wall to wall, the mansion was packed with glittering young heirs and heiresses. Tonight was the night to let down their guard and enjoy a little reckless pleasure. To reward themselves for all the hard work they put into classes, ensuring their future place in the Ivy League.

Champagne danced through the room on silver platters, music blared from the deejay booth in the solarium, there was an open bar in the billiards room, and keg stands were going on in the kitchen, for the less distinguished.

"I think your new status calls for a drink," Landon called over the heavy pounding of the bass. He snatched two champagne flutes off a passing tray and handed one to Cat.

"To the Spence Seven, may your senior year with them be everything you could wish for." They drank deeply.

"I have one," Cat shouted, "To you. Wait, no. To us — may our senior year be as entirely fabulous as we are!"

"Here, here!"

They clinked their glasses and finished the champagne in one gulp.

"I think someone's going to get drunk," Landon gave Cat a knowing look.

"Landon Jennings, I hardly ever drink. I can count the

number of times I've been drunk on one hand," she held up three fingers.

"I know," Landon smiled, "Every time you were with me. I'm just saying, tonight calls for celebration."

"Well, my mom did say I could let loose," Cat raised an eyebrow with a smirk.

"In that case, I'm going to get you an amaretto sour," Landon walked towards the billiards room.

"Two," Cat shouted after him.

She had never felt the desire to let loose quite in that sense before, so she was taking full advantage of it. Many of her friends drank and partied; most of them thought it was part of the package that came with being young and wealthy. Cat didn't agree. Alcohol held no mystery for her. She never saw the appeal of getting wasted and doing stupid things that would inevitably be caught on someone's camera phone and end up on Facebook the next day. No thank you. She would rather watch the scene unfold and be able to tell people what they had done the night before. That was how she spent her time at these parties. Watching, not joining. That, and trying to keep Landon out of trouble.

The only times when she had gotten slightly inebriated herself were when Landon had insisted that she deserved to get a little crazy every once in a while.

Meghan Taylor appeared suddenly at Cat's side. She was one of Cat's best girlfriends and a new member of the Spence Seven.

"Congrats, my friend," she said, giving Cat a warm embrace.

"And to you as well," Cat returned, "You look fabulous. Marchesa?"

"Of course, BCBG?" Meghan appraised Cat's ensemble.

"Well spotted."

"Love it!" Meghan exclaimed.

Guessing whom each other was wearing was an old game among their clique. It never grew old. Cat was very good at it, since she often attended the Bryant Park fashion shows with Landon's mother. She was an upper level exec at Ralph Lauren. Since she didn't have a daughter and Landon showed no interest in attending, she always took Cat as her date.

Meghan grabbed her hand suddenly, "Come with me! You will never guess who's been staring at you since you walked in the door."

"Who?" Cat was very curious. She had never dated anyone, and the fact that someone had been staring at her made her more curious than flattered.

"Matt Darlington," Meghan squealed.

Matt was a player to say the least, but to say he was gorgeous would not do him justice. Cat couldn't help but admit her heart skipped a beat when she heard his name.

"Oh," she tried to remain coolly unaffected, "I wonder why?"

"Because you look totally hot!" Meghan informed her, annoyed at Cat's refusal to accept how attractive she was.

Cat blushed.

"No, I really don't," Cat shook her head, "I mean this dress looks good. But I — I don't know."

"Ugh!" Meghan rolled her eyes, exasperated as Landon approached with drinks. "Landon! Landon, tell Cat how hot she looks."

"I don't think I'm allowed to say that," he replied, handing Cat her drink, "It would be weird, right?"

Cat gave him a playful poke to his ribs.

"You should go talk to him." Meghan urged.

"Who?" Landon inquired.

"Matt Darlington," Meghan shot back, as Cat opened her mouth to speak.

"Sick! You can't be serious!" Landon looked appalled.

Meghan looked at Cat, confused by Landon's strong response.

"To say Landon dislikes Matt would be a gross understatement," Cat informed.

"Why? Because he gets all the girls," Meghan asked.

"Ha! No, I am not jealous of Matt and his myriad of sexually transmitted diseases, thank you very much," Landon snarled.

"They were friends when they were little and Matt stole a Thomas the Tank Engine toy from FAO Schwartz, then blamed it on Landon and he got in trouble for it," Cat answered, "They were six."

Meghan looked back and forth between the two of them, "You two know way too much about each other."

A hand clasped onto Landon's shoulder; it was Samuel Alden — their generous host.

"So good of you to come, my man," Samuel stretched his hand out to greet Landon.

"Good to be here," Landon responded with a firm handshake.

"Cat, you look stunning as always," Samuel said smoothly kissing her hand. "Meghan, good to see you with clothes on."

"Screw you, Samuel," Meghan snapped, clearly affronted.

"I believe you already did that," he calmly replied, "Remind me to pay you later."

"What's with the bow tie, Sam?" Cat inquired trying to break the tension. "Are you trying to channel Chuck Bass with that look?" She knew comparing him to the Gossip Girl character always got under his skin. Funny enough, Samuel did favor him — both in looks and in style. One might think he watched the show for fashion advice.

"That fag has nothing on me," Samuel replied, touching his hand slightly to his bow tie; and turning to Landon, he changed the subject, "You smoke Cubans, right?"

"Who doesn't?" Landon's response had a note of sarcasm that only Cat could detect.

"Let me show you my new humidor. We'll have a smoke." Samuel turned to lead Landon up the stairs, away from the party, "Ladies."

"Samuel," Cat nodded.

Meghan turned her head away, refusing to acknowledge him.

"Wait, Landon," Cat called quickly, stepping after him. "Give me my other drink. I'll need it to loosen me up if I'm going to talk to Matt."

"Well, just don't catch the clap," said Landon, handing over the other glass.

"Oh, yes. That's just what I had in mind for our conversation, 'Hi. My name's Cat. Want to have sex in the bathroom?'" she rolled her eyes at him and took her drink.

"Touché," Landon smiled. "See you in a bit then."

"Sure," Cat smiled. "Landon," she called. He turned to her once more. "You're not going to do anything else up there, are you?" her voice was lowered so only he could hear.

"No, Cat," he squeezed her hand. "I promised you, didn't I?"

"Yeah, alright," Cat squeezed back. "Have fun."

If Cat had known that was the last time she would see her best friend alive, she would have never let go. Landon was dead. She had found him herself, only a couple of hours later. She had watched them lower his body into the ground. He was gone; of that she was certain. But if Landon was dead, who had she seen as she stepped out of Mimi's truck? The sensation of movement brought her back, strong arms were holding her. Who was carrying her now? Her eyes flickered open as he laid her gently on the bed. She stared into the greenest eyes she'd ever seen.

CHAPTER FIVE

DESPITE HER MESSY, VOMIT-COVERED APPEARANCE, SHE WAS beautiful — of that there could be no denying. But he couldn't help but think how breakable she looked, as he laid her down on the bed and stepped back to observe the scene unfold. Mimi was already rushing into the room with a cold washcloth and checking Cat's pulse. Her eyes were open but she hadn't spoken yet. Landon. That's what she had called him, right before passing out. He had been finishing up some work in the barn when Mimi had arrived home with her. He had come out to offer to help with the bags when she had turned to him and then instantly crumpled to the ground. She made him uncomfortable and he had no idea why. That was annoying. Mimi was helping Cat sit up in the bed; her eyes were burning holes into him. Why was she looking at him that way?

"Catie, this is Luke," she followed Cat's gaze to the stranger in the room. "Luke is your new neighbor, and my right-hand man on the farm. He's going to be a senior at Watauga, like you."

"Nice to meet you," Cat mumbled. She looked down at her hands to break the lock he had on her eyes. She was covered partly in vomit, partly in wet grass, and entirely in embarrassment. She wanted to crawl under the bed and never come out.

"I've heard a lot about you, Catie," he replied simply.

"Great," Cat thought. His tone offered no indication of whether what he had heard was positive or negative. She took the chance to glance at him and see whether or not his expression would give anything away.

Looking at Luke closely, she realized he didn't resemble Landon nearly as much as she imagined he did. Her eyes must have been playing tricks on her in the bright sunlight. He had curls, true. But his were dark brown, almost black and short, compared to Landon's messy mop. He was tall, maybe 6' 2". She was always bad at guessing things like that. He wasn't quite as tall as Landon, though. Luke's build was more muscular compared to lanky Landon, though he shared the same confident stride. His eyes looked like bright emeralds. He was quite possibly the most attractive male she had ever laid eyes on. She realized, quite suddenly, that she was still staring at him and she shook her head as if to break the spell.

"Luke, thank you for bringing Catie upstairs for me," Mimi offered, refolding the washcloth and pressing it to her cheeks and forehead. "Catie, what on earth happened to you?"

Luke watched as Cat struggled for words, for some explanation for her sudden collapse. He knew that whatever had overcome her had something to do with a guy named Landon, but who he was and why he had this effect on her, he wasn't certain. He found himself surprisingly very intrigued. Just having met her a few minutes ago, he was shocked to feel so sincerely interested.

"It might be the sudden change in altitude," he offered quickly.

Cat gave him a look of gratitude, "I think that must be it."

"The air is much thinner up here than you would be used to," Luke nodded.

"Well, I suppose you should just sit tight up here and I'll bring your lunch up," Mimi patted her hand. "Luke, will you sit up here with Catie till she's feeling better?"

"I'm fine," Cat spat out before Luke could respond. She hadn't meant it to sound so brusque, but considering the circumstances and how she looked, she wanted to be completely alone. Preferably hidden out of sight for at least a month.

"I think I'm just going to hop in the shower and clean up," she added in a softer tone.

"Well, just the same, I think it would be best to have someone up here. He can sit outside the door. What if you passed out in the shower?" Mimi walked towards the door, "Is that alright Luke?"

"I — I guess," he said. He didn't want to sound eager to sit outside her door while she showered, and he wasn't sure how comfortable that would be for either of them.

He dared another glance in her direction. She was broken to be sure. Her eyes told him that much the minute they'd met. Mimi had told him that she had been getting wild in New York City, that she was partying, and had become too much for her parents to handle. So, they were sending her to live in the mountains of Boone, NC. Looking at her, he sensed that there was so much more to that story. She looked nothing like the spoiled city girl he had imagined. Sure, from the look of her hands he knew she had never done work on a farm, and her chic ensemble made her quite out of place among Carhartt jeans and steel toed boots, but there was a depth to her eyes that he hadn't pictured in a rich girl from Manhattan.

They were silent for a good minute after Mimi had left the room. Luke pretended to stare out the window. Cat took off her cardigan and wiped down her neck with the cool washcloth.

"You really don't have to stay up here with me," Cat's voice was a bit curt.

She didn't mean to be rude to him, but the last 24 hours had been so hellish, she was beyond pretending to be okay. She could feel her composure slipping and when it broke, she would take her anger out on anyone or anything in the vicinity. She didn't want to do that. Not to a stranger.

Luke shifted from where he was leaning against the wall and sauntered to the old stuffed armchair by the window.

"I don't think either of us have a choice," he said as he plopped down.

Annoyed, Cat stood up and walked to the door.

"Well, I'll need clothes to put on after I get out of the shower," she snapped, "Do you think you could get my bags for me? Or do you need to ask my grandmother for permission first?"

Luke stared at her. Her eyes were like fire. He had no idea someone could be so haughty while covered in puke and grass, and with their hair all a mess. He began to laugh.

"What?" Cat demanded angrily.

Luke began to howl with laughter. She was amusing to him.

"Stop laughing," she shouted. She fought the urge to stomp her foot.

"You're funny," he chuckled while calming down, and he wiped his eyes.

"Oh, right," Cat's tone was full of sarcasm, "This whole situation is just hilarious. I get sent to the boonies against my will to be guarded by some country hick who finds me amusing. Ha-ha. Now, if you'll excuse me, I'm going to take a shower and I expect my bags to be in my room when I get out."

Cat had gone too far. She knew she had. He didn't look a thing like a country hick, a farm boy sure, but country hick, no. He had laughed at her though, and that had pushed her over the edge. Still, she felt guilt pour over her and it made her wish she could take it back.

"As you wish, your Majesty." Luke was fuming now, too. He stood up and bowed to her before brushing past her shoulder as he strode out the door. "Rich bitch," he muttered just loud enough for her to hear as he stomped down the steps.

"Agh!" Cat stomped to the bathroom door and slammed it shut, just to emphasize her frustration.

Luke heard her banging around in the bathroom as he walked out to the truck. He thought for a moment that she might be different from the New York City girls always stereotyped on TV. Nope. Just a spoiled little brat, used to getting her way.

He knew Mimi intended for him to get to know her so she would have a friend before school started. Yeah, right.

He would just as soon not have to see her again. The interest he had felt towards her upstairs had been replaced by downright dislike. Luke considered himself to be a very patient person, but being called a hick was the one thing he wouldn't allow.

He grimaced as he remembered she would be working with him on the farm each day. This was going to be just great.

"She will probably expect me to do all the work so she won't break a precious nail," he muttered aloud to himself. He would make sure she did her share.

He jerked her bags up with such force the one on the right came open, spilling its contents onto the ground. He stood there staring at her clothes for half a second and thought about kicking them around in the dirt before he bent over and began throwing them back into her duffle bag. When he came across something small and lacy, he paused for a second. He was a guy after all. Then, he shoved whatever it was, and the rest of her belongings, into the bag to keep himself from inspecting it further.

Cat leaned against the sink as she waited for the water to heat up. Why did she have to snap at him? She didn't even know him, and now she was sure she had an idea of the awful things he thought about her. His "rich bitch" comment had her blood boiling. Nonetheless, Cat decided she would have to make an extra effort to be friendly to him. Hopefully, that would keep him from going around school talking about what a bitch she was before she even had a chance to make a first impression on people. She had three weeks until school would start. Three weeks to change his mind about whatever he might be thinking. She stepped into the tub and let the water wash away her frustration. She felt her tension melting away as she breathed in the steam.

After a hot shower, she felt like a new person. She smelled like one, too. She cursed herself for not thinking about bringing some clothes into the bathroom to change into. Now, she would have to scurry across the hall to her bedroom and hope that she wouldn't run into Luke on the way. She towel-dried her hair a bit before wrapping the towel around her, under her arms, and across her chest. Cracking the door open just a sliver, she peered out. No one to the left, no one to the right--the coast was clear. Speedily, she darted down the hall on her tiptoes and looked through the door to her room. It was already ajar and she could see her bags on the bed. He had gotten them for her after all. She would have to remember to thank him for that. Peering her head through her door, she didn't see anyone. With a sigh of relief, she stepped in and closed the door behind her.

Turning, she spotted him and let out a yelp of surprise. He had been sitting in the armchair by the window, probably the one area in the room you couldn't see from peering in the door. Her squeal had startled him and the book he had been reading tumbled to the floor by her feet: *The Fountainhead* by Ayn Rand. Her eyebrows raised in surprise. Quite a sophisticated novel for someone she had called a country hick not even an hour ago. She felt herself blush.

"Good book," she commented, bending over to pick it up.

"You've read it?" he sounded surprised as he reached out to accept it from her. Not many high schoolers he knew read Ayn Rand. Then again, he was the only one he knew of...until now. If his mother hadn't been a Literature professor at Appalachian State, he wasn't sure he would have heard of her.

The astonishment in his voice irritated her. He sounded as though he thought she did nothing but shop and have her nails done or something.

"Yeah, I don't know that I necessarily agree with her theory of objectivism, but she's a decent writer," she replied, aiming to impress.

She knows about objectivism. Luke was intrigued. He didn't picture her as the philosophical type. He wouldn't let her impress him that easily though, not after what she had said to him before.

"Neither do I," said Luke, "I mean there is something to be said for being happy, but to make it the moral purpose of my life seems selfish."

They stood there, each holding one side of the book until Cat realized she still had her hand on it and let it go.

"I need to get dressed," she had just become conscious of the fact that all she was wearing was a thin towel and her wet hair was creating a small puddle on the hardwood floor.

"Sure," Luke walked around her to the door, "You're feeling okay now?"

He didn't know why he was asking. After all, he had just decided to despise her, and now he was acting as if he cared.

"Yeah, ummm, thanks," Cat attempted a smile.

Why was he making her so nervous? She watched him close the door behind him and she fell onto the bed exhausted and confused. Mimi must have brought up a turkey sandwich, since one was now sitting on the nightstand. Starving, she devoured the entire thing before getting herself dressed.

She opted for simple khaki linen shorts and a flowy tank. Not too casual but not dressy, either. She didn't want to look like she was trying too hard. Cat thought of the encounter they had after she got out of the shower. She thought about apologizing, but had been distracted by his book. Apparently, he was distracted too because he didn't seem to be angry with her. Maybe they could put their little spat behind them and start over. Maybe it would be as if their initial meeting today had never occurred; that she hadn't puked on herself and passed out. Wouldn't that be nice? That was what they needed--a clean start.

"I need a clean start, too," Cat whispered softly to herself, as she stretched out on the soft, worn quilt that covered the bed.

Perhaps, she would be able to find one here.

Feeling refreshed after a little power nap, Cat hopped down the stairs to find Mimi. Maybe she could persuade her into letting her drive into Boone and look around. She didn't have a driver's license, but Mimi didn't need to know that little detail. How hard could driving really be, anyway? Gas is on the right, brake on the left. Or was it the other way around? Having a driver was a fortunate thing growing up, but it kept her from ever having taken driver's education. Not that they even offered it at Spence. No one her age had their license anyway. There wasn't any need.

Walking through the first floor, she was just beginning to think that she was alone in the house when she heard a noise coming from out back. She opened the back door to find Luke, shirt off and weed eater in hand, trimming around the edges of

Mimi's flower garden. He had some strange plastic glasses on, she guessed to protect his eyes from anything that might fly up.

She called to him. He didn't respond. She called his name once more and then noticed he had earplugs in his ears. She sat on the back-porch swing and watched him while he finished up. Cat knew she should just go inside and wait, but she was bored and, truthfully, she was enjoying watching him work. He was certainly nice to look at with his shirt off, muscles rippling in his arms and chest, but there was something more than that. It was his precision. He wasn't just trimming away the weeds in a rush, but he was perfectly outlining the stacked stone Mimi had surrounding her flower garden. It was obvious he cared about doing a good job. Cat admired that.

Luke turned off the weed eater and looked up. He was caught off guard, seeing Cat swinging quietly on the porch swing and staring at him. She didn't look away when he caught her looking at him, but continued to stare. He felt his stomach do a flip-flop. Girls had never made him the least bit nervous before, and he had dated quite a few.

"Do you know where my grandmother is?" she called to him.

Luke realized she had said something, but didn't hear what it was with the earplugs in his ears. He took them out, pulled off his protective glasses, and began walking towards the house.

"I didn't catch that," he said, holding up the earplugs.

"Oh, right," Cat acknowledged, "I was just wondering if you knew where Mimi was?"

"She said she was going to pick up some Mellow Mushroom for dinner," he sat down on the steps and began to untie his work boots.

"Oh," Cat had nothing else to say. She felt like she should apologize for before, but she wasn't sure where to begin.

"So, you're feeling better now?" Luke inquired. Now, he felt stupid for asking again.

"Hmm-mm," Cat looked at her feet. She lifted them out to swing higher. Something told her that he knew she didn't have altitude sickness earlier. She could sense it when he said it in her bedroom to Mimi, but going along with it seemed like an easier explanation than 'I thought I saw my dead best friend.'

"So, who's Landon?" he asked.

The suddenness of his question caught Cat so off guard she nearly fell off the swing. It was as though he had been reading her mind. She clutched one hand to her chest. She always thought heart "ache" was a thing in fairy tales or sad, country love songs. But she noticed that her chest felt crushed each time someone spoke his name. Breathing was harder. There was a pressure that mounted. She exhaled slowly and looked away.

Luke remembered a few moments ago that she had said the name before she collapsed. He thought about asking a few other questions to lead into the topic, but he was a matter-of-fact kind of guy and decided not to dance around it.

"I'm sorry?" Cat felt like she might pass out again. Putting her feet down to stop the swing, she stared at him in disbelief. How on earth had he heard about Landon? Surely, Mimi wasn't sharing her sad story with everyone.

"Landon. It's what you said before you passed out," Luke clarified. The look on her face made him wish he hadn't asked. He sat on the porch and leaned against the column.

Cat swallowed, "He's my — my best friend."

"Oh," Luke didn't know what else to say.

"I'm sure you miss him, being so far away and all," Luke added. Was that why she looked so heartbroken at the mention of his name?

"Yeah, yeah I do," Cat looked down. She hadn't cried since the night Landon died. She thought she had gotten all the tears out then, so she would never cry again. The tears burning in her eyes mocked that idea.

"I'm sure he misses you too," Luke was searching for something to say, something to cheer her up.

"I don't think so."

"Why wouldn't he?" Luke pressed her.

"Because he's dead," Cat didn't look up from her hands as she calmly stated the fact.

Luke felt like he had been punched in the stomach. Putting his foot in his mouth seemed like a gross understatement to describe how he felt. More like putting an entire leg in his mouth. He couldn't think of anything, any words, any gesture that would be adequate enough to respond.

They sat there for a moment in silence until he finally stood up and came to sit beside her on the porch swing. He didn't touch her hand, he didn't hold her, or offer words of comfort. He hardly knew her, but he felt the need to sit beside her. Never in his life had he felt so drawn to someone. So many questions buzzed in his head about Cat, but he didn't ask them. He knew somehow that her story would unfold over time and he didn't want to press her for it. He regretted his last question so horribly, he doubted he would ask another anytime soon.

His presence comforted her. They sat like statues until she heard Mimi's truck pulling up the drive.

"Let's get some pizza, Catie," Luke finally said, offering her his hand to help her up.

"Cat," she replied, taking it, "My friends call me Cat."

CHAPTER SIX

THAT NIGHT, CAT LAY AWAKE IN BED FOR WHAT SEEMED LIKE AN eternity. Eyes wide open, she lay listening to the unfamiliar sounds beyond her windows. Who knew crickets could be so damn loud? What she wouldn't give for the sound of an ambulance going by? She wasn't sure what time it happened, but she finally fell asleep. It was not a restful sleep. No. Cat tossed and turned until she found herself somewhere familiar. Hadn't she been here before? She was at Samuel Alden's party. She was leaning back against the railing on the back patio. She had on her navy outfit. It was the night Landon had died.

Matt Darlington was leaning into her. He had one hand suggestively on her waist and the other on the rail, firmly pinning her in place. She laughed at whatever it was he had just said, but she wasn't really paying attention.

Since she had gotten to the party, she'd had one glass of champagne, two amaretto sours, and one shot of tequila. It was at that point that she felt courageous enough to strike up a conversation with Matt. It hadn't really been too much of a conversation, though. They had talked for about five minutes before he went in for the first kiss.

After that point, he had gotten a bottle of wine and two glasses and led her out on the patio to "talk". Cat was sure she was certifiably drunk. She kept trying to remember what Landon had said about Matt and his diseases, but it was hard to think with his tongue down her throat.

Cat had never in her life done anything like this before. She was definitely not the type to hook up at parties. She was starting to worry that she had started something Matt might want to finish in a much different way than Cat had in mind. She wasn't sure he would accept her, "thanks for making out with me tonight, but that's really all I'm up for" response if he tried to take things any further.

Wasn't kissing like this supposed to be romantic? Why did it feel like he was trying to remove her tonsils?

Cat's eyes started to wander. The party had grown a little out of control, and Cat wondered when the police would be called for a noise violation. It wasn't a question of if anymore. She needed to find Landon and get out of here before that happened.

"Let's go inside," she said suddenly, looking up at Matt.

"I think we should try to find a room upstairs," he responded, sliding his hand from her waist to her hip and around to her behind.

"Sure, sure," Cat responded absently, grabbing his hand away from her rear to lead him inside.

She might have been drunk, but she wasn't stupid. There was no way she was losing her v-card at some party, to him, especially when she wouldn't even remember it.

At least this way she could get him inside and look for Landon under the pretense of finding some place to be "alone".

If the house was packed before, she had no way of describing it now. Boys were yelling in the kitchen as keg stand competitions were being held. Cat thought she saw Meghan in the corner with a hottie from Dalton's lacrosse team, but where was Landon? Was it possible that he was still upstairs with Samuel smoking cigars?

"Let's go upstairs," she shouted to Matt over the noise.

"Awesome," came his response.

She smiled. It's a good thing he's cute because he has the brains of a lamppost.

Cat stumbled as she reached the first landing. All the doors were locked on the second floor, and Cat didn't have to guess at what might be going on behind them. She continued up to the third floor. She watched as Matt tried each doorknob.

"Everyone's getting busy tonight," he snickered.

"Yeah, hmmm," Cat replied automatically.

Where on earth could Landon be? He wasn't downstairs. Then again, she hadn't seen Samuel yet, either. They were probably together.

When they reached the fourth floor, Cat caught a whiff of the unmistakable scent of cigars. She followed it to the room at the end of the hall. As her hand reached for the doorknob, the handle turned and Samuel emerged with two younger girls in tow.

She noticed the glassy look in their eyes. They hadn't just been smoking cigars. They were doing coke; she was sure of it.

"Where is Landon?" she demanded. The thought of him lying to her sobered her up quickly. She wanted to find him that very instant and give him a piece of her mind.

"Whoa, whoa, whoa," Samuel held his hands up, "Why such a hurry?"

"Samuel, I need to find Landon," she tried to keep calm.

"I haven't seen him in the last hour or so," he slurred his reply, "Not since he got a call from his dad."

"Since what?" Cat was confused. What did his dad have to do with it?

"Yeah, his dad called to tell him he had gotten engaged or

something and wants Landon to be the best man," Samuel replied offhandedly.

"Oh no," Cat breathed, "Samuel, where did he go after that?"

"He said he needed to escape a bit, but he didn't want what I offered, so he said he was going up to the roof to chill out alone," Samuel walked towards the stairs, an arm around each girl.

"Why didn't you go with him?" Cat nearly shouted at him. Landon did not need to be alone right now.

"I'm not his keeper, Cat," he was clearly affronted, "There are stairs to the roof through my bedroom," he pointed the way, "Go and check on him yourself."

Cat took off in the direction he had pointed. Matt looked thoroughly confused by the exchange that had just occurred and he pulled her back to him.

"Cat, I thought we were going to … you know," he whispered the last two words in her ear.

"No, Matt, we are not going to 'you know.' I'm sure if you stumble downstairs there are a dozen willing girls waiting in line." Disgusted, she broke away and practically ran towards Samuel's bedroom.

When she reached the rooftop, there was no one there. She made a 360 degree turn again just to be sure. She exhaled and turned her eyes upwards. It was a perfect night. You could actually see a few stars — a rare occurrence in New York City. She moved unsteadily to the chaise lounge and lowered herself down. The effects of the alcohol were really sinking in. It would be so easy to fall asleep here. The seat was still warm, as though someone had been sitting there only moments before. She stretched out her legs and put her arms on the armrests. Perhaps Landon had gone home early. It made her a little pissed off to think he would leave without telling her.

Something hard was poking her in the lower back; she reached behind her and felt under the cushion. It was a cell phone. It was Landon's cell phone. Her heart skipped a beat. He wouldn't have left without his cell phone. He was glued to that thing. She quickly put in the code to unlock the buttons and saw that Twitter came up on the screen. He had made a post five minutes ago: "Need to escape. This time for good. Keeping my promise. I'm the one to blame. Two lives left, Cat. Take care of yourself."

Cat leapt to her feet and began to look around wildly. His cell phone was still glued to her hand.

She hadn't passed him on the stairs. Had he heard her talking to Samuel and hid in the bedroom, so he could sneak away unnoticed? She had no idea what he was planning to do, but fear reigned in her body. The thought of anything happening to him sobered her at once. She knew she had to find him and quickly, before it was too late. Darting towards the door, she retched it open just as she heard a blood-curdling scream coming from the garden below. Five stories below. She ran over to the edge and looked down.

It was dark, and people were already crowding around the body, but she knew it was him. Her best friend. Her Landon.

Her scream matched the scream of whoever had stumbled upon the body and her knees gave way as the darkness closed in around her.

Cat awoke, drenched in sweat, as thunder crashed outside and a branch thumped across her window. She was shaking. Sitting up in her bed, she drew her knees to her chest and rocked herself with her head bowed over her knees. Her pillow was wet from tears, but her eyes were dry now that she was awake. Why was she only able to cry in her sleep? She wiped her hands across her face. Cat felt that a good cry might be just what she needed, except to be awake during it. To be conscious of it and really let some healing take place. Continuing to relive the nightmare in her dreams couldn't be healthy, and yet she had dreamt that night over and over since it had occurred. Perhaps her subconscious was trying to create an alternate ending. She could've gotten to the rooftop to find Landon waiting for her and they could've talked through things. If only she'd gotten there five minutes earlier. If only, but each time the dream was the same, exactly as it had occurred in real life. The same gut-wrenching agony she felt that night, seeing his body sprawled out below, as though she was seeing it for the first time. Guilt, perhaps the strongest emotion of all, washing over her, making her wish she had taken her own life. She had tried that, she reminded herself, quite unsuccessfully.

Cat didn't want to think about that, not now, probably not ever. She pushed the covers aside and went to the bathroom to splash some water on her face. She stood there longer than necessary and stared into her eyes in the mirror. They had looked so dead the last few months, but something about them tonight was different. What had happened today, that had put some semblance of fire back into them? She knew the answer before she asked the question. Luke. Something about him had intrigued her far more than she wanted to be. She didn't want to be interested. She didn't want him to be able to get a rise out of her so easily. It was as if he knew which buttons to push, though she had only just met him. She still didn't know why she had told him about Landon. But when he asked, she answered. It had been easy, as though she wasn't capable of lying to him. She splashed more water on her face and got back into bed. Tomorrow would be her first day of working on a farm, her first full day with Luke. She was excited and terrified at the same time. How could he arouse so many emotions in her? She would have to leave that question unanswered, for now.

The sun was not yet on the horizon when her alarm started blaring. Mimi had set it for her the night before, since she didn't know how to work such an archaic alarm clock. The clouds hung low around the farmhouse and the cool gray mist swirled through the fields of Christmas trees below. She stared out her window from the comfort of her bed. She would say the sight was beautiful if it weren't so terribly early. Six a.m. was far too early to rise on a summer morning.

Mimi had said that today she would just follow along with Luke and learn the ropes. She wasn't sure if that meant she should wear work clothes. She didn't own any work clothes. She hit the snooze button on the alarm clock until Mimi came up to check on her a second time. She decided she shouldn't push her luck on her second day here, so she got up to get ready.

After putting on her oldest pair of Seven jeans and a Ralph Lauren sweatshirt over her tank top, she went downstairs.

Mimi was scrambling eggs on the stove and the smell of bacon was irresistible.

"Maybe you should pull your hair up, Catie," she said with a smile, examining her headband closely.

"Why?" Cat asked, touching her headband. She wanted to keep at least one thing feminine on.

"Well, I was going to send you and Luke over to fetch a few bales of hay from the south field and take it to our neighbors for me, and a headband isn't likely to stay on while you're doing that," Mimi looked at her granddaughter with an amused expression.

"Moving hay can't be that hard, right? I mean, what is hay? Straw? And that would weigh what, like, two, three pounds?" Cat crunched on a piece of bacon, oblivious to the fact that Luke had walked into the kitchen behind her and overheard her comment.

"You have so much to learn, city girl," he laughed.

Cat whirled around. She did not like being caught off guard, especially by Luke.

"Hay bales that weigh two or three pounds? Try 80," Luke laughed.

"I might not know much about hay, but you would be clueless in New York. Then who would be laughing?" she shot back. How was he capable of getting her blood boiling so quickly?

"Maybe, but we're not in New York. You're in the mountains now," he was clearly enjoying this playful banter a little too much.

"Don't remind me. I've been moved to the land of Christmas trees, hay bales, and hicks," she snapped back.

"Hey, now! You kids settle down and get some breakfast, then get to work. I have some errands to run, but I'll be back later. Alright?" Mimi looked from one to the other as though she was hesitant to leave, lest another world war break out right in her kitchen.

"Sure," Luke shrugged.

"Fine," Cat said as she sat at the table with her back to him.

Mimi finished up in the kitchen, grabbed her purse, and gave Cat kiss on the forehead as she walked out the back door.

"Be nice," she ordered as she left.

Luke filled a plate for himself, then one for Cat, and brought them to the table.

"You should eat more than a piece of bacon, Cat," he said as he placed it in front of her.

"Don't tell me what to do," she glared at him.

"I'm trying to be nice. You could try too, you know," Luke stated while Cat continued to sit in silence, "Fine, suit yourself." He dumped the contents of her plate onto his own and began to eat.

Cat was hungry, but she didn't want to eat simply on the principle that she didn't like being told what to do. Maybe when he got up to leave, she would sneak a couple of bites before following.

"Is this how it's going to be, Cat?" Luke eyed her slyly.

"What?" she wasn't quite certain what he was talking about.

"Every time I try to joke around, you get worked up and call me a hick?" his tone sounded more serious.

"You weren't trying to joke around. You were trying to get me worked up and you know it," Cat's voice was getting snappy.

"You think I like getting you worked up?" Luke raised his voice to match hers.

"Yes, I do!" Cat yelled.

"Well, maybe I do! But you do the same to me, and don't even pretend you don't!" Luke's voice overpowered Cat's. He stood to his feet.

"Fine!" Cat leapt to her feet, too.

They stood there, inches from each other's faces, angry, and neither one backing down.

Cat wasn't sure which one of them started to laugh first, but once they started, it seemed impossible to stop.

"Let's just agree that we enjoy pushing each other's buttons and try not to do it," Cat finally said once the laughter had died down.

"But what would be the fun in that?" Luke smirked.

"Ha, ha," Cat said. She looked at him carefully. It felt like she had known him forever. It was easy with him. Easy to get mad, easy to forget, easy to forgive. Easy. She had forgotten how easy it could be to be friends.

"Why are you looking at me like that?" he asked, startling her thoughts.

"Like what?" she said, stealing a bite of eggs off his plate.

"I don't know. It was just ... nothing," Luke shook it off.

"What?" Cat pressed him. She was curious to know what he had seen in her look.

"It's like I've known you, you know? For more than just a day, longer than that, never mind," Luke stood and took his plate to the sink. He was clearly uncomfortable.

Cat stood up and went to his side with the dish towel, drying the plate he had just washed.

"I know," she bit her lower lip. "I know what you mean," she said, putting the plate away.

Luke cleared his throat, "Yeah, well. We need to get out in the field before Mimi gets back. I don't think she's paying me to hang out in her kitchen all morning."

With that, he grabbed his baseball cap and shoved it on his head as he stepped out the back door, leaving Cat standing there dumbfounded.

Why are guys so confusing? She wondered, as she hurried to catch up with him. Here she was thinking they might be "having a moment", and he brushes her off as if she's nobody.

Who does he think he is? She wanted to shout, "Hey! You country bumpkin, what the hell do you think you're doing, messing around with my emotions like that?!" Instead, she got in the passenger side of the farm truck and slammed the door extra hard.

"Yeah, Luke, you're right. I don't want to be seen cavorting with the help anyway," she said as he turned on the engine.

Gritting his teeth to keep from saying something he shouldn't, he slammed his foot on the gas, gunning it down the gravel road.

CHAPTER SEVEN

LUKE GLANCED OVER AT CAT AS HE TOOK ANOTHER MOUNTAIN CURVE at breakneck speed. He knew she had to be getting queasy, since she wasn't used to curvy roads, but she wasn't saying a word. Her jaw was clenched tightly and her hands were glued to the vinyl seats. He knew he was being a bit of a jackass, but being called "the help" had sent him over the edge. Just as half the things she said to him did, a voice in his head reminded him. One second, he'd think she was an amazing and intriguing woman, and the next, he'd be convinced she had to be the most spoiled brat he'd ever laid eyes on. Even then, he couldn't stifle his attraction towards her. No girl had ever caused him so much confusion in so little time.

He slowed down enough to whip the car off the highway and onto the dirt road lined with no passing signs. She gasped as a bump sent her reaching across to pull her seatbelt tighter.

"This road is lined with no trespassing signs," she commented.

"So?" Luke responded.

"It says trespassers may be shot on site ... are they serious?" Cat thought signs like that only existed in *The Beverly Hillbillies*.

"I guess, or they wouldn't have put it on the sign," Luke smiled on the inside. She was so new to so many things. He had probably never even noticed the signs before.

"Maybe we shouldn't be here," there was an edge to her voice. She didn't want to be a scaredy cat, but getting shot was not on her to-do list for today.

"Cat, this is your grandmother's land," he laughed.

"Oh," she felt so stupid. She wasn't used to being clueless about things. She was used to being the smart one. She enjoyed knowing more than other people, and she had yet to have an opportunity to show him just how intelligent she could be. Cat doubted she would have that opportunity as long as they were doing anything farm related. She would just have to create her own opportunity. Maybe she would see if there was an art museum on the nearby campus of Appalachian State, where she could take him to show off a bit. Cat needed a self-esteem boost after being made to feel so silly about so many things.

The truck hit a rut in the dirt road that sent her head bumping up into the ceiling above. She felt as though she might puke, again.

"Hang on," Luke said nonchalantly.

Cat was certain Luke knew she was carsick. Her green complexion made it pretty clear, she thought, as she caught a glimpse of herself in the side view mirror. The truck slowed as they reached an open field dotted with large square bales of hay.

"These things don't look like they could weigh eighty pounds each," Cat thought aloud.

There were probably 200 of them, though. Cat's eyes scanned across the field. There was no way they could get all of them. The truck bed could only hold maybe ten without stacking them, from Cat's estimation. Well good, she thought to herself, maybe that means it won't take long.

"I'll hook up the trailer," Luke said, breaking Cat away from her thoughts.

"The what?" She didn't see a trailer. Weren't those the little houses on wheels? She'd only seen them in movies, usually occupied by some deadbeat dad who didn't pay child support. She'd never been in one herself.

"Over there," he pointed, and Cat followed his line of sight to where a flatbed trailer stood with railing up the sides and a few ropes hanging down to tie the bales in place.

"Ahh," Cat didn't like the looks of it. It meant they would be spending a lot more time and energy loading bales of hay than she desired, which was none at all.

"You didn't think we could load all of them onto the truck, did you?" The tone in his voice was one of amusement.

Cat ignored it. All she had heard was that they would be loading all of them.

"We are loading ALL of them?" her voice could not hide her shock and disgust.

"That's right. Onto the trailer," Luke repeated. He hated whiners, and hoped she wouldn't complain the whole time. It would make for a very long day.

"I thought a trailer was a house on wheels," she said absently.

Luke smiled. "Well, there are several types of trailers. This one is for loading and transporting things like timber, Christmas trees, or hay," he paused. "I bet you've never been in a trailer home, have you?"

"No," Cat responded, she didn't want to sound snooty so she quickly added, "I don't have a problem with them or anything … I just have never had the opportunity."

"Well, it won't be too hard to change that … now that you live here," Luke responded.

When they backed up to the trailer, Cat hopped out. She needed some fresh air. She needed to find a restroom. Not only did she still feel nauseous, but the bumpy road had not been kind to her bladder.

"Where's the restroom?" she asked, turning to Luke.

"I'm sorry?" He was looking at her as though she had two heads.

"The bathroom. Restroom. Where is one?" she felt suddenly as though she was asking something stupid again. She only hoped he wouldn't laugh at her, as he'd done before.

Luke smiled. He started to laugh, but quickly played it off as coughing. He didn't want to get into another tiff so early in the morning.

"Well," his eyes searched the woods that surrounded the field. "You could pick behind that tree, or that one, or that one over there."

"Very funny," Cat snapped at him and began stomping off towards the woods.

"Cat, wait!" he called.

"What now? Are you going to recommend another tree for me to squat behind?" Cat snarled at him.

"No, there's some Kleenex in the glove compartment, and don't get near any poison ivy," Luke said, as he attempted to be civil.

"Fine," Cat stomped over to the truck, took out the Kleenex and headed towards the woods.

"Luke, wait!" she turned back to him. "What does poison ivy look like?"

"Leaves of three, let it be!" he replied as he worked to attach the trailer to the hitch.

Cat made her way into the woods.

"Leaves of three, let it be. Leaves of three, let it be," she muttered to herself.

Leaves of three … half the plants she saw had three leaves on them. She gasped; maybe she was walking through poison ivy. She started hopping through the brush, careful not to touch any plants at all. She looked ridiculous, not to mention the fact that it was impossible to avoid touching plants.

"If only they didn't all look the same," Cat thought aloud as she looked for a place to relieve herself.

Luke checked that the hitch was secure. He looked towards the woods and thought of Cat. She was so perplexing. He didn't know why they were always at each other's throats. Was it because they were so different? He knew their backgrounds were like night and day, but he didn't think that was it. Luke realized he was enjoying pushing her buttons a little too much ... but the look in her eyes when she was mad at him. They were so alive. They had looked so dead the day before, when he first met her. They looked so dead when she told him about her best friend. Not even sad eyes, just dead. As though she had pushed the emotion so far back, and buried it so deep, that she wouldn't feel anything ever again. Making her angry was his way of showing her that her emotions still existed. Maybe, Luke thought, if I'm able to get a rise out of her enough times, that wall she has carefully built around herself will start to crumble. Then, Cat will realize she is capable of other emotions, too. She could deal with her sadness and move on. Maybe move on with me? Luke shook his head to clear his thoughts.

He grabbed his work gloves and an extra pair out of the workbox on the back of the truck. He looked up to see Cat running at him, full speed. Her eyes were full of terror. He took off towards her.

When he reached her, he grabbed her shoulders.

"Are you okay?" he brushed the hair from her eyes. She was panting so hard she could barely speak.

"I — I was — and then it attacked me- oh God! I was — then I ran — I — I — was — so — so scared!" she broke into sobs.

Luke wrapped his arms around her tightly. He thought of his rifle only 20 yards away in the back of the truck. He should go and grab it before whatever attacked Cat came charging at them from the woods, though that wasn't likely. Bears and other animals were usually more scared of humans than humans were of them.

"Was it a bear?" Luke bent down to look her in the eyes.

She shook her head; she was crying hard. Her eyes got wide at the word bear.

"A bobcat?" Luke asked. Again, she shook her head.

"A panther? A snake? A fox, turkey, opossum?" he pressed. She shook her head to all.

Luke was curious.

"Cat, what scared you so bad? What attacked you?"

"A — a," she sniffled, trying to catch her breath.

"It's okay. It's alright. Take your time," Luke soothed, pulling her close again.

He stroked her hair and let his hands rub up and down her back, consoling her. He couldn't help but notice how her hair smelled. Not flowery or of perfume, like so many other girls, but like warm vanilla, and something else. Mint? He breathed it in. She was intoxicating. He usually hated when girls cried. He just wasn't the mushy type. Cat, on the other hand, could cry as often as she pleased as long as he could hold her.

"Luke, it was vicious," she whimpered, catching her breath.

"Cat, WHAT was it?"

"A squirrel," she said with a dead-serious look in her eye.

Luke pushed her away to get a good look at her. She was serious. He burst out laughing. He slapped his knees. He fell to the ground and literally rolled with laughter while Cat screamed at him for making fun of her.

"Stop! This instant!" she screamed again, adding a foot stomp to prove how irate she was.

He was unbelievable. He was adding insult to injury. She was terrified of squirrels to begin with; their beady little eyes and mischievous grins, always chattering like evil little imps up in the trees. Then, to have one leap down on her head as she finished peeing; she almost had a heart attack.

"Did you just stomp your foot?" he asked, before doubling over in laughter once more.

She instantly regretted the foot stomp. Why did he have to be so mean?

"You weren't there, Luke! It jumped on my head! It attacked me!" she squealed.

"It was a killer squirrel?" he asked.

"Yes, it was!" she insisted.

"Oh, I suppose it went high-ya!" Luke began a very bad karate chop impression that stopped Cat in her tracks.

"What did I do?" Luke asked quickly. Her face had gone blank and empty the second he did the karate chop.

"Nothing," she turned from him, wiped her eyes, and then spoke in the most professional tone. "We should get to work. I want to get this over with."

"You should put these work gloves on," Luke said, handing her a pair.

He watched her as she put on the gloves and stalked off towards the closest bale of hay. He had no idea what he had said or done to cause the unexpected change in her behavior, but he felt that he knew where it stemmed from. Landon. He wasn't going to ask her about it. Not now. But he knew that if he was ever going to get to know the real Cat, she would have to open up to him. Otherwise, he just couldn't deal with trying to create a friendship with someone whose demeanor was as ever shifting as the wind. The strangest things set her off.

When Cat reached the hay bale, she sized it up. It came up to just above her knee and was about four feet long. Should she just pick it up and carry it to the truck? Would he laugh at her if she couldn't lift it herself? Luke had told her they each weighed about eighty pounds. She couldn't comprehend how a rectangle of straw could be so heavy. She was still figuring out the best way in which to lift the bale when she looked up to see Luke pulling up alongside her with the truck.

He hopped out, strode up to the bale, and bending down in the squat position, heaved it up and tossed it onto the trailer.

"Why don't you stand in the trailer and push them to the back and stack them while I toss them to you?" he asked.

"Don't give me the easy job just because I'm a girl, Luke," she narrowed her eyes at him. "It didn't look that difficult."

She walked about fifteen feet to where the next bale sat. She eyed it. It was her nemesis, her challenge. She must overcome it, or she was sure to be the subject to more of Luke's mockery. Squatting down, she hoped she was still in shape from running track. She typically ran every morning in New York, around the reservoir a couple of times. It was an easy 5K and she could run it in twenty minutes or just under. Of course, she hadn't run as consistently since Landon died.

Lifting with all the strength in her legs, she heaved it onto her shoulder. She nearly collapsed under the weight, but forced her legs to move forward. She took a few quick short breaths as she walked towards Luke, keeping her eyes on the truck. She let it slip off her shoulder, onto the flat bed.

Dusting her hands, she turned to him, "No sweat."

Luke nodded, "Great. Two down, two hundred or so to go. Try

to keep up."

"Watch me."

And he did. Luke watched in awe as Cat lifted and hauled bale after bale of eighty-pound hay bales. Not once did she complain or groan. Sweat was dripping from both of them by midday and the field was half cleared. Luke watched as Cat began to struggle with the weight of the bales. He knew she was exhausted. He was pretty damn tired himself, and yet, she didn't slack off. She had a look of determination on her face.

Probably wants to prove me wrong, Luke thought to himself. Well, she's done that.

Cat's legs ached to the very bone. Her thighs felt like they were on fire and with each squat they burned more. Her right shoulder had been killing her from where she was balancing the bales, so she switched to her left. Now, it was hurting just as bad. Yet, somehow, this physical exertion had been therapeutic for her. She was no longer angry. She had burned that off with the workout she was getting. Her mind felt free. Free from the pain and sadness that came with the thought of her best friend, free from the anger towards her parents for sending her here, free from frustration at Luke for being so damn confusing. Free. It was nice to work, just work, and not think of anything else. The sweat felt cleansing, like tears, but pouring from every pore in her body.

Cat lifted another bale onto her shoulder. Her arms had started to itch like crazy a few minutes before, and she had taken her sweatshirt off, thinking it had probably been the sweat that was aggravating them. Now, as she set the bale onto the flat bed, she realized she had been wheezing for the last few minutes. Her throat felt awfully scratchy, too. She lifted her hand to rub at her throat when she noticed the red welts up and down her arms.

Luke came to the trailer with another bail and threw it up. Cat was looking at her arms and he caught a glimpse as he passed. She was covered in hives. They were even on her face and neck.

"Cat, good Lord!" he exclaimed. "Why didn't you tell me you were allergic to hay?"

"I — I," she wheezed, "I didn't know," Cat looked taken aback. "I've never touched hay before today. How could I have known?"

"I guess that's true," Luke nodded.

He wanted to keep her calm. Allergic reactions to hay were usually not serious, but hers was the worse he'd seen.

"Can you breathe okay?" he asked, holding up one of her arms to take a closer look.

"Well, my throat's kinda scratchy. I've been wheezing a little the last few minutes. I think it's getting worse," Cat took a deep breath in and listened to the wheezing sound it made.

She didn't know if it was because Luke had said she was allergic or if she was really getting worse, but suddenly she felt itchy all over. Her eyes burned and felt watery.

"We need to get you some Benadryl and quick," Luke led her to the truck and opened the passenger door for her. "I'm going to tie down the bales really quick, and then we'll head over to the McKinney's farm."

"Who?"

"They're the neighbors we're taking the hay to. Mrs. McKinney's a nurse and I'm sure she'll have something to give you."

"But, what about the rest of the hay?" Cat inquired. "Shouldn't we get that first?"

Luke was dumbfounded. Here she was, covered in hives and wheezing, and she was thinking about finishing the job.

"I'll come back later and finish," he answered.

With that, he closed her door and set about to quickly tie down the bales. Cat watched him in the rearview mirror. He had kept his long sleeve shirt on while he was handling the bales so the hay wouldn't scratch at his arms. "Smart call," thought Cat as she examined her own. She was quickly distracted, though, as Luke peeled his shirt off and set about pulling the ropes across, tying them in precise knots Cat didn't know the names of. His biceps flexed as he pulled the ropes firmly into place, and gave them a good jerk to make sure they weren't going anywhere. She realized her mouth was hanging open. She closed it and tried to focus on something else. The paint on her nails was badly chipped. She was in serious need of a manicure after today. She glanced up to see him sliding into the seat beside her and revving the engine. He was still shirtless. Cat tried not to stare. She took a deep breath to try to steady her heart rate, but ended up in a coughing fit.

"Are you okay?" Luke began to pat her on the back as he swung the truck around in the field and headed back in the direction they had come.

"Fine, fine," Cat lied. "It's just getting a little harder to breath."

"Cat, Mimi is going to kill me if I let something happen to you on the first day," Luke joked.

"Mimi can't blame you if I'm allergic to hay," Cat replied reassuringly.

"No, but she can blame me for not noticing sooner."

"That's silly," Cat said with a shake of her head.

The truck hit the paved road. Luke hit the gas and the truck lurched forward towards its destination. He quickly glanced back to ensure the hay bales hadn't shifted from their place.

"No, I should have noticed earlier. I would have noticed earlier but," he paused. "But I was making a point not to look at you."

He said the last part quickly.

Cat felt her heart skip a beat.

"Why?" she asked with feigned indifference.

"Well, let's just say I find you ... distracting," he said, mumbling the last part a bit.

Cat wasn't sure if she should be flattered or offended. After a moment, she responded to his admission.

"I really don't know what to think about that, Luke," she looked at him, wheezing quite audibly now.

"Neither do I," Luke replied, eyes glued to the road. "We're almost there," he added.

The rasping of Cat's breath was the only sound for the next couple of minutes, while the truck wound through the charming little community of Valle Crucis. They finally pulled onto a long drive dotted with Bradford Pear trees. The sign at the entrance read "Valle Crucis Stables."

Luke parked in front of the barn, since they had the trailer attached to the truck. He had already hopped out and made his way around when Cat opened the door.

The small pale-yellow home had a porch on the front and a couple of rocking chairs. It was well kept with petunias lining the sidewalk to the door. It was very quaint, yet Cat felt at home here the second she stepped out of the truck.

A female about their age, Cat guessed, came out of the door before Luke even had her around the truck.

"Luke, I know my father ordered more hay than that," she said as she skipped down the steps.

Cat got a better look at her. She was stunning. Tall, blonde, and incredibly tan. She was the closest thing Cat had ever seen to a real live Barbie doll. She suddenly was very self-conscious of the fact that she was covered in hives, sweaty, stinky, and generally a mess.

"Oh my," the gorgeous stranger exclaimed, as she saw Cat.

"Rachel, this is Cat. Cat, Rachel," Luke made quick introductions. "Cat is Mimi's granddaughter. She seems to be allergic to hay."

"I'll say!" Rachel exclaimed. Then, she hurried forward to usher Cat inside. "You poor thing! We'll take care of you. My mom's a nurse." She pulled Cat gently by the elbow through the door.

"You will be just fine," she said as she pushed Cat into the Lazy-Boy. "MOM!"

"Thanks. I'm so sorry to intrude like this," Cat stuttered. She felt so bewildered by how quickly she'd been received. I guess this is what people mean when they say "Southern hospitality".

"Yeah," added Luke behind her.

"MOM!! Oh, Luke, you hush! You're not the least bit sorry to intrude," she scolded him in a sisterly manner. "Luke has been making himself at home here since we were in kindergarten," she said to Cat with a smile. When 'mom' didn't materialize, Rachel pulled Cat up and marched her towards the small hallway.

The living room was small and it opened to the dining area. Rachel led them through to the hallway where there were bedrooms on either side. The house wasn't messy per se, but it definitely looked lived in. Toys had their place in toy boxes and bins on the sides of the living room, and children's photos lined the walls as Rachel led them towards the back.

She saw Cat eyeing the photos as they passed.

"I have one sister and two brothers," she said, "It's a little cluttered in here. Sorry."

"No, no," Cat assured.

"This is the first trailer Cat's ever been in," Luke said pointedly.

She felt herself blush intensely, even under the red blotches that already covered her face. She wanted to kick him in the shin.

"Oh, really?" Rachel raised an eyebrow. "I guess you don't

find trailers in Manhattan."

"Well, I —," Cat struggled for what to say. She hadn't realized it was a trailer. She just thought it was a cute little house.

"This is a double wide, though, so you're in the Cadillac of trailers, Cat," she said with a wink.

Cat breathed a sigh of relief.

"I want to hear everything about New York, Cat. Especially the shopping," Rachel sighed dreamily. She banged on the back-bedroom door, "MOM! We need your expertise!"

Cat smiled, "I will be happy to tell you all about it." She wondered how Rachel already knew so much about her. It seemed that word traveled fast in small towns.

A groggy voice came from behind the door, "Come on in. Was that Luke's voice I heard?"

They stepped into the dim room. The woman was wrapping herself up in a housecoat and had turned the bedside light on. She was tall like her daughter, but her blonde hair was streaked with bits of gray.

"Oh, my!" she exclaimed at the sight of Cat, "What are you allergic to, my dear?"

"Mom, this is Mimi's granddaughter, Cat," Rachel made the introductions. "She and Luke were loading hay."

"I see that," Mrs. McKinney nodded, sitting Cat down on the bed. "You'll have to excuse my appearance, Cat; I just woke up."

"Mom works the night shift at the hospital," Rachel added.

"I'm so sorry to have woken you," Cat apologized.

"Not at all. Not at all," she put on her glasses and began looking at Cat's arms. "Luke, will you go grab my bag out of the front seat of my car?"

"Yes, ma'am," he said, exiting the room.

"Let's see," she said, "Open your mouth for me. Yep, throat's swollen, too. I'm going to give you a shot to reverse your reaction. It's an antihistamine, a drug similar to cortisone. Do you have any other known allergies?"

"No," Cat responded nervously, "but I didn't know I was allergic to hay until today, either."

She could hear her wheezing was getting worse. She knew something had to be done. If only that something wasn't a shot. Today had not been a good day. She was having to face all of her greatest fears in the same day. What were the chances of that? First squirrels, now shots … if she had to deal with worms at some point today, she would really lose it.

"You'll be fine," Mrs. McKinney patted her hand, sensing her distress.

Luke hurried back in the room with a large medical bag.

"You have the shot in there?" Cat's voice was shaky. She thought they would drive to a doctor's office to get one. She didn't realize she was going to get it right then.

"I do a lot of house calls. I'm the only nurse practitioner on this side of the county," Mrs. McKinney said, sorting through things in her bag, and finally pulling out a case and two glass vials.

Cat should have turned her head, but she watched as she pulled a large syringe out of the case.

"I'm going to have to give you the shot directly into a vein to prevent anaphylactic shock," she said, calmly filling the syringe first from one vial, then the other.

Cat felt the edges of her vision beginning to blur, she felt very hot and dizzy. She slumped forward, dropping her head between her knees.

"Cat!" Luke was by her side in an instant.

"Cat? Cat, can you hear me?" Mrs. McKinney called, lifting Cat's face to meet her own.

Cat was so embarrassed. She could see Rachel standing calmly by the bedroom door. Mrs. McKinney was still beside her and Luke was kneeling in front of her. She wasn't comfortable being the center of attention, not at a time like this. She started shaking and lowered her head back down between her knees.

"Does it have to be a shot?" she whimpered.

"I'm afraid so sweetie. And it needs to be right now, so you don't get any worse."

"Here. I'll hold your hand Cat," Luke said, taking hers in his.

What Cat couldn't see was the curious grin that spread across Rachel's face when he did this. She only noticed the way he looked at her.

"Don't look at the shot. Just keep your eyes on me," he brushed some loose waves of hair from her face.

As if I could look anywhere else, Cat thought. She had her eyes locked on nothing else but him.

"Okay, just hurry," she whispered.

Gazing into his green eyes, she felt a peace wash over her. She was sure she would get lost in them, until she heard Mrs. McKinney say, "All done!"

"That's it?" Cat broke her trance.

"I'd like for you to stay here about an hour or so, so I can keep an eye on you. Make sure you don't have any reactions to the shot, but yes ma'am, you're through," she patted Cat on the shoulder.

"I'll go get the rest of the hay," Luke released her hand, and just like that, their connection was broken. "I'll be back for you in a bit."

He smiled at her quickly and was out the door.

"Rachel, why don't you fix Cat some lunch? I'm going to get a little more sleep before work," Mrs. McKinney said, as she put her things away and disposed of the syringe.

"Thank you so much," Cat said standing up. She was still a little wobbly on her feet.

"Not at all," Mrs. McKinney smiled genuinely. "You feel free to come over as much as you like. I'm sure Rachel is dying to talk about New York fashion with you."

"Mom," Rachel said reproachfully, as she led Cat out of the room towards the kitchen.

"She's right, though!" she added with a laugh. "I would give my right eye for a pair of Christian Louboutins!"

"They are fabulous," Cat agreed.

She watched curiously, as Rachel gathered a ripe tomato, Duke's mayonnaise, and white bread and set about to make them sandwiches. So, this girl from the mountains of North Carolina knew about Christian Louboutin shoes? Life was full of surprises. She felt an instant kinship with Rachel, and not just because they shared the same affinity for fashion. It was because she was so welcoming, so genuine, and Cat rarely felt that in the people she had known back in New York City. Everyone there was typically so closed off to those around them. What a strange world where people would pull a stranger in, and make them feel welcome (while shooting them up with meds). Cat smiled as she eyed her tomato sandwich somewhat suspiciously. Tomatoes were pretty high on her list of most-loathed vegetables. She chose courage and took an enormous bite; in part because her gracious hostess was watching, but also because Cat was just plain starving. Juice from the tomato dripped down her chin; it was delightful. Rachel grinned and Cat couldn't help but laugh at herself. She would be okay here after all.

CHAPTER EIGHT

CAT PUT DOWN THE LATEST ISSUE OF VOGUE. SHE HAD BEEN READING it at Rachel's insistence that she critique Marc Jacobs's Fall Collection. When Rachel had heard that Cat had attended New York Fashion Week, the questions were non-stop, but Cat didn't mind. Not too much, at least. Unfortunately, Cat couldn't recall each collection she saw to the specific detail Rachel required. She had been given the latest issue of Vogue to refresh her memory on what she had seen.

"Well, I really liked his use of color in this collection. Last Fall had far too much gray and black for my taste," Cat said sitting up in the rocking chair and leaning over the porch so she could see Rachel better.

"I couldn't agree more," Rachel looked up, smiling. She dusted the dirt of her knees and climbed up the steps to sit in the chair beside Cat.

"Those flowers look lovely," Cat examined the new additions to the flowerbed lining the sidewalk.

"Thanks," Rachel beamed, "I don't have the money for fabric to design my own clothes … but I do design the flower beds."

"Very nice," Cat nodded. She was feeling one hundred percent better now that all her hives had disappeared and she could breathe normally again.

"Can I get you some more lemonade?" Rachel asked, taking Cat's empty glass from the small table between them.

"Hmmm, yes please," Cat nodded.

She rocked back and forth, enjoying the mountain breeze as it cooled her face. Luke had been gone two hours so far. Rachel didn't think he'd be back for at least two more. Cat imagined him driving the trailer around the field and loading all the hay himself. It was exhausting just to think about. She wished there was something she could do.

Rachel came back out with a full glass and handed it to Cat.

"Well Cat, now that I've asked you to analyze every Fall collection coming out, I only have one more question."

"Go ahead," Cat said, taking a large swallow of lemonade.

"What do you think of Luke?"

The question made Cat sputter and choke on her lemonade. It had caught her so off guard. Rachel died laughing at her reaction.

"Well, I guess that answers that," she said with a sly grin.

"No, no. You just caught me by surprise," Cat said, trying to recover. "He's fine, I guess. I hardly know him. Why?"

"He's crazy about you," Rachel leaned forward in her chair, waiting to gauge Cat's response.

"I doubt that," Cat's heart had begun hammering in her chest. She willed it to beat steadily. "I think I drive him crazy."

"Cat, I've known Luke my entire life. I've seen him with girls. Even with Clarissa, his girlfriend, he's never acted the way he acted with you today."

"How's that?" Cat tried to ask nonchalantly.

"Like he didn't care for anything in the world except taking care of you. It was, well, let's just say, he was different with you. Good different," Rachel said matter-of-factly.

"Wait. Did you say he has a girlfriend?" Cat asked, just piecing together what Rachel had said. She didn't want to sound disappointed. She tried to alter her voice to sound interested, instead of upset.

"Oh, I should have said he *had* a girlfriend. Word on Facebook is that he broke up with her last night," Rachel judged Cat's response. Apparently pleased at what she saw, she smiled widely, "I think you should totally ask him out."

"Oh, I don't think I could do that. I've never really dated anyone. I wouldn't know what to say," Cat began. "Not that he would say yes anyway."

"Please, Cat. Don't be ridiculous!" Rachel straightened up in her seat. "The boys at Watauga will be going gaga over you. He'll be so jealous he won't want anyone else to get you."

"I doubt that," Cat couldn't hide the excitement in her voice. She had attended an all-girl school since her freshman year of high school. She wasn't used to being around boys — with the exception of Landon. But it wasn't the thought of other guys that made Cat excited, it was the thought of Luke.

"I hear she's furious," Rachel said abruptly, taking the conversation in a new direction.

"Who?" Cat asked, confused.

"Clarissa, Luke's ex. When he got home last night, she was waiting for him. I hear she was going to surprise him or … something. And, he just broke up with her! No explanations or anything," Rachel added mischievously. "So, when did you get into town?"

"Umm," Cat hesitated. "Yesterday."

"And when did you meet Luke?" Rachel leaned towards her.

"Yesterday," Cat felt her heart beating faster.

"I KNEW it!" Rachel cried, jumping to her feet.

Her sudden exclamation made Cat jump in her seat and slosh lemonade onto her jeans.

"Rachel, be serious. Luke just met me yesterday. That wouldn't be the reason he broke up with — umm,"

"Clarissa," Rachel nodded.

"Right, Clarissa," Cat finished.

She couldn't help but think that maybe, just maybe, Rachel was right. That Luke had feelings for her like that. Not that it would matter, she quickly reminded herself. He drove her crazy anyway. They would just drive each other mad if they ever dated. But there had been something. Something in the way he held her when she had cried this morning, something in the way he looked into her eyes that made everything and everyone else melt away.

"So, why did you come to live with Mimi?" Rachel asked.

Her question was innocent enough, but Cat had no idea how to go about answering it. It was too complicated to give a brief answer to, and she really didn't feel like going into a three-hour conversation of her life during the last three months.

She must have had a very contemplative look on her face because Rachel added, "Oh, you don't have to tell me. No worries."

"No, I don't mind. It's just really complicated," Cat said with a smile. She was sure she looked relieved at the thought of not having to explain herself.

"You'll have plenty of time to tell me later. All senior year," Rachel said happily, "I can't believe I'm a, I mean, we're seniors. It will be the best year. You'll see, Cat."

Cat watched as Rachel finished off her glass of lemonade. She'd only known her for a few hours, but she felt like they'd been friends forever.

"So," Cat began, leaning towards Rachel with a sly grin, "What is Luke's ex like? What is my competition?"

They both laughed.

"She's a cheerleader. Really petite. Cute," Rachel winked, "but not nearly as pretty as you."

"Ha, ha." Cat responded.

"And she will be pissed when she hears he's been spending time with the new girl from New York," Rachel added bluntly.

"Great," Cat thought, "Just the way I want to start the year. With some girl out to get me."

"She's vindictive, slutty, petty … and a brown-noser," Rachel added, wrinkling her nose. "Can you tell what I think about her?"

"Not at all," Cat laughed.

"So, that means I'm going to have to start getting the word out about how fabulous the new girl is; and with me as your new best friend, you'll be golden," Rachel laughed.

She picked up her phone and her fingers began to fly on the buttons.

"What are you doing?" Cat leaned in to see.

"Sending out a tweet, and a post on Facebook: Just met Cat, new girl from NYC. She is fabulous! Party at Watauga Lake tonight at 8pm. Come one, come all, and see for yourself," Rachel pressed send before Cat could object.

"Oh, Rachel … I don't know that my grandmother will let me go. I was getting into … well, a little trouble in New York … and going to a party is definitely something my parents would have forbidden her from letting me do," Cat hated to be a party pooper, but she knew what Mimi's reaction would be to this.

"Cat, no worries," Rachel patted her arm, "My mom and Mimi are like this," she said, crossing two fingers, "My mom will call and let her know that Luke and I are just going to introduce you to some people before school starts, so you won't be nervous on your first day."

It did sound like a great plan. Cat couldn't help but get a little excited at the thought of meeting her new classmates. She wanted to make a good first impression. She wanted this year to be a new start. She was putting the past behind her. She didn't want to deal with it anymore. She wanted a chance to be happy again, to feel again. She had decided all of this earlier today, when she was pouring sweat out in the field. Sweat. She looked down at her clothes. There was no way she could make a good first impression like this. She was filthy.

"Rachel, I'll have to go back to Mimi's and get ready!" Cat exclaimed looking at herself.

"You'll have time. I'll text Luke and see how much he has left." Rachel's fingers went to work on her phone at once.

"You could take my car if you wanted and then just drive back when you're ready," Rachel said looking up.

"I — I don't think I know my way back," Cat replied, looking away. She didn't know her way back, that was true. It also sounded better than saying she didn't know how to drive.

Rachel's phone beeped.

"Ah! He's finished. Seems he conned my little bro, Roman, into helping him," Rachel put her phone away.

So, Luke would be back soon. Cat would get ready and before she knew it, she would be enjoying a party thrown in her honor. This day had been full of so many surprises. She leaned back in the chair and smiled as Rachel began to fill her in on all of the cliques, girls, and guys that made up their senior class at Watauga High. Her new school.

CHAPTER NINE

CAT HAD LAID OUT FIVE OUTFITS. SHE HAD TALKED TO RACHEL THREE times and she had modeled for Mimi in two of them. She still wasn't sure what to wear. What did one wear to a 'casual' party at a lake to meet a bunch of people for the first time? Too dressy says, "I'm a rich snob from New York." Too casual says, "I don't care enough to look nice for you people." She finally decided on a crisp pair of BCBG white shorts and a blue lace tank. She slipped on her silver Jack Rogers sandals, and she was ready to go. And, not a moment too soon, she was just skipping down the stairs when Luke pulled up in his truck. He had run home to shower while she got ready.

He jumped out of the truck and started towards the door before he saw her. He stopped for a second and fought the urge to whistle when she came skipping through the door. She was stunning. Her caramel waves were down loose around her shoulders. He hadn't seen her hair down yet, unless you counted when it was dripping wet and fresh out of the shower the night before. He liked it down. The light brown color had just a shimmer of gold in the sun. He hadn't noticed that before.

"What?" she looked down at herself, he had apparently been staring too hard.

"Hmm?" he faked confusion.

"Is there something wrong? Am I too dressy? Too casual?" She looked at her outfit self-consciously. "I can run back up and change."

"No. You look … fine," Luke wasn't sure if this response was unkind. But he felt saying, 'you look amazing,' would make things uncomfortable.

He offered his hand and walked her around to the passenger side of the truck.

This whole act of being walked to her side of the vehicle felt new and strange and made her stomach do back flips. Was it being walked to the car door or the person who was doing the walking? Cat had a feeling it was the latter.

Cat slid into the seat wondering if she should have changed after all. She didn't want Luke to think she looked just 'fine'. She wanted him to find her tempting, irresistible even. She sighed as she watched him walk around to the driver's side. He was wearing khaki shorts, a white button up with the sleeves rolled up, and Birkenstocks. His short curls were tousled in a messy, yet utterly sexy way. It was Cat's turn to be caught staring.

"You okay?" Luke asked, eyeing her suspiciously as he got in.

"Umm hmm, fine," she turned her eyes forward.

They drove for the first ten minutes in silence. Each one always seemed to be on the verge of saying something, but then stopped when they opened their mouths. Cat caught him staring at her twice and had been caught looking at him three times. Each time, they gave an awkward smile and pretended to be staring at something just beyond the window.

Finally, Cat couldn't stand the tension any longer.

"So, Rachel told me you have a girlfriend?" Cat asked nonchalantly, keeping her eyes forward so they wouldn't betray her.

"Had," came Luke's one-word response.

"Oh?"

"I, um, broke up with her recently."

"How recent?" Cat was dying to know the details, but thought playing it cool would get her further.

Luke looked at her for a moment, before turning his attention back to the road, "Last night."

"What happened?" Cat was genuinely curious. Was it her arrival that had been the catalyst, or was that her wishful thinking?

"I guess I was tired of pretending that I cared. I haven't cared for a long time. Each time I'd try to break it off, she would cry and want to talk things out. Then, before I knew it, we'd be back together. I finally just did it," he said with a shrug, as he turned onto a gravel road.

"How long did you date?" Cat inquired.

"Ten months or so," he was clearly looking for a change of subject.

"Wow. You guys must have been serious," Cat raised her eyebrows. She wondered what it would be like to be in a relationship lasting longer than an hour.

"Clarissa liked to think so," Luke sighed. "I would've broken up with her months ago."

"So, I know she cried and made you feel bad; but, if you were so miserable, why didn't you just end it sooner? It couldn't have been worth it … or was it? I guess if you guys did … things. Maybe it was?" Cat wished she hadn't asked such a personal question, but she did want to know.

"Oh, no. Well, I mean. Yes, but no," Luke stumbled over his response. He felt so guilty all a sudden. He didn't want Cat to think badly of him.

"Ahh, that makes a lot of sense," Cat had this icky feeling in the pit of her stomach. Was it jealousy? She had only met him yesterday. How could she be jealous of some girl he may or may not have slept with before they had even met?

"Cat," he reached across the seat and grabbed her hand, "we didn't."

"You don't have to tell me," Cat pulled away.

"And I haven't," he said, not releasing her hand.

"Okay," Cat looked down at his hand still on hers, "Luke … why are you telling me this?"

"I — I just thought, maybe if I show you that I can open up to you, you'll realize you can open up to me," he let go of her hand and shrugged. "You just seem like you could use someone to talk to."

"I don't know what you're talking about," Cat swallowed the lump rising in her throat and got out of the car.

How did he see her so clearly? For a moment, Cat wanted to tell him everything, to cry and let out all the pain and anguish that she had worked so hard to bury and forget. She had told herself today that the pain of her past was gone. That today was her fresh start. Why did Luke threaten to make her remember, when all she wanted to do was run away from it all?

Luke hurried from the truck to catch up with her. Again, he regretted his moment of honesty with Cat. Confused was not adequate enough to describe how she made him feel.

She let him catch up to her. Partly because she didn't know where she was going, but mostly because she liked being close to him.

The path wound through a small bit of woods and opened up to a sandy beach along a perfect mountain lake.

Rachel already had a bonfire going and was popping up camping chairs around the fire beside large logs that looked like they were used for benches.

"Hey!" Rachel came running up and greeted Cat with a warm hug, almost knocking her over, "You're early!"

"Oh. I'm sorry," Cat began.

"Don't be silly," Rachel grabbed her hand and pulled her towards a card table still flat on the ground. "This just means you get to help me set up."

"I'm happy to," Cat bent down to help Rachel set up the table.

It wasn't too long before the first guests arrived. Before the first hour was up, Cat counted nearly 60 people milling around on the beach. She had met everybody. Some greeted her with handshakes, some went straight for a hug, but everyone wanted to hear about New York City and how she came to be in Boone.

Cat had already practiced her response.

Her parents were too controlling and she needed a change of pace.

It was simple, and surprisingly everyone was able to relate on some level.

The fire grew bright as the sun went down. Someone had brought their iPod and speakers to hook up for music. A few others had been happy to supply beer. Apparently, they knew Rachel would not be bringing any. Cat had asked her when they arrived if there would be alcohol and Rachel had responded with one sentence, "Cat, my dad is a Baptist preacher." Then she laughed when Cat asked what being Baptist had to do with it. Apparently, Cat had a lot to learn about the South.

Cat hadn't planned on drinking anyway; she had just been wondering what kind of parties they had here in Boone.

"Okay," Rachel said, "That's Troy. He plays basketball. Matt, super smart. Ford, he's our best linebacker. He's like a big teddy bear."

Cat followed her gaze to where Rachel was pointing out each of the guys. Trying to remember their names was quite a feat. They all knew her name, but of course, they only had one name to learn.

She felt like she had most of the girls' names down, based on where they were sitting around her. Of course, more people were arriving, so it was making it challenging when they kept trading places. Remembering them in order had not been a good idea, Cat decided.

"Uh-oh," Carey piped up from where she sat on the log beside Cat, "bitch alert."

The heads of all the girls in their circle turned to see four girls walking onto the beach.

They were all wearing cutoff jean skirts and polo tops. Thankfully, not all the same color.

"Did they plan to dress the same?" Cat directed her question to Rachel, yet the entire circle erupted in laughter.

"Good Lord, I hope not," Rachel smiled. Then, she looked at Cat and mouthed the word "Clarissa."

Cat nodded knowingly.

The small blonde led the way. Her hair was bobbed short and stacked in the back. She had a look on her face as though she had just smelled something nasty. Other than her expression though, Cat thought she could be considered quite cute.

"So that's Luke's ex," Cat said thoughtfully.

"She's so sneaky," Sarah said with narrow eyes. "Best to stay on her good side."

"Really?" Cat didn't like the sound of that.

"No one likes her," Rachel lowered her voice, "But her family has money and so she invites everyone for ski weekends at their chalet all winter. Apparently, it's easy to buy friends."

The girls all watched Clarissa and her posse grab beers from the table and turn to approach them.

Sarah spoke first, "Hey, C! You look so good."

"I try," Clarissa looked over her shoulder to Luke, "He'll be seeing what he's missing out on."

"We were all so sorry to hear about you guys," Carey added.

Cat was shocked at how quickly all the girls poured on the compliments and the sympathy. The ski weekends must be an important invite for everyone to go through this much trouble, Cat thought.

"You must be Cat," Clarissa turned to her with a half-smile. The pitch of her voice had gone up noticeably.

"Hi, nice to meet you," Cat stood and extended her hand.

"You're living with your grandmother? Is that what I heard?" she inquired.

"That's right," Cat nodded.

"Why would anyone leave New York to come here?" Clarissa smirked. "Unless, you didn't have a choice."

"Well — I," Cat didn't know what to say. She couldn't believe this girl she didn't even know was being so confrontational. "I guess I just needed a change of pace."

"You must find this place so backwoods compared to what you're used to," Clarissa added. It was as though she wanted Cat to say something snooty and come across as the snob from the city.

"No, we visit my grandmother every year. So, I've been coming to the mountains my whole life," Cat smiled forcefully.

"Oh, who's your grandmother?" Clarissa took a swig from her beer.

"Martha Wilson, she lives near Valle Crucis. Everyone knows her as Mimi, though," Cat could see Luke staring at them out of the corner of her eye.

"Mimi. That's who my boy — I mean my ex-boyfriend works for," there was a sudden edge to Clarissa's voice.

Rachel stepped beside Cat before she could say anything,

"Cat already met Luke. Yesterday."

Cat wanted to clamp a hand over Rachel's mouth, but the damage was already done.

"If you'll excuse me," Clarissa turned away from them and stomped towards the fire. Stopping a few feet from Luke, she motioned for him to follow her. Luke stepped out from the safety of his guy friends to follow her, but not before shooting a deadly look in Cat's direction.

"Rachel, now he's going to be pissed at me," Cat spun around to face Rachel.

"No, Cat. Now you have an excuse to go over to him," Rachel informed slyly.

"What?" Cat asked.

"You can go rescue him, Cat," Rachel took her arm, "Come on, let's go sit on that log and see if we can hear what she's saying to him."

Cat pressed her lips together — torn between her desire to know what was going on and the guilt of eavesdropping. Curiosity won and she nodded. Rachel was good at this game. But she was certain there had to be an easier way of hitting on Luke than this. She was such a novice at this.

Once settled on the log, they could hear nearly everything Clarissa was saying, or yelling as the case may be, at Luke. It seems as though being in the cover of the nearby trees had given Clarissa the false impression that they couldn't be overheard.

"Tell me, Luke. Say it to my face. Why did you break up with me?"

"Clarissa — I"

"I know it's that new girl, whatever her name is."

"Cat?"

"I knew it!"

"Clarissa. I haven't been happy in a long time, and you know it."

"Don't lie to me, Luke. I know you loved me. I was prepared to do anything for you … ANYTHING!"

"Clarissa, I'm sorry that you're hurt."

"Have you kissed her?"

"What?"

"Have you kissed her? I know northern girls are sluts, but I would've done whatever she did to steal you."

"Don't talk that way about her. She hasn't done anything to you. She just got here yesterday."

"Yeah! YESTERDAY … as in the day you dumped me. Asshole! You are an asshole. Both of you are!"

Cat's face burned red. Half the party had gone silent to better hear the argument. Cat felt dozens of eyes watching her. She kept her eyes glued to the fire. Rachel was pinching her arm to the point that Cat had to ask her to let go.

"Sorry, Cat. But did you hear that? He's crazy about you!" Rachel breathed in her ear.

"Why are you sticking up for her, Luke!" Clarissa's voice shrieked.

"I'm not sticking up for her, I," Luke began.

"I blame her. I will make her pay for this. I forgive you, Luke. Oh, Luke," she crooned. Her voice dropped quieter and Cat leaned back on the log, straining to listen.

"Baby, I still love you. I'm willing to give you another chance," her voice went on silkily. "If you say you're sorry and that you love me, I'll take you back."

Luke didn't say anything.

"I'm waiting," the sweetness in Clarissa's voice began to wane.

"Well, I'm not going to lie to you," Luke said quietly.

"Luke, this is your last chance. If you don't apologize right now,

I will believe that you cheated on me with that Yankee whore."

Anger flared in Cat, and she lost her balance, falling backwards off the log. Embarrassed, she leapt to her feet. Rachel stood up after her. By now, the entire party watched silently as this strange love triangle unfolded. There were whispers and friendly nods towards Cat. She felt her cheeks burning and it wasn't from the bonfire.

Rachel gave her a nudge, "I think Luke could use some help." She winked.

Cat turned before she could change her mind and marched into the shadows where Luke and Clarissa stood. She cleared her throat. Luke had no idea what Cat was up to, but he was glad to have her there. He was so close to telling Clarissa that he was crazy about Cat. He couldn't tell her that yesterday; he didn't realize it was possible to have such a longing for another person. Not just physically, but wholly. He longed to know all of Cat — her quirks, her secrets, all of her. He would have told her all of that if he didn't know that half of the senior class was listening a few yards away.

"Excuse me, Clarissa," Cat said from behind.

"What?" she shouted without turning around.

"We just met. Cat, the Yankee whore. I just thought, since I was a topic in this argument, I would set the record straight," Cat walked around her and stood beside Luke. "Luke hasn't done anything. He hasn't hit on me. He hasn't kissed me. He just met me," Cat touched Luke on the shoulder.

"I don't believe you," Clarissa snapped at her.

Cat saw a window of opportunity to make Clarissa leave Luke alone and leave her insanely jealous in the meantime. It may have been wrong, but she took it.

Cat spoke up, "Well, Clarissa. Since you already think the

worst of me, since you already believe that Luke and I have hooked up, I might as well make it a reality."

And with that, Cat was on him. Luke was completely taken aback. The force of her kiss nearly made him stumble back; but he recovered in a millisecond, and hoisted her body up against him, her legs wrapped around his waist. Luke heard a scream of frustration from Clarissa and catcalls and whistles coming from everyone else around the lake. But all he saw was Cat. All he felt was her body firmly against his own. Her lips parted just enough that he could taste her tongue against his. Never before had he been kissed so passionately. And certainly, never in front of so many people.

What have I done? This was all Cat could think as she threw herself onto Luke. Literally, threw herself. I don't even know if I'm doing this right. What if I've embarrassed this poor guy? Will he be humiliated? Will he be angry? No, Cat told herself. No, the hands that lifted her off the ground and returned every ounce of passion were not embarrassed by her. She had this crazy notion to kiss him in front of Clarissa and had acted on it without a second thought; so unlike herself. Cat was thankful that for once in her life she had just acted. She allowed herself to get swept up in the moment, the heat, his touch; it wasn't until she heard Clarissa shouting and whistling coming from onlookers that she realized just how carried away she'd allowed herself to become.

Cat pulled her face away and held his cheeks between her palms. She had no idea what just happened, yet she didn't regret it. She had only turned to kiss him and the next thing she knew, she had her legs around him. He let go of her legs and her body slid down, until her feet touched the ground. The moment had only lasted a few seconds, well ten at most, but

Cat felt all the underlying tension that had been present since they had met melt away in an instant.

His eyes looked into hers as she opened them.

"I think I made her jealous," Cat smiled.

"You think?" Luke laughed.

"Should we join the group?" Cat turned her eyes to where the rest of the party was watching Clarissa stomp angrily back to her car.

"Yeah, just give me a minute," Luke smiled, embarrassed.

"Okay," Cat laughed.

Once she started laughing, it seemed difficult to stop. She buried her head into his chest until she could control her giggles. She hadn't laughed so heartily in several months.

And then it hit her again. Why did she deserve to be laughing when Landon couldn't? He was dead and she was standing here laughing. Her laughter ended abruptly.

Luke saw the shadow cross Cat's face and she looked at him with those dead eyes — the ones that shouldn't belong in a person so full of life.

"I need to go," she said suddenly, and with that, she was running into the woods. Into the dark.

What am I thinking? Cat chided herself, as she ran through the thick brush. Branches swiped at her hair. Her sandals didn't make running away any easier.

Where am I going?

It's not like she could run all the way back to Mimi's. She didn't even know what direction the parking lot was from here.

There could be bears in these woods, or snakes, or, God forbid

... squirrels. It was this thought that caused Cat to slow down.

She heard the footsteps of Luke catching up to her. Putting her hands on her knees she dropped her head down to catch her breath.

"Good grief, Cat," Luke came up behind her. "You're pretty fast."

Cat turned to him. The humor of the situation was not lost on her. They had just shared an amazing kiss. Then, she ran away without explanation and he catches up to tell her she runs fast. She bit her lip to keep from laughing.

"Thanks," Cat folded her arms across her chest. "I used to run. Before —"

Luke made a mental note of that. He would be captain on the cross-country team this year and they could use some more runners. But now was not the moment to ask her about her times, or whether she preferred Asics or Saucony.

"What's the deal, Cat?" his voice turned serious as he slowly approached her.

He walked towards her as though she was a frightened animal, afraid she might dash off again.

Cat knew what he was asking, but didn't answer his question.

"Let's get something straight, Luke. The only reason I kissed you was to help you out and make Clarissa leave you alone," Cat announced.

"You're not answering my question," Luke took another step forward.

They were close enough now that he could reach out and touch her, but he didn't.

"I was embarrassed from kissing you in front of all those people, so I ran away," Cat lied badly.

It's a good thing he can't see my face in the dark, Cat thought to herself.

Then he would be able to see how she truly felt about him. It was written all over her face. She only hoped it wasn't coming through in her voice. She couldn't let herself be happy. She didn't deserve to love like that. To be swept up in something so completely that it would take her pain away. Her pain connected her to Landon. She wasn't ready to let go of it yet ... it would be like forgetting him.

Luke touched her hand, "You can do it, Cat. It's okay."

"What?" she was confused.

"You can let yourself be happy. You can laugh and not feel guilty. You ..."

Cat interrupted, "You don't know what you're talking about, Luke!"

Wrenching her hand away from his, she turned and began to stomp away.

"Cat! Cat, where are you going?" Luke wanted to grab her, and laugh at her, and let her go all at the same time. Instead, he just followed as she continued to stomp deeper into the woods.

"Away from you!" came her snappy reply.

"You can't grieve forever, Cat. It's not healthy. You deserve to be happy," he called after her.

She continued to stomp away.

"Landon would want you to be happy," he tried this approach, knowing that what he said was true.

Cat stopped, but didn't turn.

She knew he was right. Landon would have been furious to see her behaving this way. To see how she beat herself up every time she smiled or laughed. She sighed heavily. She was so scared that forgiving herself would mean forgetting Landon.

Luke walked up behind her. His hands went to her shoulders and gave them a squeeze.

"No one blames you for his death Cat," he whispered.

"That's not true," a tear rolled down her cheek.

"I don't know what happened, but you can't keep blaming yourself," he wrapped his arms around her.

If she was going to let herself be happy, she would first have to be honest. Luke needed to know what happened, everything that happened, before he decided to get mixed up with someone as messed up as Cat had been the last few months.

"You don't know," she began, turning around to face him.

"Then, tell me," he pushed her hair from her eyes.

She looked up at him through her tears and, though it was dark, she saw understanding in his eyes. She saw someone she could trust.

He caressed her cheek with his fingertips. When he got to her chin, he tilted her head up and kissed her. Slowly, sweetly, Cat felt weak in the knees.

"Wait," she pushed him away, "I want you to know everything first. Then, you can decide if I'm worth getting to know better."

"I already know," Luke answered assuredly. "But if it will make you feel better to tell me your story first, then you should. I want to know everything about you. Everything."

The sincerity of his answer left her a little breathless.

"Where's a good place for us to go?" Cat looked around, the woods kind of creeped her out.

"Let's head back to the campfire, before a million rumors start flying about what we're doing in the woods. Then we can leave," Luke smiled.

Taking his hand, Cat let him lead her out of the woods and back to the beach. She had no idea she had run so far. She was about to ask Luke if he was sure they were headed in the right direction when she heard voices in the distance.

Whistles and cheers erupted when they emerged from the woods. Cat felt her face turn beet red.

"Oh, come on guys, we were only gone for like five minutes," Luke brushed them off.

"That's long enough," yelled one guy, the football player whose name Cat couldn't quite recall.

Luke shook his head and laughed them off. He was still holding Cat's hand, until Rachel came bouncing up to her.

"So? Are you guys official?" Rachel asked, looking from Luke to Cat.

Cat wasn't sure exactly what to say. They hadn't ironed out any details of their relationship. Cat didn't want to say they were dating until he knew everything.

"We're going to spend some more time together and then Luke can decide," Cat said thoughtfully.

"Oh," Rachel looked disappointed, "okay."

"I think I'm going to go ahead and take Cat home," Luke said, "I promised Mimi I'd have her back early."

They said their goodbyes. Cat tried, with some difficulty, to remember all the names she had learned tonight. As she left, she wondered what they all thought of her — the new girl who kissed Luke in front of his ex. Did that make her somewhat of a bitch?

"They all think you're great, you know?" Luke appeared at her side to walk her to the car.

How did it seem like he was always able to read her mind?

"I don't know," Cat tilted her head to the side thoughtfully.

"I do. You're the only girl they've ever seen who could put Queen Clarissa in her place," he held the door open for her to get in the truck.

"It was kind of awesome, wasn't it?" Cat smiled.

Leaning in, he pecked her quickly on the cheek, "Damn straight, it was!"

She threw her arms around him, pulling him in, and leaned her head back with a burst of laughter. Luke couldn't help but kiss her in that moment. The way she had smiled, her face all flushed, the desire just overcame him.

With one hand behind her neck and the other on her waist he leaned in to where she sat in the truck. He knew he had taken her by surprise by the little gasp she gave right after he kissed her. It was so innocent; he couldn't help but kiss her again, only this time holding it for just a bit longer.

When he pulled away, he smiled at her and closed the truck door. Cat leaned back against the seat and tried to catch her breath. She placed her hand over her heart, only this time it was not aching; it was swelling with joy. How can the human heart be capable of so much feeling? One moment she's sinking, the next soaring, and all in a matter of 24 hours. She didn't know if this was the roller coaster of emotions she needed in her life right now, but she didn't want to get off.

This is going to be difficult, she realized, as she thought about the task that lay before her.

How did she begin to tell him about Landon's death? Or what had happened to her in the aftermath?

Luke had said earlier that no one blamed her for what happened. She shut her eyes, trying not to remember that what he said was entirely untrue. Someone did blame her, and because of that, she also blamed herself.

CHAPTER TEN

MIMI HAD BEEN UP READING WHEN CAT GOT HOME.

She and Luke had already planned it out. She would go in, chat briefly about the get-together, then exclaim how crazy tired she was and go upstairs to bed.

Meanwhile, after Mimi had seen Luke's truck drive away, he would park on the other side of the barn and carry the ladder around to her window. She would then climb down and they would find a place to be alone and talk. Simple.

It sounded like something out of a movie, Cat thought. She giggled to herself as she hopped out of the car and called loudly, "See you tomorrow!" just in case Mimi was watching or could hear.

She had butterflies in her stomach as she climbed the steps of the porch. She was a terrible liar. Anyone who knew her knew it. Of course, Mimi didn't really know her. So, Cat had that working in her favor.

"You're home early," Mimi smiled, looking up from her book, when Cat came into the living room.

"I know, I'm exhausted!" Cat yawned loudly; she hoped that didn't sound super fake.

"Well, Catie you had an early morning," Mimi nodded.

Good, she bought it, Cat thought.

"I had fun tonight. It was nice to meet some new people," Cat smiled. "But I think I'm going to bed. Another early morning tomorrow, right?"

"No work tomorrow," Mimi chirped.

"Awesome," Cat was filled with glee.

"Church tomorrow. I'll wake you up around 8am, okay?" Mimi looked back at her book.

"Oh, um, okay," Cat responded and went to climb the stairs.

She had never attended church other than an occasional wedding. Her dad was Catholic and her mom used to be Baptist, but they had never decided in which denomination to raise their daughters, and as such, they rarely went. Except for holidays, or weddings ... or funerals added a voice in the back of Cat's mind.

She was so lost in thought she had forgotten about Luke, until she heard a rapping at the window and let out a squeal as she nearly jumped out of her skin.

"Catie? Catie, are you okay?" Mimi's voice called up the stairs.

Cat looked at the window where Luke stood on the ladder with wide eyes.

"I — I'm fine!" she called, "I thought I saw a mouse, but it was my-uh-my shoe! I'm going to bed now! Good night!"

"Night!" Mimi called back.

Cat listened until she was certain Mimi's footsteps led her into her own bedroom downstairs before she crossed to open the window.

"What the hell, Cat?!" Luke hissed.

"Sorry, you scared me," she hissed back.

"But you knew I was coming," he snapped as he climbed into her room.

"Well, I forgot okay," Cat retorted in his face.

Then she softened. Would it always be like this with him? She grabbed his face, and pressed her lips against his, catching him completely off guard. He stumbled back, making the window rattle slightly in its frame. A floorboard creaked.

"Shh!" she said, pulling away and putting a finger to her lips.

He pushed her hand away and kissed her with equal if not greater force than what she used on him, causing her to stumble backwards to the bed.

She allowed herself to lay back, pulling him with her. Obliging, he lay down with her, and holding himself up with one arm, he cradled her head with the other. He kissed her — her lips, her cheeks, even the tip of her nose, down her neck, across her collar bone, until he pushed himself away, quite suddenly, and sat up.

Cat was confused.

"What-what's wrong?" she sat up as well, straightening her hair.

"This is just too dangerous, Cat," Luke smiled at her. "I want you too badly to be in your room, in your bed, alone with you."

"We were just kissing," Cat felt ashamed.

"I know," Luke leaned in and kissed her cheek, "but I think you are too special for me to take advantage of you like that."

Her heart swelled with admiration.

"I think I was the one taking advantage of you," she laughed.

"You wanted to talk to me before we got serious anyway, remember?" Luke smiled in the way that revealed a dimple in one cheek. Cat melted. Maybe this was too dangerous. He pushed himself away from her and stood, extending his hand to help her off the bed.

"Do you have somewhere we could go?" Cat accepted his hand and walked to the window.

They had planned her escape perfectly, but she had no idea where they were going to go afterwards.

"I have the perfect place," Luke kissed her hand before hoisting himself noiselessly through the window. He was so much better at this sneaking thing than Cat was, she decided. She followed after him with considerably less stealth, but thankful, at least, that Mimi wasn't disturbed.

Fifteen minutes later, Luke pulled the truck to a halt. Even though it was nearly 11pm, Cat could see the outline of an old barn against the night sky. The half-moon provided ample light on the field before them. Allowing her gaze to track upwards, Cat held her breath. The stars were unlike anything Cat had ever beheld. Other than visits to the planetarium at the Museum of Natural History near her home, she had never seen the stars so clearly. It was astounding. The touch of his hand by her side brought her gaze back down.

"Is that a barn?" she asked curiously, nodding towards the hillside.

"It is," Luke hopped out of the truck and came around to open her door.

By now, Cat had learned not to open the door herself. She could get used to this kind of chivalry.

"Aren't you forgetting something?" she asked as he helped her out.

Luke looked around, "I don't think so."

"I'm allergic to hay, Luke."

"There's not any hay in this barn, Cat. You'll be fine," he smiled and led her up the worn dirt path to the side door.

Cat had never heard of a barn without any hay before. But, then again, she had never spent time in any barns so what did she know?

He opened the tack room door and turned on a desk lamp that was sitting on a table, illuminating the small room.

Cat could see an old couch against the wall that was covered with a colorful quilt. She saw the table by the door that held jars full of paint brushes of every imaginable size. Floor to ceiling shelves housed every possible color of paint, and then some. Cat saw a few easels on the other wall and stacks of canvases. She shook her head; she thought, this was a barn not an art studio.

"Where are we?" she turned to Luke.

"This is my barn. Well, you know, my dad's barn," he said, as he looked to his feet. "You're the first person I've ever brought here."

"Your barn?" she looked around. "You paint?"

"First, your story, Cat. Then, we can get to mine," he said as he led her to the couch.

Then, he pulled up a desk chair from the corner and sat in front of her.

Cat wasn't sure where to begin.

The beginning is always a good place to start, right?

Luke listened as she described Landon, their first meeting, the shenanigans they used to get into. He laughed as she recounted dropping Landon's Pomeranian down the laundry chute. He held her hand as she told him about suspecting Landon's involvement in drugs, and when she found out it was true. By the time she got to the part where Landon died, Luke felt that he had somehow known him, too. Cat spoke with such love and admiration for him. It was easy to see why her life had been turned upside down by his death.

He held Cat as she cried and found that his own eyes were moist with tears. A first.

Luke pulled away from her saying, "Cat, no one blames you. You have to forgive yourself if you're going to heal."

He thought he sounded a bit like a bad Oprah episode, but he knew he was saying the truth.

Cat shook her head.

"Stop it, Cat," he looked into her eyes. "You can't keep doing this to yourself! You came here to move past this, right?"

"Oh, Luke," Cat wiped her eyes with the sweatshirt Luke had given her in the truck, "if only that were true."

"What do you mean?"

"You think I came here to get over Landon's death? That I'm blaming myself?"

"Yeah?" Luke was uncertain of what she was saying.

"Luke, I came here because of what happened after Landon's death. Maybe I do blame myself, but that's because she blames me, she told me so herself!" Cat began to sob.

"Who?" Luke wrapped his arms around her.

"His mother. Landon's mother told me that I am the reason her son is dead," Cat stopped crying and looked at Luke with a face that had gone numb.

"Tell me, Cat," Luke urged. He didn't want to lose her again.

"Alright," and with a sigh of defeat, Cat allowed herself to remember everything she had been carefully locking away in her mind — every sorrowful and sordid detail.

CHAPTER ELEVEN

CAT SAT IN HER HOSPITAL BED. SHE WAS STILL SHAKING UNCONTROLLABLY.
She had grown more aware in the last hour and scenes of what
had happened were flashing in her mind. Only pieces though,
she had been in and out of consciousness since they had found
Landon's body sprawled out in the garden where he had leapt
to his death.

She remembered screaming, and then she remembered
Samuel carrying her down the stairs. Her legs had been shaking so that she found it impossible to walk. When the
ambulance had placed Landon's body on the gurney with a
sheet over it and brought it through the house, Cat had clung
to it. It took several grown men to pry her off, and that was
when she had hyperventilated and had to be put in an ambulance herself. After that point, she didn't recall much of
anything, until just now.

She examined the crisp white linens on which she lay. The
beep-beep of the nearby machine told her she was hooked up
to a heart monitor. She looked down at the hospital bracelet
around her wrist. Lenox Hill Hospital.

Did they bring Landon to the same hospital? Cat closed her
eyes. Some floors beneath her, Landon could be lying in a morgue,
in one of those fridges they keep bodies in. She puked. She managed to turn slightly, so it ran down the side of the hospital bed
and onto the floor.

She hadn't seen his body, except from where she stood five floors above it looking down. No one would let her go outside. It was probably best. She wanted to always remember him as she knew him, not like that.

Cat heard footsteps and voices coming down the hall. It was her mother and someone else, a nurse maybe?

"Oh, my baby," Cat's mother came running to her side.

Cat stared blankly at her, not speaking.

"My sweet daughter. I am so sorry," her mother was sitting beside her on the bed and rocking her back and forth.

Cat stared absently at the woman in the nurse's uniform as she went about checking her blood pressure and calling for an orderly to clean up her vomit.

Her mother's tears were wet against Cat's face and dampened her hair.

"Is she okay?" her mother directed the question at the nurse.

"She's still in shock. It would be best to keep her here overnight. But the doctor has cleared her to go if you want her to," she said. The nurse's tone was very much business as usual.

"No, no. She should stay. If she hyperventilated or something … it's better that she's here," Cat's mom smoothed her daughter's hair and patted her head.

Cat looked her mom in the eyes for the first time since she entered the room.

"Do they know yet?" Cat's voice was barely audible.

"Does who know, sweetie?" her mom leaned in.

"His parents. Do they know?" Cat watched as her mother's eyes filled with tears.

That was her answer.

"I want to see them," she began to get out of bed.

"No, sweetie. Now is not the time," her mother pushed her

back down with more force than Cat expected.

"Why?" Cat's voice broke.

"Because they are in shock, too," her mother hugged her. "I think you will both need time before you see each other. It's best."

Cat closed her eyes and retreated from reality into a deep, dreamless sleep. When she woke, the nightmare would be over. She was sure of it. It would be gone and Landon would be alive. Everything would be okay.

The next few days passed in a blur, but Cat never cried. She hadn't cried since that night when they had taken his body out of the garden. Maybe, she thought, she had cried all of her tears then. She didn't take any calls. She turned her cell off when it kept beeping that she had 54 unread texts. She just sat in her room, in her bed, or on her window seat staring into nothing. Praying that any minute she would wake up to find it had all been a very bad dream.

There was a knock at her door. She turned her head in that direction, but she couldn't bring herself to say, "Come in." She didn't have the energy.

There was another knock. She turned her head back to the window. She didn't care who it was; if they really needed her, they would come in anyways.

The door creaked open. Lili poked her head through. Her eyes were red from crying. She wore a black dress and a black hat with a veil that had belonged to their dad's mother in the 1940's. Always fashionable, even in mourning. Landon had been like a big brother to Lili. She was taking it very hard; not nearly as bad as Cat, though.

"Are you ready, Cat?" Lili asked, though it was clear that Cat was not ready for anything.

Still in her pajamas, hair unwashed, Cat looked down at herself.

"Ready?" clearly, she was missing something.

"The funeral," Lili said gently. "Mom said she has come up two or three times to remind you to get ready."

"Oh," Cat was feeling nauseous again. They couldn't bury Landon. They just couldn't. Because then it would mean he was really dead. And if he was really dead, Cat feared she might die, too.

"I can help you get ready," Lili stepped into the room.

"Okay," Cat nodded, and turned her head to stare out the window. It was a beautiful spring day. How cruel.

With no time to shower, Lili washed Cat's face with a washcloth. Combed through her hair, pulled it back with a thin black headband, and then into a bun. She carefully applied Cat's makeup, substituting water proof mascara for Cat's usual Bad Gal Lash.

When Lili came out of the closet bearing her typical black "funeral" dress, Cat spoke up, "No, not that one."

Lili put it back, "You can't wear your pjs, Catie."

"My green dress. The one I got at Intermix last month. Landon was with me then. He liked it. Green was his favorite color."

"I think he would like that," Lili nodded, and then finished helping her sister get dressed.

They arrived at the funeral a little early, but it was already crowded. People came to hug Cat and give their condolences. She nodded and accepted them. She didn't know what else to do. She still hadn't seen or spoken to his parents, and it had been five days since his death.

She wanted to see his mother. They had always been close. She was the only other person Cat could think of that would be feeling as awful as she did.

An enormous arrangement of white roses sat upon the casket. The sermon was lovely, as funeral sermons go. But the entire time, Cat didn't believe she was actually at Landon's funeral. Her Landon. He was only seventeen, he couldn't be dead. People don't die when they're seventeen, it has to be against the law of nature or something. It wasn't until after the funeral, when his mother and father were leading the processional out of the church and Cat caught his mother's eye that she knew it — he was really gone. She swallowed back the tears and the terror of this realization and walked out to their car.

A long line of black town cars, all with headlights on, crossed into Brooklyn. Cat felt like an iron hand was wrapped tightly around her throat, making it difficult to breathe. Her sister was holding her hand on one side and her mother on the other when their car pulled onto Bushwick Avenue. When they entered Evergreen Cemetery, she started taking deep breaths to keep from passing out.

The car finally came to a stop along with all the others in the shade of a large oak. It was a beautiful place to be laid to rest. How ironic, Cat thought, that so much time and attention had been paid to creating a park-like landscape for those who couldn't enjoy it. Maybe it isn't for them, Cat thought, maybe it is for the ones who loved them. However, she didn't feel any better about Landon's death because he was buried by a flowering dogwood tree.

Holding tightly to her mother's and sister's hands, she willed her feet to move until she reached the large hole in the ground. The hole where Landon would rest from this day forward. Cat felt a lump rising in her throat. She swallowed it down.

The preacher said a few words, the casket was lowered, it was over so quickly. Cat clenched her fists and squeezed her eyes tight when they started to fill the hole in with dirt. She couldn't watch this. Landon had never liked the dark. When they were little, he would always make her keep the night-light on during their sleepovers. She didn't want him to be down there in the dark, all alone. She wanted to dive in there with him and shout, 'Let me stay here, too! If Landon is down here, I need to be with him!' He needed her. Tears started to form in her eyes. He needed her. He had needed her that night and she was on the patio with Matt Darlington. Damn her! He had needed her and she had abandoned him. If she had been there, Landon would still be alive. It was her fault. Everything was her fault.

When she opened her eyes most of the crowd had cleared away. Many were already in their cars or half way there. Her family was milling over to the side, exchanging regards with others Cat didn't bother to look at. Directly across from Cat, on the other side of the grave, stood Landon's mom. When Cat opened her eyes, she saw Mrs. Jennings staring at her. Not a sad stare or an understanding stare, but a look that told Cat she wished it was her in that grave instead of her only child.

With some speed, Mrs. Jennings came around the grave until she was face to face with Cat.

"Mrs. Jennings," Cat began. She had rehearsed, over and over the last few days, what she would say to Landon's mother and father when she had the chance.

"How could you?" Landon's mother spat at her.

"I — I — I'm so terribly sorry," Cat's eyes swam with tears. "He was my best friend."

"Is that how you treat your best friend?" her voice was shrieking now, drawing attention from all those left to hear. "You killed him! You deserted him and you killed him!"

Cat didn't know what to say. There were no words. Silent tears poured from her eyes. Her shoulders heaved as she accepted whatever abuse that his mother wanted to heap onto her.

"I — I'm so, so sorry," Cat repeated. But, before she got the last word out, she was knocked sideways by the force of Mrs. Jennings full hand slap.

Cat remained on the ground as people came rushing forward. Mr. Jennings tried to take his ex-wife to the car.

Cat's mother, father, and sister ran to help her up. Cat felt humiliated, guilty, and ashamed. She looked into Landon's grave with a longing to join him.

"I blame you! I blame you!" Mrs. Jennings shouted until she was tucked safely in her vehicle, but even then, her muffled cries carried to Cat.

"So do I," Cat muttered as she looked down where dirt was beginning to fill in the grave. "So do I."

CHAPTER TWELVE

CAT EXAMINED THE LEFT SIDE OF HER FACE IN THE MIRROR. A VERY clear reddish-purple handprint was visible, even through the three layers of foundation she had carefully applied. It served as a visible reminder of the slap she had received three days ago in the graveyard.

She stepped back to look at herself. Her uniform was neatly pressed, her hair was tidy; she looked completely different than she had the previous week, staying in pajamas all day and even neglecting to shower. But on the inside, she felt the same. The bruise on her face was nothing compared to the pain that had been inflicted within.

After the scene at the graveyard, both of her parents had words with Mr. and Mrs. Jennings. Mr. Jennings was very apologetic of his ex-wife's behavior. Mrs. Jennings remained resolute in her belief that Cat was to blame for Landon's death. The thought of that wounded Cat to the very core of her being. The last thing she wanted to do was to get out of bed and get ready for school. However, according to her parents, she had no choice. Spence had excused her absences for one week, but any longer would hurt her perfect G.P.A.; and the school year was coming to a close.

Cat couldn't care less about her G.P.A. It's funny how it can take a tragedy to put life into perspective. According to Lili, Meghan had stopped by three times to see if Cat wanted to join her in what she called retail therapy. Somehow, Cat didn't think the Alexander McQueen sample sale would make her feel any better.

There was a soft knock at the door. Accustomed now to Cat's silent response, her dad peeked his head in the room.

"I'm heading to an early meeting," he informed her. "I thought I could give you a ride over to Spence."

"That's not really in your direction," Cat responded.

"That's alright," her father insisted. "I can just have the driver take the FDR all the way downtown."

Cat knew that this would most likely make him late for work. Her father hated being late. This was his way of showing how much he cared.

"That's sweet Dad," Cat smiled at him and turned away to grab her bag, "But, I already told Meghan she could pick me up."

It was a lie. However, since he couldn't see her face when she spoke the words, he might just buy it.

"Alright," her father began to close her door. "Call if you need anything today."

"I will," Cat forced a thank you smile in his direction as the door closed.

When she heard his driver leave, she walked solemnly downstairs. Her mother heard her footsteps and came around the corner to see her off.

"Is Meghan's car here?" her mother looked at her with uncertainty. "Your father said she's picking you up. When did you talk to her?"

Damn, Cat thought.

When Meghan had come calling last night, Cat had asked her Mom to take a message. She had said she wasn't ready to face people yet.

"I called her this morning," Cat lied. "I decided I needed some support for the first day back and she wanted to give me a ride."

Her mom paused for a moment. Cat knew she was trying to appraise whether or not her daughter was being honest. Cat was not in the habit of lying to her parents. They always took her word on things; she had never given them any reason to think otherwise.

Her mother's face broke into a wide smile, "I'm so glad, honey. I think having support from friends is important to healing."

She hugged her daughter and looked out the window, "But, where is she? Meghan should be here by now, then."

"Ummm, I told her I would walk down to her place," Cat headed for the door. "I'm actually supposed to be there right now. She's probably wondering where I am."

"Do you want me to walk with you?" her mother hurried after her.

"No," Cat forced another grateful semi-smile, "I think I'll be okay. Really."

"Alright," her mother hugged her again, "I'll be thinking of you today."

Cat nodded.

She wished there wasn't a reason for everyone to be thinking of her. She wished Landon was here. She wished this morning, like all of the past mornings, that they were eating breakfast at Eli's and she was scolding him for making her late.

She set off to the end of the block and then turned right to walk in the direction of Meghan's townhouse, which was two blocks down, just in case her mother was watching.

After going two blocks, she leaned against the side of the building. Decision time. Was she going to school?

She heaved a sigh and crossed the street to begin her walk

through the park. It was a beautiful May day. Only five weeks of school left. Finals were being held over the next two weeks and then the last three weeks would be spent preparing and presenting their portfolios to show the evidence of learning that had occurred their junior year.

She reached Fifth Avenue quickly. She didn't even remember walking there; she had been so deep in thought.

Staring to her right she saw The Met. If only it wasn't Monday, she would slip inside and lose herself for a few hours in art. It was one of her favorite hobbies — a pastime inherited from her mother. Before her mother had kids, she had worked at Sotheby's and was an Art History major in college. Cat was not an artist herself, but it was something for which she had always had an appreciation.

She turned left to walk the ten blocks up to 91st street. When she reached the 90th street reservoir entrance, she paused for a moment before climbing the steps to the track that circled the reservoir. She began to walk around it alone.

She ran here most every morning, though she hadn't in the last week. The scene was a lot different from when she and Landon had walked around it in January. They had been the only ones out that day. Today, Cat walked around it leisurely while dozens of joggers darted around her. The sun warmed her skin as she continued to make her lap. When she reached the bench that she and Landon had sat on that day, she took a seat.

Cat wasn't sure how long she sat there. She only knew she was starving and her bladder told her she needed to go to the bathroom. Deciding it was pointless to continue sitting there and risk peeing on herself, she marched herself to Le Pain Quotidien, where she stayed until school let out, so she could walk home under the pretense of coming home from school.

Cat continued this charade until Wednesday.

She walked in the door after spending most of the day perusing the new exhibit at MOMA when she was suddenly approached by her two very flustered parents.

"I'm in trouble, aren't I?" Cat said simply. She didn't even try to play the "whatever could be wrong?" card.

Her father said, "Yes" at the same time her mother answered, "No."

They looked at each other.

"No," her father surrendered. "But you have some explaining to do."

"I got a call from your school this morning asking why you hadn't been there yet this week. I told them I'd watched you leave every day," her mother rubbed her temples. "Cathleen, you must know how worried we were!"

"I came home from work, missing a very important meeting," her father added.

After Cat's mother shot him a look, he amended his statement.

"That's not important," he sighed. "What's important is that you're safe. But we were frantic with worry. After what Landon did to himself ..."

"I'm not going to kill myself," Cat practically shouted. "I just wasn't ready to go back yet. I'm still not ready!"

"Well, I'm sorry. We're both sorry. But it's time for you to go back. You don't have a choice," her father's voice was firm.

His Blackberry beeped.

"I need to take this," he said. With that, he retreated to his study, leaving Cat and her mother in the foyer.

"They're going to let you retake the tests you've missed," her mother said, as though that would make her feel better.

Cat looked at the tile flooring.

"I'm supposed to make sure you're there tomorrow by seven a.m.," her mother added. "I'll be riding with you."

Cat nodded. She knew there was no further discussion on the matter. She knew she should probably retreat to her room and study. She hadn't picked up a textbook in over a week. Instead, she laid down on the couch mindlessly flipping through channels until she ate dinner and abruptly went to bed.

The week passed and Cat remained in her zombie-like state. She was certain she had flunked her tests. She hadn't even paid attention to what bubble she was filling in on the scantron forms. She made the pattern of a flower on one, and the other was a waterfall with rocks at the bottom. She was certain she had filled in more than one oval per line several times.

They would probably call her parents, Cat realized. But she felt too numb to have any worry about that.

She walked through the halls like a ghost. It wasn't until the next week, on Wednesday, when Meghan approached her cautiously in the hall that Cat felt some emotion stirring inside her.

"There's a party this weekend," she said apprehensively. It was the first big party since Landon's death.

"It might be good for you to get out, Cat," she added.

Cat was suddenly overcome with the desire to go to a party. Anything. Anything that would help her to forget the sadness she'd been drowning in. She wanted to bury the pain. Bury it so deep that she would forget about it.

After all, Landon had said she had two lives left. She wanted to live them recklessly.

"What time could you pick me up?" Cat faked an excited smile.

"Don't you want to know where it's going to be?" Meghan looked at her friend curiously.

"Oh, sure," Cat backpedaled. "Where is it?"

"Only at Matt Darlington's" Meghan shrieked. "He still likes you, you know?"

"Really?" Suddenly, Cat had another way to lose herself in mind. She set her thoughts on this party and meditated on it all week. It would be a night to remember, she told herself. A night that would help her forget.

CHAPTER THIRTEEN

HER MOTHER AND FATHER HAD HAPPILY AGREED TO ALLOWING CAT A night out. They said it would be good for her to surround herself with friends during this difficult time. If only they knew what Cat had in mind.

Meghan picked her up at 8pm sharp. The party had officially begun at seven, but Cat always believed in being fashionably late. She had left her house in a classy Ralph Lauren sundress, but had asked Meghan to bring her something scandalous to change into. She quickly changed into a barely-there, sequined dress by Zac Posen in the backseat of the car. Meghan had even brought her a pair of her mother's five-inch Brian Atwood heels to complete the ensemble.

"Cat, you look fab," her friend beamed, as they stepped out of the town car and stared up at the Fifth Avenue mansion.

"Thanks," Cat felt her stomach doing somersaults at the thought of what she had planned for the evening.

"You know Ralph Lauren only lives a few blocks north of here," Meghan said knowingly.

"Yes, I know," Cat tried to feign interest, but she had known that fact for years.

Once inside, Cat walked straight to the bar. Forgetting Landon seemed like such a daunting task. Maybe after a few shots it would seem more easily achievable.

Meghan took two shots of tequila with Cat, before flitting off after her latest love interest.

"Trying to get drunk, Cat?" a familiar voice spoke.

Cat turned to see Samuel standing there with a shot in hand.

"This will get you there faster," he said.

"What is it?" Cat eyed it suspiciously.

"Do you really want to know?" he smiled coyly.

Cat took a deep breath. Knowing Samuel, it was probably laced with some sort of drug. Cat shrugged, ignoring the screaming voice in her head, and downed it in one gulp.

"Now, let's go enjoy the party," he said as he took her hand and led her into the oversized living room that served as the dance floor.

The beat of the music seemed to pulse through her very veins. The flashing lights and the spinning of the disco ball all seemed to swirl together. She felt lighter than air.

Cat couldn't remember what she was doing or where she was exactly. She knew she had a mission, but that too seemed to elude her. All she could think was how free and relaxed she felt, as though floating. Is this what it felt like to be high? Cat guessed it was, but she had never tried any sort of drug before.

Samuel took her hand again. He was leading her somewhere. There were steps and she stumbled. At one point, she took off one of the five-inch heels and carried it as she hobbled along, laughing nonsensically. Cat couldn't think straight enough to care or to wonder where she was going. The music seemed further away. The lights had faded. She felt like she was suddenly falling. It was an uneasy sensation. She stopped to hold on to the wall to keep herself upright.

"Wait," she pulled back, leaning heavily on the wall. "I'm falling."

"It's all good, Cat," Samuel hissed in her ear. "You'll feel better when you lay down."

"Good idea," Cat agreed.

She needed to lie down. To sleep. She didn't like this feeling at all. Like she was spinning and free falling at the same time. She could barely walk straight.

When Samuel laid her down on the bed, she closed her eyes.

Cat opened them again to find Samuel, half on top of her, groping her. Where was she? Oh right, a party. Cat began putting things together. She had taken a shot of whatever he had given her, and after that, her memory was fuzzy. The drink had obviously been a poor decision on her part.

Samuel's hand was up her dress, on her chest; his mouth was on her neck. This felt disgusting, like being slobbered on by a big dog. But, then again, Samuel had much more experience in this area than Cat did. Maybe this was what fooling around was supposed to be like. She closed her eyes and tried to enjoy it for a moment. Thus far, she had been quite successful at forgetting. She congratulated herself. Landon was completely forgotten. At the thought of his name, pain started seeping back in. It was a duller pain, not quite as sharp or intense as before.

Cat took a deep breath. She needed to throw herself more into this awkward make-out session if she was to forget Landon again. She desperately wanted to forget him. And soon.

Samuel was obviously drunk himself, as he was fumbling with the buttons on his shirt. He was completely on top of her now.

Samuel grabbed her hand and moved it into his pants. Cat tried to pull it away, but he wouldn't let her hand go.

Suddenly, with panic, she realized what she had gotten herself into. She didn't want to do this. She only prayed it wasn't too late to get out of it.

Again, she tried to pull her hand away. And again, Samuel

held her hand in place.

"Let's go back downstairs," she tried sitting up.

"I don't think so," he said, rubbing her hand against himself.

Cat was mortified. She pushed against him harder; but this time, he pushed her back roughly onto the bed.

She formed her hand into a fist, "You can't make me do that to you! You're sick!"

Suddenly, he had both of her hands pinned above her head.

"Fine!" he shouted back; his breath reeked of liquor. "I'll just have to find another way to finish!"

His free hand was undoing his pants. Cat kicked him as hard as she could. She tried to dig the other five-inch heel right through his shin.

He shouted a stream of profanities and slapped her hard across the face. Suddenly, his hand was around her throat as she gasped for air.

"You try that again and I'll beat the shit out of you," he hissed, with his face an inch above hers.

Releasing his hold on her, Cat gasped for air and began to sob.

"Please, Samuel," she stuttered. "Please let me go!"

She tried to sit up once more and was backhanded across the other cheek.

Cat bit her tongue; she could taste the blood in her mouth. She wanted to reach and make sure all of her teeth were still there, but Samuel still had her hands painfully pinned above her head.

He had gotten his pants down now and was violently pushing her dress up; he pulled down her panties.

Please, please God make him stop, Cat prayed with all her might.

When he pushed himself against her, Cat felt another wave of nausea. Turning her head towards Samuel, she puked all over him, herself included.

"You nasty bitch!" he pushed off the bed and ran into the bathroom to wash the vomit off.

Cat didn't care about the fact that she was covered in her own sick, she got out of there as quickly as she could. Running down the stairs, with both shoes in her hand at this point, she bolted out the door before anyone could even comment on her appearance. She ran to the end of the block, turned, and ran three more blocks south. Only then did she decide it was safe to stop and catch her breath. She crossed Fifth Avenue and sat on a park bench. She wasn't sure what time it was, at some point she remembered her cell phone reading 12:45am. She didn't know how she was getting home; Meghan was supposed to be her ride. She hadn't seen her since they'd first arrived.

Leaning her head into her hands, she began to sob. How could she have been so stupid? Landon would have been furious with her if he had seen the way she'd behaved. She couldn't believe she had actually tried to get drunk, or that she had accepted that drink. She shook her head at her own foolishness. She was ashamed. She felt so guilty and alone. It was her fault that she couldn't see straight. It was her fault that she was nearly raped tonight. Burying her head further into her arms, Cat let out a cry of agony. It was her fault that Landon was dead.

Cat let herself cry for another moment before she decided it was time to go home. There was something she had to do. Coming into the front door, she opened it as quietly as she could. On tiptoe, she crept towards the stairs and found a note waiting for her on the landing.

"Cat, we hope you had a great time at the party. Your father and I are going out with Dave and Kim on their new yacht. Be back very late! Love you, Mom"

"Perfect," Cat thought to herself. This would make the task at hand that much easier.

Cat no longer felt the need to tiptoe as she climbed the stairs with steadfast resolve to the third landing, where her parents' bedroom was. Opening the double doors into their huge master bath, Cat went to work. They had to have some prescriptions somewhere in here. Something that Cat could take enough of in order to never wake up again. Cat searched for thirty minutes, but all she found were muscle relaxers from when her mom had sprained her ankle last fall.

Cat examined the bottle. This would have to do. She took three and waited a few minutes. Nothing. She popped in three more. She realized that if she was going to do this, she might as well get it over with already. Turning the bottle up, she swallowed several more capsules.

She laid down on the bathroom floor. She could feel her heart and her breathing slowing down, when somewhere in the distance, she heard someone screaming her name. It was like trying to hear someone underwater. There was a lot of noise, but none of it made sense.

She tried to open her eyes to see what was going on but she couldn't. She couldn't move at all for that matter.

She wanted to shout, 'Hey you! Keep it down, I'm trying to die here!' But alas, her mouth wouldn't work, either.

The fog was getting thicker, the noises were sinking further and further away. Perhaps she was dead. Being dead meant all her pain would be dead, too. Cat smiled on the inside at that thought.

CHAPTER FOURTEEN

SHE WAS NOT DEAD. DEAD PEOPLE DIDN'T CONTINUE TO THINK, AS far as Cat knew. Dead people certainly didn't hear things, of that Cat was quite sure. She had been hearing noises for some time now. Some were voices, shouting, loud mechanical sounds, the wailing of a siren, all sorts of sounds.

Cat was just beginning to realize that she must be alive when she noticed she was now able to move, too. Carefully, she opened one eyelid and then another.

Light green walls, white sheets, medical equipment. "Another hospital," Cat groaned.

"Oh well, if at first you don't succeed, try, try again," Cat murmured to herself.

Somewhere in her mind she heard Landon's voice laughing at her. "You should have remembered you had two lives left, Cat," it seemed to say.

"One life left now," she said aloud.

The loudness of her voice in the still room startled her. It sounded dry. Cat realized she was quite parched. She tried to move her hand towards the call button on the side of the bed, but found that her hands and arms were strapped down.

Seriously? Cat looked at the straps. What do they think I'm going to do?

"Kill yourself," the voice in her head answered her before she'd even finished the question.

Cat laughed. Her laughter immediately turned to sobs. She knew she wouldn't try it again. She hadn't really wanted to die in the first place. That was why she had started taking the pills so slowly to begin with, so someone could find her and stop her before it was too late. Death wasn't the answer. She'd been foolish enough to trick herself into thinking that it could be. The pain of Landon's death was unbearable. How did people get through circumstances like this?

Did they pray? Did the thought of a God listening to them and being there so they weren't experiencing it alone make them feel better? The thought of it did sound nice. Cat had never been a particularly spiritual person. She had been to church for some of the major Christian holidays at some point in her life and occasionally she would accompany her father to mass, but that was about it. She knew the Lord's Prayer. Cat said it in her head. She didn't feel any different.

"God, I'm so alone," Cat prayed. "Be with me. Ease my pain. Please."

Cat didn't feel that was polite enough so she added, "Thanks, I mean, thank you."

Surprisingly she felt a little bit better. Was it admitting the fact that she was in pain that made her feel better? Was it the thought of having someone there to take this burden from her? Cat wasn't sure, but she did feel better.

Cat was just in the midst of deciding she should try this prayer thing more often when the door opened.

"Cat?" Lili asked, "Mom! Dad! She's awake!"

Lili hurried to her side.

"Cat! I was so scared when I found you!" Lili sniffled; her eyes were brimming with tears.

"I'm so sorry," Cat whispered. She wanted to reach out to her sister, but again found she was tightly strapped down. She didn't like the feeling of having her arms held down. It made her think of the last time, which was still all too fresh in her memory.

Looking from her sister to her parents' worried faces, she realized the agony she had put them through. She felt another wave of guilt wash over her.

"I'm so sorry," Cat repeated, looking into her mother's eyes.

The nurse who had entered with them had busied herself checking all of Cat's vitals.

She cleared her throat, "I'm going to have to ask you a few questions about last night, Cathleen." She was looking at her clipboard. "I will need the minor to leave the room," she glanced towards Lili.

Cat could see her sister's reaction was quickly defused by her father's offer to sit with her in the waiting room. Cat's mother took a seat beside Cat and held her hand.

"Alright," Cat turned her attention to the nurse.

"You were brought in by ambulance for an overdose of muscle relaxers found in your parents' bathroom," the nurse gave a quick glance to Cat's mom, as if to say she was responsible. "Is this correct?"

"Well, my parents were gone," Cat began; she didn't want her mother taking any blame for her actions regardless of who the pills belonged to.

"A simple yes or no will suffice," the nurse interrupted curtly.

Cat swallowed, her throat felt drier than ever, "Yes."

"Upon your arrival at the hospital, your stomach was pumped. Your examination revealed bruises to your wrists and both sides of your face. Your blood tests also revealed high levels of alcohol and Rohypnol, a date rape drug commonly called "roofies." Did you realize you were taking this drug?" The nurse's stare was icy. It seemed to say, 'You prep school kids think you have such a tough life with all your parties and easy access to drugs and alcohol.'

Cat blushed with anger under her stare.

"I said," the nurse repeated herself slower, "Did you realize you had taken this drug?"

"Not *that* drug in particular, no," Cat responded.

Her mother was shifting uncomfortably.

"But you did realize you had taken a drug?" the nurse stared at her emotionlessly.

"Yes," Cat said quietly.

"And were you raped?" she asked. The bluntness of the nurse caught Cat a little off guard.

Cat didn't answer. If she said she was almost raped, she would be asked to say who did it. Pressing charges against Samuel Alden would be ludicrous. They wouldn't win. He would be able to bring witnesses that saw Cat getting drunk and dancing with him, and going upstairs with him of her own will. It would be no use.

"There are no signs of forced entry," the nurse informed her.

"If you knew that, then why did you ask?" Cat snapped.

"Procedure," the nurse responded. "Mrs. Rhodes, may I speak with you and your husband?"

"Of course," Cat's mother remained seated.

"In the doctor's office, if you don't mind," the nurse walked to the door and held it open for Cat's mother to walk through.

An hour passed but Cat still couldn't move and was thirstier than ever. What was taking them so long? Cat wondered what would happen if she needed to go to the bathroom, then she noticed a thin tube that led from under the sheets to a clear bag of urine that hung on the side of the bed. She had a catheter in. That thought only slightly grossed her out.

The door opened and a doctor came in, followed by the snarky nurse who had been there earlier.

"Where are my parents?" Cat craned her head to see around them.

"They will call you this evening," the doctor smiled. "At our recommendation, they've agreed to place you in our Teen Therapy Group. It's for teens who, like yourself, have tried to commit suicide. It will give you time to grieve your loss, and share your thoughts, in both an individual and group therapy setting."

"So? What are you saying, I come back a few nights a week or something?" Cat couldn't understand why her parents had left her.

"No, oftentimes, circumstances like the ones you've endured the last few weeks need more intense therapy to overcome. Particularly, if the grief has caused one to become suicidal," the doctor's voice was unnaturally pleasant and calm.

The nurse chimed in, "Your parents have informed us of your situation. Many of the teens that go through our program have experienced a similar loss."

Cat couldn't believe what she was hearing, "You mean ... I have to stay here a few days?"

The doctor paused, "Our program lasts a minimum of six weeks, but can be extended if it's thought to be necessary."

"What the hell?" Cat was shouting over the doctor's voice. She didn't hear him go on about the benefits of the program and how much better she'd feel once she'd allowed herself to grieve properly.

"Are you f-ing kidding me?" Cat yelled over him. "I won't stay here. There's no way! You can't make me stay against my will!"

"Actually, Cathleen, your parents signed your admittance papers. You are a minor," the nurse's voice made Cat want to scream.

"Look," Cat tried to remain calm, "I'm sure your program is great for people who really need it. But I don't need it. I didn't really want to die. I just want to go home."

"Well, it's a little too late for that realization," the nurse said as the doctor left the room.

Cat began to cry. "Wait!" Cat called as the nurse turned to go. "I'm really thirsty. Could I please have some water?"

"Your I.V. supplies all the fluid that you need," the nurse replied haughtily. "Your lunch will be brought in two hours and you'll be allowed to get up to eat and walk around the room — with supervision, of course. Then, you'll have to get back in your bed."

"I have to stay strapped in like this?!" Cat squealed in horror.

"You're on suicide watch for 24 hours from when they brought you in ... you only have 16 and a half more hours left," and with that comment, the nurse left Cat alone to sob herself to sleep.

CHAPTER FIFTEEN

THE FIRST WEEK IN THE PROGRAM, CAT'S EMOTIONS RANGED FROM angry, to irate, to positively livid. There wasn't room for any sorrow at this point. How could her parents have deserted her like this? She didn't need group therapy. She needed to be home, to have some sense of normalcy. In the few weeks since Landon's death, her entire world had turned upside down. It was as though the universe, as Cat knew it, was revolting against his passing. Cat had gone from being a happy, confident, trustworthy, straight-A student to someone who bombed her finals, attempted suicide, and got locked up in the nut house. Her social status as one of the Spence Seven was surely in jeopardy. They had probably already replaced her. Not that Cat cared about that anymore.

Cat refused to eat the disgusting stuff they tried to pass off as food for the first four days. When she was threatened with being tube fed, she grudgingly obliged. The nurse who had been there when Cat woke up the first day was there every other day. The other nurse, who insisted Cat call her Nurse Misty, was actually quite sweet. Cat made a point to be kind to her. Maybe she could get Cat something better to eat. The other nurse, Cat found out, was named Nurse Nibyzik. Cat just called her Satan. She also thoroughly enjoyed muttering things about her under her breath, while in her presence, and then pretended to be confused when the nurse asked her what she had said. It was Cat's only form of entertainment in this place.

It was in the middle of week two when Cat realized that she probably should start playing nice if she wanted to get out when the six weeks were up. From that point on, she tried to be the perfect patient. Though, Nurse Nibyzik made it challenging.

Each Friday, she was allowed a five-minute phone conversation with her parents. According to the program, complete isolation from every part of one's life was necessary to pinpoint the area of turmoil. In Cat's case, they knew her trouble was not related to her parents, so they made an exception.

The first phone conversation was mainly comprised of Cat screaming, "How could you do this to me?" Subsequent phone calls had been much calmer. Cat still hadn't forgiven her parents, but she understood that it was fear for her safety that had driven them to such extremes.

The group therapy sessions weren't as bad as Cat had expected them to be. She had gone into them with plans of boycotting them entirely. She wouldn't speak and they couldn't make her. To her relief, she wasn't forced to talk or asked any direct questions. Listening to the stories of others somewhat helped. It made her feel that there were actually other people out there who were dealing with a pain as acute as her own. It was nice to know she wasn't completely alone in her suffering. Not that she would wish this feeling on anyone, but it was nice to have others who could understand.

Six weeks had seemed like an eternity when Cat was first admitted; and though the monotony of the days got to her at times, Cat was pleasantly surprised when she had only one week left.

Cat walked into the group therapy room. Four days left. She could do this. She sat in the same blue plastic chair in the circle that she had sat in every day prior. The other teens were filling in their seats. Cat hadn't really had a chance to get to know any of them outside of these therapy sessions. They took their meals in their rooms. They weren't really given an opportunity to talk unsupervised. Perhaps they're afraid we'll share suicide tips, Cat mused.

"So," Mr. Simmons, their group therapy leader, spoke up, "Who would like to get us started today? Cathleen Rhodes? How about you?"

"What?" Cat was a little taken aback. They had never called people out before.

"Well," he smiled politely, "You are the only one in the group who hasn't shared yet. We like to give everyone the opportunity. Would you like to?"

"No," Cat said bluntly.

Mr. Simmons nodded; he didn't seem offended.

"Maybe tomorrow, then," he said, before continuing on.

Cat suddenly became aware of the fact that she would be expected to share tomorrow. Did she have to? Would saying 'no' work a second time? Could she just keep saying 'no' until she was discharged? She only had a few days remaining.

Cat gasped as the thought crossed her mind — what if not sharing means I have to stay longer?

Cat realized she couldn't bear that alternative. She'd better find the guts to share something, just a little bit. She didn't have to go into a whole sob story like some people did. That's what she would do, she decided. She would share just enough to appease Mr. Simmons and ensure her ticket home. Easy.

Walking into the room the next day, Cat's mouth felt dry and her tongue felt fuzzy. She could already hear herself tripping over her words. She was not a fan of public speaking. Once, during her sophomore year, she had been forced to give a speech in English and had run from the room only to puke in the hall. Cat threw up a lot.

It occurred to Cat that some people puke when they feel sick, but she puked for a variety of reasons and emotions: sad, angry, worried, car sick, or drunk. When it doubt — puke it out. Could she have that made into a bumper sticker?

Cat was still making a list in her head when Mr. Simmons spoke her name.

"Cathleen?" he repeated.

"Yes?" Cat responded quietly. She was surprised her voice even worked at all.

"Would you care to share today?" His tone was still polite, but there was a definite urging behind it.

"Umm, okay" Cat breathed in deeply, "I guess."

"Go right ahead." He nodded.

Cat felt the eyes of everyone in the room on her at once.

"My best friend died. And then ... then I tried to commit suicide," Cat was quiet for a moment.

They still stared as though they expected more.

"And then my parents enrolled me in this program," Cat shrugged, "That's about it."

"How did he die?" It was a younger girl with short spiky black hair that spoke.

"He — He killed himself," Cat looked at the floor.

"How?" Another girl spoke, but Cat didn't look up to see who it was.

Cat paused.

"He fell ... well, he jumped off a building," Cat felt a lump rising in her throat.

She didn't want to cry here. She thought the pain was subsiding. Talking about it made it feel fresh again.

"What was his name?" asked the girl with black hair.

"What?" Cat looked up.

"Your friend? What was his name?" she asked again.

Cat couldn't say his name. Her tongue was plastered to the roof of her mouth. Her jaw felt defiantly locked in place. If she said his name, the tears would come for sure.

"Landon," she spoke, barely above a whisper.

Just as she predicted, the tears started spilling over and running down her cheeks.

"That sucks," it was a younger teenage guy, a boy really, who spoke up.

His statement, so accurate and to the point, made Cat laugh.

"Yeah, it does," she smiled. "It really sucks."

The conversation led into others speaking up about their own situations, and Cat was allowed to slip into the background once more. She felt so much better, though. As if a giant weight had been lifted. It hadn't come from the few words she had spoken, but from that one boy who had articulated what no one else had said to Cat since Landon's death.

Cat was tired of hearing people say the pain would pass or that he was 'in a better place.' She just wanted someone to call it as it was and just say how shitty the whole situation was. It sucked. Having that guy say it made a difference. Cat knew that the pain she was facing was far from over, but she felt like she was going to make it. With time, all wounds heal, right?

CHAPTER SIXTEEN

CAT HAD BEEN HOME FOR TWO WEEKS AND WAS GOING ABSOLUTELY stir crazy. She had expected her parents to be overprotective but this was madness. Her mom wouldn't even let her go to the bathroom by herself. When she arrived home from her stint in therapy, she found that every potentially dangerous object in her room had been removed for fear she might relapse. Cat had gone to take a shower to find her razor missing. When she asked her mom for a razor, her mom had refused and had gone out to buy her Nair, instead. Cat was beside herself. She had made a mistake. She could admit that. But all she wanted to do now was move on.

She thought going home was what she had wanted for the last six weeks, but now she wasn't sure. Every time she walked into a room, there was a hush. Cat got that sick feeling in the pit of her stomach that told her they had just been talking about her. To make things worse, Cat wasn't allowed to leave without a chaperone. The school year had ended, but because of Cat's poor performance on her finals, her parents were making her study to retake them the first week of August. The school was making an exception for Cat due to the traumatic circumstances in her life the last couple of months.

Home didn't feel like home anymore. She couldn't stand the sound of her bedroom door creaking open several times in the middle of the night to make sure she was okay. She knew things weren't going to be the same as they had been before, but if this was the new normal, she just didn't think she could take it. She had to get out. The only problem was how?

If only she could get in touch with Meghan. Then, she would be sure to find some way to break out of this prison. Without her cell phone, and with the constant supervision, Cat hadn't found a spare moment. Her mother wouldn't even allow her on the computer without watching her. What did she think she was going to do? Look up other methods of committing suicide? Cat would just have to be patient. They had to leave her alone sometime. Even for a few minutes. Cat would just bide her time until an opportunity arose.

That Thursday morning, Cat agreed to help her mother make quiches for her ladies' luncheon. They had just begun when her mother realized she couldn't find her recipe.

"Cat," she said sweetly, "Would you mind getting on the computer and getting the recipe for me?"

"Sure," Cat hopped off the stool where she was perched. "What website is it on?"

"Food Network," her mother called after her. "I think it's one of Emeril's ... or maybe Giada De Laurentiis?"

"I'll find it," Cat called back.

She felt her heart start to race as she sat down in the computer chair.

"Chill out," she told herself. "It's not like you're planning a jewelry heist, you're just emailing your friend."

Quickly, her fingers flew on the keyboard. Within a few minutes, Cat had successfully emailed Meghan, looked up the recipe, and then erased the computer's history ... just in case someone decided to check.

"Got it!" Cat proclaimed happily as she re-entered the kitchen.

"Oh, you were quick," her mom said with a smile. "It takes me forever to look up things on the computer."

"Well, Mom," Cat's voice grew quite serious, "that's because you're old."

Then she burst out laughing, her mother's musical voice laughing with her. For just a moment, it felt like old times. Just a moment.

"Oh, Cat," her mother stopped laughing and began pouring out measurements, "I've been meaning to talk to you."

"What about?" Cat wasn't sure she wanted to know. Her mother's suddenly serious tone told her it could only be one of two things: Landon's suicide or her own suicide attempt. Either one was not a pleasant subject.

"Your father and I have been thinking lately ... about ... about letting you go stay with Mimi for a bit," her mother didn't look up to see Cat's reaction as she began cracking eggs.

"That could be fun," Cat tried to sound pleasant, "I haven't seen her in almost two years. It would be nice to visit for a week or two."

"Well, he thought ... I mean, your father and I thought that with everything that's happened the last few months, it might be good for you to stay there a bit longer than that," her mother still hadn't looked Cat in the eyes. To Cat, this was not a good sign.

"How much longer?" Cat's voice grew apprehensive.

Her mother continued, speaking as though she hadn't heard the question, "It would just be so hard to return to Spence after all this. By now, I'm sure other students and parents know, and that would be very difficult for you to deal with."

"You mean difficult for you and Dad to deal with," Cat's voice dripped with disdain, "your perfect straight-A student, ruined."

"That's not fair, Cathleen," her mother's voice rose.

"What's not fair is that I make one stupid mistake and I'm being treated like a prisoner in my own home! Oh, and after being sentenced to SIX weeks of group therapy, let's not forget that fun little detail!"

"What were we supposed to do, Cathleen? Drugs, alcohol, a suicide attempt — all in one night!"

"It was one terrible, crazy night! Am I going to be punished for it for my entire life?"

"Think of what this did to your father and me, Cathleen. Just think of someone other than yourself for one second!"

"Don't you think I feel guilty enough for, for … EVERY-THING? HOW MANY FREAKING TIMES DO I HAVE TO SAY I'M SORRY?"

"Do not raise your voice like that to me, young lady."

They stared at each other in silence.

"Mom, I'm sorry," Cat spoke slowly and calmly, "I love you … very much. I have been through a lot and I wanted one crazy night to forget it all. It was the biggest mistake of my life. I didn't want to die. I was stupid; I admit it. I take full responsibility. But you have to learn to trust me again. You can't just send me away for one mistake."

Her mother paused, "Maybe you're right. I'll talk to your father about it."

"Thank you," Cat breathed a sigh of relief. Cat couldn't imagine being sent to live in North Carolina for God knows how long.

"This is your chance to show us how responsible you can be, like the old Cathleen was," her mom nodded grimly.

"Mom, I'm the same Cathleen. I'm just going through something difficult. Can't you see that?" Cat felt so betrayed. Her own parents couldn't look at her or think of her as the same person after what happened. Who was she supposed to lean on for support without their trust?

"Well, I have to warn you, Cat. Anything that reveals otherwise will have your father putting you on a plane to Mimi's for your senior year. We love you. But we, your father in particular, just can't tolerate rebellion."

Cat sighed. She knew her dreams of breaking out for a night were over. She would be perfect, because anything less than that would mean a one-way ticket to North Carolina.

CHAPTER SEVENTEEN

ANOTHER WEEK AND A HALF WENT BY WITH CAT PLAYING THE PART of the perfect daughter. She had always been good before, but then she didn't feel like she *had* to be. She was allowed some freedom to come and go as she pleased and was always trusted. Cat wondered if she would ever have that relationship with her parents again. Since her semi-suicide attempt, it seemed that they truly looked at her as a different person. That hurt Cat most of all. At least Lili still treated her the same.

Cat sat on her window seat staring outside. She was dying to go on a jog, it was the perfect morning. But every time she asked, her mother seemed to find some excuse or something she needed Cat to do. Cat didn't know what they thought she was going to do? Jump in the reservoir? She had been home for four weeks now and things seemed to be getting worse.

"Cat?" Lili called from down the hall.

"I'm in my room!" Cat replied.

"Can you come here for a sec?" Lili called back.

Sighing, Cat got up and shuffled down the hall to her sister's room.

"So, there's this party tonight," Lili was going through her closet, "And Mom and Dad are actually going to let me go!"

"You made me come in here so you could tell me that you get to go out and I don't? Thanks." Cat turned to go.

"No, wait!" Lili rushed to her.

"What?" Cat felt impatient. The fact that her soon to be sophomore little sis was getting to go out while she had been told she had to stay in and fold laundry was absurd.

"I need to borrow something to wear," Lili saw the look on Cat's face and quickly added, "I'll figure out a way to get you out for a bit if you let me."

"How?" Cat was skeptical but intrigued.

"I'll tell mom that I want you to take me back to school shopping. That it will be healthy sister-bonding time, and that I won't let you out of my sight." Lili smiled mischievously. "And then I'll go shop by myself and you'll have free time to do whatever."

Cat smiled, "I have a cute dress by French Connection that will look great on you!"

"Personally, I had your new Marc Jacobs dress in mind," said Lili, walking around her and down the hall towards Cat's room.

Cat pursed her lips. That was one of her favorite dresses. But it would be worth it for a day of freedom.

"Deal!" Cat called and followed her into the room.

Cat even helped Lili with her hair and makeup that night. She had to admit it — her sister looked fabulous.

"So, where's the party?" Cat asked as they stood in the foyer, waiting on the car to pick Lili up. Cat hadn't thought to ask earlier; she just assumed it was at some sophomore's place. Someone she probably didn't know anyway.

"It's Samuel Alden's party on the rooftop of the Gansevoort Hotel!" Lili exclaimed, excitedly.

Cat swallowed hard. She couldn't breathe for a second. The last time she had seen Samuel she had puked on him, right after he'd nearly raped her.

"Lili, I need to tell you something ..." Cat began, but didn't get any further because her parents came in.

"Lilienne, you look fantastic!" their mother proclaimed proudly.

"Just lovely, sweetheart," their father said before kissing Lili on each cheek.

Cat watched them. She remembered not too long ago it had been her receiving all of their parents' praises. It felt so strange to be on the other side now.

"Cat helped me get ready!" Lili winked at Cat.

"That was sisterly of you, Cathleen," their dad smiled, with some difficulty, at her.

"Well, have fun tonight, sweetie! Your car is here," their mom held the door open for Lili.

"I'll walk her to the car," Cat said quickly, grabbing Lili's elbow and leading her through the door before her parents could protest.

"What was that about?" Lili turned to her and jerked her elbow away.

"Lili, be careful tonight. Please. Samuel … Samuel …" Cat couldn't get out the words she wanted to say. "Just stay away from him, okay?"

"Okay," Lili said with a confused tone.

"Promise me," Cat tried to fill her voice with sincerity and importance, but she wasn't sure if it came across.

"Okay, I promise," Lili still looked uncertain, but Cat was pretty sure she had made an impression.

She watched her little sister get in the car and waved as she went to her first 'real' party of her high school career. Cat couldn't shake the fact that something wasn't right. Why did Samuel invite Lili? He never invited younger girls, unless he wanted something from them. Cat shuddered. She knew this wasn't good. She needed to be there. She needed to protect Lili. But how?

Cat trudged back up the stairs and inside to her prison. There was no way she could ask her parents if she could go to the party. The idea of her doing so was laughable. But ... somehow, she had to get down there.

Her mother interrupted her thoughts, "Cat, will you put this laundry away for me?"

"Mm-hmmm," Cat took the basket of laundry and dutifully climbed the stairs.

Ever since the economic crisis, their housekeepers had only been coming twice a week, instead of their usual three times a week. It was strange to have to take on chores, but Cat didn't really mind if that was what her family needed.

She began sorting through her mother's clothes and putting them away. Socks in this drawer; t-shirts in that one. She was just putting her mother's underwear away, when she noticed something. It was her iPhone — her beloved iPhone. Cat ran to the door to look over the railing and make sure her parents were still safely downstairs, then ran back to the drawer and picked it up.

She turned it on, praying that it still had some battery life left. It did. She checked her email, her Facebook, Twitter ... all while putting laundry away, of course.

On Twitter, she came across Samuel Alden (his name was @scotchandsex) and clicked to look at his most recent tweets. Her stomach hit the floor when she read, "One Rhodes sister in the nuthouse, I guess the other will have to do."

She had to get to Lili. Her parents would never let her leave; and though the thought of being caught and sent to live in North Carolina scared her to death, it didn't worry her nearly as much as what might happen to Lili if she didn't haul ass down to the Meatpacking District ... and quick.

Hurriedly, she put the rest of the laundry away and went downstairs to tell her parents goodnight.

With her iPhone hidden in her bra, she made her way back to her room and got ready as quickly and quietly as possible.

Arranging pillows carefully under her sheets and turning off the lights, she prayed this old trick would be enough to fool her mother if she checked in on her. It always worked in the movies.

She checked her phone yet again. She had sent like ten texts to Meghan and a dozen more to Lili, and hadn't received anything back.

Finally, a response from Meghan. "B by N 10. Meet me @ corner."

The message had been sent five minutes ago. Cat gritted her teeth. Somehow, she had to find a way to slip past her parents and make it to Central Park West in five minutes. She had to think fast.

With her shoes in hand, she tiptoed out the door and carefully down the steps. She could see straight through the foyer into the living room where her parents had opened a bottle of wine. It looked like they had almost finished the bottle, which meant her mother would be sufficiently tipsy. Maybe she could make it without being caught.

Not wanting to risk it, she dropped flat to her stomach in an army crawl, and crawled across the tile foyer and to the door. They couldn't see the door from where they were seated, Cat knew. Gingerly, she turned the knob, and silently she slipped out into the night. Meghan was waiting. Cat prayed she wasn't too late for Lili's sake.

When she and Meghan arrived at the party, it became evident to Cat quite quickly that her stint in therapy had become public.

"Oh, Cat! Wow! How are you? No one expected to see you here!" was the response of many people she saw.

"Have you seen my sister?" seemed Cat's only line of response.

Everyone had seen Lili. With Samuel. But no one seemed to know where they were now.

Cat panicked. She ran around the rooftop three times just to make sure they weren't up there. Suddenly, she was hit with the realization of where they were. A hotel. Meghan had already made herself cozy with Matt Darlington. Go figure. Cat was completely on her own. She took the elevator down to the lobby to check at the front desk and see if any rooms had been reserved in Samuel's name.

Of course, the Penthouse Suite was his for the night. Cat closed her eyes in prayer as she took the elevator back up. It seemed to take an eternity. She just hoped against the odds that she wasn't too late. That she wouldn't find Samuel molesting her little sister.

She knocked hard on the door, despite the 'Do Not Disturb' sign. No answer. She rapped on the door even harder. She continued knocking a minute, maybe longer, until the door opened.

"Well," he slurred his words, as he looked her up and down with mild surprise, "Did you come back so I could finish what I started? Just take your clothes off and get on the bed with the others."

Cat looked past him to see two half naked sophomores lying on the bed, obviously strung out.

"I'm here for my sister," Cat tried to push past him into the room.

"Bitch would hardly get near me, so I sent her home. Do I have you to thank for that?"

Cat didn't respond. She turned and headed back to the

elevators. She felt relief wash over her. Lili was safe. She wouldn't play Samuel's game and he sent her home. Thank God!

Cat took the elevator all the way down to the first floor and walked out onto 9th Avenue. She would just have to catch a cab and get home before anyone knew she was gone. Cat pulled out her iPhone and punched in Lili's number.

One ring, two rings, three …

"Hello," her sister's voice sounded strained.

"Lili, I've been calling you for over an hour! Are you home yet?" Cat asked nervously.

"Cat! Where are you? They're about to call the police!" Lili hissed into the phone.

"What?" Cat felt her heart stop.

"They know you're gone! Where are you?" Lili was whispering now.

"I came down to the Gansevoort. I found out what Samuel was planning for you and I came to save you," Cat felt tears burn in her eyes.

"Oh, Cat! You didn't!" Lili exclaimed. "I mean, thanks, but when I caught him putting something in my drink, I was outta there!"

"I was so worried about you. God! They know I'm gone? What am I going to do? I can't come back!" Cat rubbed her temples in deep thought.

She had been walking since she walked out of the Gansevoort, but she hadn't really paid attention to where.

"Cat they're coming in here … I have to go!" Lili hissed. "Just text me where you are, and stay there. I'll send the car back!"

With that, she was gone. Cat continued to walk. Even when Lili sent the car and she got home, she would have to explain to her parents why she had snuck out. The whole situation was beyond frustrating. Would they accept her reasoning that she had only left out of sisterly devotion to Lili? Would they believe her? Would they even listen at all? They would threaten to send her to Boone again. And that just wasn't an option.

Cat continued to walk. She looked up to see where she was. Greenwich Avenue. She didn't know where she should go. Directly beside her was a little hole-in-the-wall bar. She wasn't even sure what the name of it was. There was just a neon sign over the door that said 'Bar'. On the sidewalk, by her feet, was writing in chalk: $2 tequila shots. This would do.

She texted Lili and went inside to wait. After a dozen, "No thanks, I'm not interested" later, Cat was beginning to regret coming into this place. It smelled like smoke, despite New York City's no smoking law, and she was the only girl there. All around, it seemed like a pretty shady place. She was just about to leave and find someplace else to go when she got a text from Lili: "The car's here. Come outside."

"Thank God," Cat breathed. She thanked the bartender for the free shot he'd given her, and then she hurried outside.

She had just walked out of the bar when the door to the town car opened, and her father stepped out with Lili's phone in hand.

"Cathleen," he said, holding the door open for her.

"Dad, I can explain everyth- ..." Cat began.

But he interrupted, "Don't speak. I forbid you to say another word. Get in the car immediately, young lady."

After closing the door behind her, he went around the car and got into the passenger's seat, leaving Cat in the back by herself.

When she got home, all the lights in the house were on. Lili and her mother were sitting in the living room. Her father still hadn't spoken a word to her.

"Dad, can I talk now?" Cat asked, after they had walked into their home.

"No," her dad didn't look in her direction.

"Lili, Cat, go to bed. We'll talk in the morning," her dad said with a tone of finality.

Cat was shaking as she climbed the steps with Lili to the second landing. If only she could explain. If only he would give her a chance to tell him why she'd snuck out.

"Don't worry, Cat," Lili grabbed her hand and squeezed it when they reached her room. "I told Mom why you were coming down there. It'll be okay."

"I hope so," Cat squeezed her hand back and went into her own room.

After getting ready for bed, she laid there forever unable to fall asleep. Three a.m., three-thirty a.m. Sometime around that point, she must have drifted off to sleep.

"Cathleen? Cathleen, time to wake up!" it was her mother's voice.

"What time is it?" Cat raised her head groggily. She was utterly exhausted.

"It's four-thirty a.m., but you need to pack and get ready for your flight. We're leaving in half an hour," her mother switched her lights on, blinding her completely.

"What flight? What are you talking about?" Cat tried to retreat from the light by pulling the pillow on top of her head.

The pillow was ripped away and the bed sheets torn back.

She looked up to see her father standing there looking grim and grumpy.

"I'm counting to three," he said, something Cat hadn't heard him say since she was in grade school. "One, two ..."

"Okay, I'm up!" Cat shouted at him getting out of bed. "Now, what's going on?"

"You are getting ready and packing for your flight to North Carolina. We'll take you to the airport in half an hour."

"What?" Cat's voice was shrill. "I've been perfect! I've abided by every ridiculous rule! The only reason I snuck out last night was to save Lili! You have to believe me!" Cat was full on begging at this point. She looked at her mother for pity, who just looked down.

"Oh, I know," her father said sarcastically. "You were trying to save her from Samuel Alden. Cathleen, I know the Alden family. I make deals quite frequently with Samuel's father. They are decent, upstanding folks. To think that my own daughter would try to smear their son's good name to make an excuse for sneaking out to a party is … well, it shames me."

"He tried to rape me!" Cat blurted out. "The night I tried to commit suicide, he tried to RAPE me!"

Her mother looked up with terror in her eyes.

"THAT'S IT!" her father shouted. "You are leaving for your entire senior year! I can't believe you would stoop to telling these lies so that you won't get into trouble! You have thirty minutes!"

With that, he turned and stomped out. Cat crumpled to the floor in tears. They didn't believe her. Her own father wouldn't even listen to her.

She felt her mother touch her shoulder, "Your father thinks this is best. I'll start packing for you. Remember, you'll be going to public school, so no need for designer clothes."

Cat continued to sob. She couldn't believe this was happening.

"Mimi will need your help on the farm. It'll be good for you. It will help put all the luxuries you've had here into perspective. I'll send the rest of your things in a week or two. This time away will be good for you … you'll see."

Cat cried the entire time she was packing. She cried on the

way to the airport. She only stopped crying when her mother pulled out *Call of the Wild* just as they came to a stop by the curb at LaGuardia.

"What is this?" Cat was confused.

"It's your summer reading for Watuaga High. You'd better get started, since you start classes there next month," her father answered, tersely.

"How did you get it so quickly?" Cat asked. But the answer came to her before they responded. There had never been any deal. Whether she behaved herself or not, they had planned to send her to North Carolina all along.

"When did you book this flight?' Cat asked.

Her mother was silent.

"Two months ago," her father's voice was cool, "While you were in therapy."

"What about our deal?" Cat asked, looking directly at her mother.

"Well, you broke that last night, didn't you?" her dad responded.

"Cathleen," her mother looked up, "You can use this as your purse in Boone." She handed Cat her old Longchamp bag. "Girls at Watauga won't be carrying Louis Vuittons. It'll only make you stick out."

Cat's mouth hung open in shock. Not from her bag being taken away, that was the least of her worries, but from her life being ripped away. Just like Landon had been torn from her, so had everything else. She had nothing.

"And we'll be taking your iPhone, too," her father added, removing it from the bag before her mother could hand it to her. "If you need to call, you can use Mimi's land line. You need to get away from everything."

The driver had put her bags on the curb, in the rain. From the way her parents were glued to their seats, it was obvious they weren't walking her inside.

"Here's your ticket," her mother put it into Cat's hand. "We'll be thinking of you, Cathleen."

"Mmm-hmm," her father added and turned away to face the other window.

Cat took the ticket and got out. She didn't say goodbye. She couldn't open her mouth to say anything.

They had planned this all along. The thought kept repeating in her mind. She felt betrayed on the deepest, most intimate level. She stood there in the rain as they drove away. She stood there watching her world shatter to tiny, irreparable pieces.

There was no longer a way to put things back together. She was beyond that. Now, all she could do was start over.

CHAPTER EIGHTEEN

CAT FOLDED HER ARMS ACROSS HER CHEST. SHE HAD FINISHED HER story a minute or two ago, but she hadn't looked up at Luke yet and he hadn't said anything.

I come with too much baggage, Cat thought, as she wiped her eyes with the sleeve of the sweatshirt she was wearing.

Her throat was sore from talking and she felt that she had cried enough tears that night to flood a small village, but for the first time in three months, she felt like a whole person again.

The sky was just beginning to lighten, Luke noticed, as he looked out the window. He still felt uneasy with the weight of the story he had just been told. He felt uneasy and he was pissed as hell. He stood up and marched to the one window in the room. His hands curling into fists and uncurling as he stared out at nothing in particular.

His heart felt heavy for Cat. For all she had endured — the pain, the betrayal, the heartbreak of it all. She had been wronged by so many people. By her own parents, no less. Abandoned when she had needed them the most. Luke felt the anger inside of him burn at that thought. Then, he remembered what Samuel had nearly done to her and something inside of him snapped.

"Damn it!" he growled as he punched his fist against the wall.

Cat jumped. These were the first words he had spoken to her. It must all be too much, she thought. She didn't blame him. She squeezed her eyes shut from exhaustion and opened them up again to stare hopefully at Luke. Who would want to get involved with someone who'd just gone through so many traumatic experiences? At their age, it was all about having fun, keeping things lighthearted, nothing too serious. None of this fit into that category.

Cat quietly stood and walked towards the door. She would just wait in the car until he cooled down enough to drive her back to Mimi's. She wished she hadn't told him anything. It had been a mistake. A huge mistake.

Suddenly, and without warning, Luke seized her hand just as she was reaching for the doorknob. In one swift and fluid motion, he gathered her into his arms. He didn't say anything, but his touch told Cat everything she needed to know. He cared deeply. He accepted her. He felt her pain.

It felt as though a thousand bricks had been lifted off her back; or like a corset that had been laced up too tightly, had finally been cut away. Cat could breath. She felt lighter than air. She hadn't even realized she was crying until Luke pulled back and looked down at his now wet t-shirt.

"I guess I make a good tissue," he laughed.

"Sorry," Cat wiped hopelessly at her cheeks.

She didn't want to imagine what she looked like. Her makeup was probably running down her face in streaks, mascara and all.

"Why were you trying to leave?" Luke held both of her hands.

"I — I thought you were mad at me," Cat began.

"At you?" Luke looked dumbfounded. "Cat, after everything you told me, how could I possibly be mad at you?"

"Well, for being so messed up. For the stupid mistakes I've made. For coming with so much baggage." Cat was about to list off a dozen more things, but Luke held up his hand to silence her.

"I wasn't mad at you. I couldn't be mad at you after that," he said soothingly.

"Well, punching the wall doesn't exactly show me that you accept me," Cat said with a hint of sarcasm.

"Yeah, sorry about that," Luke ran his hands through his short dark curls.

Cat loved it when he did that.

"I was mad … I am mad. But not at you," he added quickly.

"Go on," Cat walked back towards the couch. Hand-in-hand Luke sat down with her.

"Honestly, I'm pissed, Cat," Luke looked at her with such intensity in his eyes. It matched the tone of his voice. "I wish I could go to New York and kick Samuel's ass for what he did to you! I would rip his throat out, Cat. I swear to God!" Luke stood and looked ready to act on his claim. Cat touched his arm. He drew in a breath through his clenched teeth and relaxed some. "I wish I could tell your parents how wrong they were to abandon their own daughter. I wish I could show them how good and genuine you are."

Cat smiled, "Luke, you've only known me for two days."

"And do you doubt what you know about me?" Luke asked her seriously.

"No," Cat was beginning to understand. "I've known you for two days, but I know you. You're intelligent, passionate, and," Cat wanted to say, "and I love you," but she thought that would scare him away completely.

"And?" Luke looked at her curiously. He had a twinkle in his eye.

"And, I know you must be an artist," Cat added, looking around the room. "Though I don't know much about that yet."

Luke smiled. "You will."

He extended his hand to help her up.

"Right now, I need to get you home, before Mimi wakes up and finds you gone."

Cat took his hand. There was so much more she wanted to say. So many questions she had for him. He knew her life story and she didn't even know what his favorite ... well, anything was.

They rode back to Mimi's in silence. But it was a comfortable silence, not like the tension that had been between them before. His arm rested easily over her shoulder. Cat scooted to the middle seat of his pickup truck and leaned her head on his shoulder.

She was exhausted. And for the first time in months, she knew she would sleep soundly.

Luke tapped her on the shoulder, "We're back."

Cat must have dozed off. Silently, they walked hand-in-hand around the house. Cat climbed the ladder and Luke followed.

"Would you like to come in?" Cat asked him hopefully.

"I would fall asleep, Cat. And then, Mimi would skin me alive when she found us asleep in bed together ... even if we hadn't done anything," Luke added.

Cat blushed.

"Get an hour or two of sleep," he touched her cheek. "I'll see you at church in a few hours."

Cat nodded. His touch made her breathless.

Gently, he kissed her lips. Then he was gone, into the early dawn light. Cat spread out on her bed. She felt relief, and freedom, and exhilaration all at once. She felt happy. Closing her eyes, she smiled, knowing that this is what Landon would have wanted for her.

If she only had one life left, she would live it fully.

CHAPTER NINETEEN

THE NEXT TWO WEEKS WERE SPENT IN UTTER BLISS. CAT NEVER thought she would describe getting up at six o'clock every morning to do manual labor as blissful. Even though she was spending every waking hour with Luke, it wasn't enough. The time spent with Luke was like medicine to her soul. She felt love in the laughter that was so plentiful when she was in his presence. It was healing to her. They worked side by side. Oftentimes, Cat provided the entertainment with her lack of knowledge in farm related chores. She no longer minded Luke's teasing. The loving manner in which he did it only made her find him more endearing. They worked in the mornings, went on runs together in the evenings, and stole a kiss whenever they could. Behind the barn, in his truck, in the Christmas tree fields. Cat felt like she was living in a country music song, minus any rolling around in the hay. Cat didn't want another allergy shot. That wouldn't be romantic.

Everything was perfect. Well, almost everything. Luke had begun to open up to her, but whenever Cat mentioned his barn, or asked him about his artwork, he instantly became mute. He would change the subject or say that they would talk about it some other time, but then he never brought it up on his own. To top it off, Luke had asked Cat not to mention his barn or artwork to anybody. She had agreed. It's not like she could really divulge any information. She didn't know anything herself.

The secrecy only piqued her interest further. She felt like a child wanting the toy she couldn't have — and what she wanted was for Luke to open up to her. After all, she had told Luke everything. He would tell her about it when the time was right … she hoped.

They had just walked in the house from trimming trees when Mimi called to them from the kitchen.

"Catie, a package just arrived for you!" she hollered.

"I bet Mom finally got around to sending the rest of my clothes," she commented as they made their way to the kitchen.

"You mean that closet full of clothes you have upstairs isn't everything?" Luke teased.

"Haha," Cat smirked at him. "How am I going to make my name as the fashionista of Watauga High with only a few dozen designer outfits?"

"You have a point there," Luke laughed. "But I don't think you have many outfits in that package."

Cat looked to where he had motioned and agreed. It was too small for clothes. Maybe a book or two, but no clothing.

"I bet it's an early birthday gift," Mimi looked up over her copy of the Asheville Citizen Times.

"What?" Luke exclaimed. "Cat, when is your birthday?"

"What day is it?" Cat asked. The time had gone so quickly this summer, and in the midst of all the changes, she hadn't even thought about the fact that her seventeenth birthday must be right around the corner.

"It is August 12th," Mimi nodded.

"My birthday's the 16th. That's this Saturday! I honestly hadn't thought about it." Cat exclaimed.

"And then you kids start school on Wednesday, the 20th," Mimi added.

"That's so soon," Cat hadn't realized the time had passed so quickly.

"Open your present," Luke handed it to her.

Cat accepted it, but she froze in place when she saw the return address label: 'Mr. and Mrs. Jennings'.

"What is it?" Mimi asked.

"Cat, are you alright?" Luke looked alarmed.

Cat couldn't breathe. She had to sit down.

"It's them. His parents," was all Cat could manage to get out.

Mimi looked at Luke for further explanation.

"Landon's parents," Luke said somberly.

"I'll just go to the living room and give you some privacy," Mimi patted her on the shoulder as she made her exit.

"I'll be in the other room if you need me," Luke said quietly, and turned to go.

"No, wait," Cat called after him. "Could you stay with me?"

"Of course," Luke seemed pleased that she had asked him to remain by her side.

He held her hand as she tried to rip away the brown packing paper with the other.

"I think I'm going to need both hands," Cat smiled.

Luke laughed and moved his hands to her shoulders and he stood behind her.

Opening the box, Cat gasped. A small, shiny silver object had fallen into her lap. It was a class ring from Allen Stevenson. Landon's class ring. Cat picked it up carefully as though it might burn her. Then, she peered into the box for some sort of an explanation or card.

A plain white index card was all there was; and written in the unmistakably perfect penmanship of Mrs. Jennings were a few words: "I had it resized. He would want you to have it.

Happy Birthday."

Cat began to cry. It didn't say I'm sorry. It didn't have to. The gesture said it better than anything else could have. Cat was forgiven. This gesture made Cat realize that she could now fully forgive herself.

Luke bent over and wrapped his arms around her.

"It's nice," he said as he slipped it on the ring finger of her right hand.

Cat noticed he hadn't placed it on her other hand. Maybe he could put another ring on that hand someday, Cat thought giddily. Then, she chided herself for getting too caught up in her daydreams.

Cat looked at the ring and realized that she now had a piece of Landon with her always. It was comforting. She twisted it around on her finger and squeezed her eyes shut. There was such peace in knowing forgiveness. Like a prisoner whose cell was opened for the first time in years, Cat felt free.

As part of their daily routine, she and Luke went on a run after lunch. He said she was bound to be one of the best runners on the cross-country team. He said he could make her the best if she'd let him train her. *If* Cat would let him train her — that was the problem. Cat wasn't fond of being told what to do, and neither was Luke. Those were the times when they fell back into pushing each other's buttons. Gah! No one had the ability to make her smile or scream as quickly as Luke did it seemed. Cat was pretty certain he enjoyed pissing her off. In fact, she thought half the time he did it intentionally.

"Sprint these last hundred yards," he panted, as they rounded the last curve in the road.

"Can't," Cat could barely speak. She was running out of steam.

"Come on. Don't give up! Push, Cat! Push!" He yelled at her, sounding much more like a drill sergeant than a boyfriend.

"Arggh!" Cat groaned as she tried to push herself faster, but her legs had just had enough.

She slowed down to a stop.

"Cat, you can't give up! You have to push through!" Luke continued.

He was starting to get on her nerves.

"Do you want to go to State? You could be the best! You can't wimp out on me like that," Luke reprimanded.

"I don't think I want to run cross country anymore!" Cat gasped, clutching her side.

"Why not?" Luke asked, clearly affronted.

"Because, I'm not so fond of Captain Luke," Cat responded, mockingly giving him a salute.

"You don't want me to push you? Fine! See if you get any better on your own," Luke glared at her.

"I think running a 5K in twenty minutes is plenty good on my own, thank you very much Mr. I-run-in-under-seventeen-so-bow-down-and-worship-me," Cat snapped.

"I don't see you bowing," Luke snarled.

"Yeah? Well, you won't," Cat turned her nose in the air and marched towards the house.

"I think you should kiss my big toe and tell me I'm the best runner you've ever seen," Luke caught up, wrapping her in a bear hug from behind and swinging her up over his shoulder like a sack of potatoes.

"Lucas Presnell, you put me down this instant," Cat fought back her giggles and tried to sound haughty.

"Or what?" Luke swung her to the front and caught her behind the back with his other arm so he was now cradling her.

"Or I won't run cross country!" Cat shouted.

"But you already said you won't do that," Luke began to spin with her.

"Then, I will never ever kiss you again!" Cat laughed.

"I'm not putting you down till you agree to run cross country," Luke began to spin faster.

"No!" Cat squealed.

He spun faster.

"Fine! Fine! I'll do anything you want!" Cat laughed.

Luke stopped abruptly and set her down by the side of the gravel driveway. Cat plopped down on the grass, too dizzy to stand.

"You shouldn't say things like that, Cat," Luke sat beside her.

"Like what?" Cat looked up at him. She felt like she'd missed something.

"You said you would do anything I want," Luke smiled at her.

Cat's heart skipped a beat. She wasn't quite sure what he was getting at.

"Yeah, well … I think I might," Cat looked into his eyes, knowing that she spoke the truth.

Luke paused for a moment in thought.

"What if I said I wanted you to be with me … sleep with me?" he watched Cat carefully, gauging her response.

Cat felt the blood rush to her face. She had never really wanted that before, not really. It just always seemed like something scary before she met Luke. Suddenly, she found herself longing for that sense of closeness, of knowing someone so completely. A voice in her head told her that she was going crazy, she'd only known him a few weeks. Yet, her heart knew that she had found her match. Much in the same way that she knew she and Landon were destined to be best friends.

"I wouldn't ask you, you know?" he whispered. "I just wanted to see what you'd say." Luke leaned in and kissed her sweetly.

"I still haven't answered," Cat whispered back.

"Don't," Luke's voice became serious. "You're hard enough to resist as it is."

"What do you mean?" Cat laughed.

"I'm waiting 'til I get married, Cat," he answered seriously. "Or at least that was the plan 'til I met you. I see you are going to make that a challenge."

Cat laughed. Then, she was quiet. She hadn't met a guy before who was serious about waiting. It was so, so … honorable. Cat sighed and realized with shock that she was a little disappointed. Not that she was ready to take that step now, but in a year or so …

"Are you okay?" Luke asked.

"I'm great," Cat lied. Then changing the subject, she asked, "So what do you have planned for my birthday this weekend?"

"Ah, oh, well …" he looked at the ground. "Well, I feel bad 'cause I didn't know it was your birthday until today."

"Luke! I'm totally kidding!" Cat leaned on him, "Pizza and Blockbuster would be fine with me. I really don't care, as long as I'm with you."

"Well, now I really feel bad, Cat," he grimaced. "I already have plans with the guys. It's our end of summer camp out. We do it every year the weekend before school starts back."

"Oh," Cat knew her voice and face gave away how disappointed she was. She quickly tried to mask it, "That sounds like fun! Where are you camping?"

"Down in the gorge," Luke replied. Then he hesitated, "I can tell them that I won't be able to go. I'm sure they wouldn't really care."

"No, Luke," Cat tried to sound reassuring. "This is your tradition. You shouldn't miss it. It's your last chance anyway."

"Well, that's true," Luke agreed, and the subject was dropped.

"Hey! Maybe we can go out Friday," Cat exclaimed, as they reached the back porch and pulled off their running shoes.

"We're leaving on Thursday. It's a long weekend camp out," Luke looked genuinely sorry.

Cat didn't say anything more. She didn't want to make him feel bad, but this was the first birthday in her life that she actually had a boyfriend. It was kind of lame to spend it alone. Now that she thought about it, she wondered if Luke thought about her as his girlfriend. They hadn't really figured that part out. They were together all the time. Did that mean they were 'together'?

Cat didn't have a chance to ask that question.

"Hey! Can you do me a favor?" Luke asked suddenly.

"Of course," Cat looked up at him as she rubbed her feet. All this running had caused a blister to develop on her left foot. She would have to ask Mimi to drive her out to Wal-Mart later so she could buy insoles for her shoes.

"I have an appointment to get the oil changed in the truck. I'm supposed to be there in thirty minutes. I completely forgot about it. Follow me in Mimi's truck and give me a ride back?" he asked.

"Ummm," Cat didn't want to admit she didn't know how to drive, it was too embarrassing. "Mimi should be home soon. Why don't you just ask her to take you?"

"Cat, she went to one of her Red Hat meetings. She won't be back for an hour at least. What's the big deal? It won't take but five minutes to drive there," Luke looked impatient as he spoke.

"Well, I haven't driven before … around here," Cat said. Well, it was the truth, she told herself. At least partially. "I would probably get lost."

"Cat, you would be following me," Luke reminded her.

"But I haven't driven on curvy roads before!" she implored.

"Cat, seriously, it's not that hard. I'll drive slow." Luke now seemed annoyed. "Are you doing this cause I'm going to be gone for your birthday?"

Now it was Cat's turn to be ticked off. "Luke, do you really think I'm that petty?"

"No. But, you sure are making a lot of lame excuses not to follow me five minutes down the road," he frowned at her.

"Fine! Let's go already!" Cat stomped off towards Mimi's farm truck.

"Cat, you need the keys!" he called after her.

"Oh," Cat turned around. "Actually, I have no idea where they are."

"I do. I'll grab them," Luke ran inside the house.

Cat did know where they were, but she thought she would try just one more attempt to get out of this 'favor'. She sighed. She hoped she wouldn't make a fool of herself. More than that, she really hoped she wouldn't hit another car, or wreck and roll down the mountain. Her mind started churning through all the possible outcomes, none of them positive. Cat had just pictured flames coming out of the engine when Luke emerged from the house with the keys. He tossed them to her.

"Just follow me," he shot Cat a smile. As always, that smile made Cat's knees feel weak. She was putty in his hands.

"Uh-huh," was all she could say in response, and she strode to the old farm truck parked by the barn.

Once inside, Cat took the time to do all those important things people do in movies. Adjust the seat, check. Fix the mirrors, check. Seatbelt, double check. Now, the only thing to do was turn it on and drive. Cat inhaled deeply. She tried to center herself like she would in yoga, but then she heard a horn honk at her. The noise made her jump; then it made her irate. She turned to Luke and flipped him off. He stuck his tongue out at her and made her shake her head. Is this why people say love makes you crazy? So crazy that she would risk driving without a license in a farm truck on curvy mountain roads. Breathing in deeply once more, she said a quick prayer that went like, "Dear God, don't let me die or kill anyone else ... or wreck. Amen," and on the exhale, she turned the key in the ignition.

The old engine rumbled to life. It made Cat smile. Success!

Come on now, Cat. Let's not get carried away. You just started the truck. Now you have to drive it, Cat told herself.

She shifted into reverse and ever so slowly the truck began to roll backwards. Which was the brake? Which was the gas? Cat felt panic as she looked at the pedals. She pressed the one on the right. It increased her speed a little too quickly — she was about to back into Luke. She slammed on the brake and nearly gave herself whiplash when the truck jerked to a halt.

Luke honked at her again and raised his hands up as if to say, "What are you doing?!" Cat motioned for him to go so she could follow.

Cat felt quite pleased with herself as she followed him down the long driveway. She was staying on the road. She was doing great. She wondered what she could have been so worried about to begin with.

When Luke turned onto the highway at the bottom of the hill, Cat grew anxious. She couldn't even see around the curve. What if a car was coming? She waited. Then, realizing that if she waited any longer she would lose sight of Luke, she hit the gas and squealed onto the road. Immediately, she hit the brake and jerked the wheel to keep herself from going into the other lane. This was tricky. She decided she would go extra slow just to be safe. Fifteen miles per hour seemed perfectly fast enough. She rounded another curve, hoping that Luke would come into sight soon enough.

Luke had slowed down around the curve and was waiting for her. Cat closed in, slowly. He leaned out his window and shouted something Cat couldn't make out before he began speeding up. She passed a 55-mph speed limit sign. They couldn't be serious. Fifty-five miles per hour on these roads? That was ridiculous! However, if she didn't speed up a least a little bit, she would lose Luke for sure. Cursing under her breath, she watched as the speedometer crept up to 25, 35, 45. That was as fast as she would go, Cat decided. Luke slowed down to accommodate. Cat could see him shaking his head in the rear-view mirror.

"I tried to tell you!" Cat yelled aloud to him even though he couldn't hear her.

Another curve was ahead. Cat turned into it, maintaining her speed. She turned too sharply. When she felt the right tire go off the road, she jerked it quickly to the left. This action sent the truck completely into the other lane. Seeing another car coming towards her, she screamed and jerked it once more to the right. This time, there was a guard rail that the truck bumped against and Cat slowed down to 20-mph until she had control.

Luke had slowed down as well and was turning around to look behind him. He was yelling and throwing his hands in the air with even more fervor than before. Cat did not want to hear what he had to say. Soon, he was slowing down and put on his right blinker. Cat saw the sign ahead for Bob Young's Auto Shop. She followed suit and slowed down even further. Ignoring the line of cars behind her, she slowed down to 5-mph before she carefully turned and eased the truck into a parking space.

Victory! She had even parked perfectly between the lines. There were no cars on either side of her, but Cat wouldn't let that small fact ruin her moment. At least she had done something right. She was just unbuckling her seat belt when the driver's side door was wretched open.

"What the hell were you doing?" Luke demanded.

"Driving," Cat said pointedly.

"That was not driving!" he yelled. "Honestly, Cat, were you trying to kill yourself?"

"I parked in the lines," Cat said. Certainly, he could admire her fine parking job.

"Whoo-hoo. You parked in the lines," he said sarcastically. "Cat, you went off the road, and then into the other lane, and then into the guardrail. Thank God this truck is so old Mimi won't know the difference."

"I thought I did okay," Cat's voice was beginning to quiver.

Luke snorted.

"I'm going to run inside and give them my keys. Why don't you scoot over so I can drive back," Luke said, and with that, he slammed the door and marched away.

Cat bit her lip and blinked back the tears. She would not be a crybaby, she told herself.

When Luke got into the car, Cat didn't acknowledge him. She turned to look out of the passenger side window.

"You know you would have gotten a ticket if the police had been around," Luke informed her, as he pulled back onto the highway.

Cat pretended that she hadn't heard him.

"I just can't believe that you were all over the road like that!" he continued.

Cat felt tears prickling behind her eyes once more.

"I mean, I know you're used to driving in the city, but geez,"

Luke shook his head at her.

That was the last straw for Cat. She burst into tears.

"No, I'm not!" she wailed.

Luke was caught completely off guard.

"What?" he looked at her warily.

Cat sniffled as tears poured down her face, "I'm not used to driving in the city! I'm not used to driving, period! I'd never driven before!"

Luke looked at her dumbfounded.

"Why didn't you tell me?" he asked gently, as he patted her back.

"I was embarrassed, I guess. I didn't want you to make fun of me," Cat said quietly as she wiped her tears with tissues from the glove box. "People in the city don't learn to drive."

Luke turned back onto Mimi's drive and pulled the truck up to the barn. When he had turned the truck off, he scooted over to Cat and wrapped his arms around her.

"No," she pushed him away. "That won't work! I'm mad at you. You hurt my feelings."

"I'm sorry," he said as he kissed her cheek, his arms still secure around her shoulders.

"Not working," Cat fought back her smile and turned away from him.

"So, so sorry," he said as he kissed her neck.

"You really hurt my feelings," Cat pouted, sticking out her bottom lip.

"I know," Luke said, kissing her cheek once more. "I feel really awful for going on like I did." He kissed her nose. "For your first time driving, you did just fine." He kissed her forehead.

"Really?" Cat beamed up at him.

"Yes," Luke smiled at her.

"Honestly?" Cat tilted her head to the side.

"Honestly, no. You're a terrible driver. But I am really sorry that I hurt your feelings," Luke smirked.

"Uggh! Luke!" Cat hit him on the shoulder and hopped out of the truck before he could stop her.

In an instant, he was out and by her side. He took her hand and spun her around till she was face to face with him.

"I'm still mad at you," Cat said, trying not to smile.

"That's okay," Luke laughed. "I like you mad."

Then, he kissed her. Not soft and sweet like before, but with an edge that made Cat feel that he wanted so much more than he would let himself take. His kiss left her weak in the knees, but just when he pulled away, she pressed herself against him. Twisting her fingers through his hair, she made it impossible for him to escape. She thought he might pull away as he had every time before when their kisses began to heat up, but he didn't. His hands held her firmly against him. They went under her t-shirt to her back. He walked her backward towards the truck where the passenger side door was still open. Lifting her up into the seat, he remained on the ground and began to kiss down her neck. She wrapped her legs firmly around his waist and began to scoot back. He obliged, stepping up into the truck and laying on top of her. His hands supported his weight, lest he come down on her completely. She kept her legs around him as she began to pull at his t-shirt. They were both still sweaty from their run earlier, since neither had changed or showered. Normally that would deter Cat, but since she was sure she smelled as bad as he did, she didn't mind. She pulled at his shirt until she got it stuck on his head. Laughing at her, he pulled it off with one hand, letting the other hand hold himself above her. Her fingers ran over his chest. She kissed his neck, his shoulder. Salty — she parted her lips slightly and teasingly nibbled his collar bone. She had just begun to pull on her own shirt when Luke stopped her suddenly.

"It's Mimi!" he hissed as he grabbed his shirt.

He pulled Cat up to a sitting position and had his shirt back on just in the nick of time. Cat had barely had a chance to register what had happened when she heard the wheels of her grandmother's Jeep Cherokee on the gravel and saw it rounding the curve.

He offered his hand to help Cat out and turned away. Cat hurried to catch up with him. They were both a little flushed. Cat wondered if he felt as flustered as she did.

"Well, that was ...," Cat remarked.

"Yeah," Luke cut her off.

She sighed. He gave her a wink as they approached Mimi's car, which had just come to a halt.

"Where have you kids been?" Mimi asked as she glanced back at her truck. "I thought you were going for a run, not a drive."

"We went on a run, Mimi," Luke answered her as he took the bags out of her hands. "Then, Cat followed me over to Bob Young's so I could drop my truck off."

Mimi looked up in shock. "But Catie doesn't have her license!" she exclaimed.

Cat blushed. Apparently, Mimi did know.

"Well, I didn't know that," Luke said quickly. "But it was okay. She did fine."

Cat looked at him in disbelief.

"Well, let's wait till after she takes driver's ed. before letting her drive again," Mimi smiled at Cat.

"Driver's Ed!" Cat exclaimed. "I refuse to take that class with a bunch of fourteen-year olds. I'm going to be seventeen this week!"

"Cat, you have to take it to get your license," Luke informed her. "How on earth will you get anywhere?"

"I haven't had a problem with that so far," Cat replied.

"Well, there aren't too many Lincoln Towncars in Boone. How do you plan to get to school?" Luke joked.

"That's what you're for," Cat caught him in the ribs with her elbow.

Mimi cleared her throat. Cat and Luke looked up at her.

"I've been meaning to talk to you two ... I know Cat's parents wouldn't approve of her dating anyone right now," Mimi hesitated as though she wasn't sure how to continue.

"We're not like that Mimi," Luke answered quickly. "Cat's become like a sister to me." With that, he playfully punched her arm.

Cat was completely confused. Was it common to make out with your sister in rural Appalachia? She knew she was in the boonies, but seriously!

Luke gave her a look to silence her from asking questions as they walked Mimi inside with the bags.

"Well, that's a relief," she sighed. "I hate to run back out kids, but I'm actually having dinner with ... someone tonight," Mimi said quickly.

Luke and Cat exchanged glances.

"Mimi, do you have a hot date or something?" Cat joked.

"Well ..." Mimi hesitated.

"Ah!" Cat shrieked. "That's awesome! I'm so excited for you! Who is it?"

"Well, it's Pop's old fishin' buddy, Jim Buchanan," Mimi smiled. "I've known him as long as I knew your Pop. We were all in school together. But his wife, Mary Sue, passed two years ago from cancer. So, we have both been there for each other."

"Yay!" Cat jumped up and down like a little girl, taking Mimi's hands and causing her to bounce along. The kitchen erupted with laughter as Cat continued, "This is great! You're still so young. I think this is wonderful."

Mimi blushed brightly and turned to put the groceries in the cupboard.

"Just get home by midnight!" Luke laughed.

"Now, y'all stop!" Mimi laughed. "Oh, Lordy, will you look at me! I'm just a mess. I better hop in the shower and wash up if I want to look half decent for dinner."

Scurrying around the kitchen to put her things away, she hurried down the hall to her bedroom to get ready.

Cat waited until she was well out of ear shot before she rounded on Luke.

"Since when do you kiss your sister like that?" she narrowed her eyes at him.

"Cat, I had to say that! Do you think she would let us spend so much time together *alone* if she thought there was something more going on?" Luke remained calm.

He had a point.

"I'm sure your parents told her to make sure you didn't get involved with anyone," Luke put his hands on her shoulders.

"Alright, I'll go along with it," she shrugged, "as long as you give me a ride to school every day."

"You want me to be your chauffeur?" Luke wrapped his arms around her waist.

"I won't make you wear the little hat, unless you want to," Cat winked.

"Alright," Luke pushed her against the counter and lifted her onto it so she was sitting, facing him. "As long as you let me teach you how to drive."

"Ohhhhh," Cat tilted her head to the side. "Fine."

She kissed him on the nose.

Luke held his hand up, "And you have to take Driver's Ed."

Cat stuck out her bottom lip.

"Cat, you have to learn to drive," Luke held her face with both hands.

"Oh," she sighed, "I guess you're right."

"I know I am," he smiled and kissed her neck, her chin, and then her lips.

Cat sighed, "Oh, I think this is close to where we left off."

Luke pulled away.

"I think I was getting a little carried away before. I'm sorry for that," he ran his hands through his hair and looked away.

"What are you talking about?" Cat tried to pull him towards her.

"I find you hard to resist, Cat. It scares me. It scares me because I care about you," his voice dropped and became suddenly serious. "I don't want to take advantage of you."

"Luke, it's not taking advantage of me if I want you to," Cat whispered with a mischievous grin.

Luke took several steps away, "Cat I'm serious. I don't want you to talk to me like that."

Cat frowned and hopped down from the counter.

"Cat, I care about you," Luke said as he put his hands out to take hers, but kept her at arm's length. "You're not ready to do that yet, and I'm not either."

Cat wasn't sure what to say. She knew she didn't want to get too serious too soon, but she still wanted him to want her. She wanted to be pursued, so then she at least had the chance to say 'no'. Wasn't that how it worked?

"I should get back home and shower," Luke said. "I'll see you tomorrow."

"But Mimi's going to be gone all evening," Cat looked shocked.

"Cat, we've been spending everyday together, one night apart will be good for us," Luke gave her a peck on the forehead and sprinted out the door before Cat could protest.

One minute he's on top of her with his hand on her thigh; and the next, he's calling her his sister and kissing her on the forehead. Cat felt she could get whiplash from shaking her head with confusion. She needed a shower, preferably a cold shower, and now.

Mimi knocked on the door to let Cat know she was leaving. She also added, "Don't wait up!"

Great, Cat thought. My own grandmother is getting more action than I am.

Cat dried her hair and went downstairs to watch some TV. Since her grandmother didn't have cable, Cat had to play with the antenna for a minute to get "Friends" on TBS. She watched two episodes before deciding she would just go to bed early. It was only 9 o'clock. Every night prior, she had spent with Luke. Either she would sneak out or he would come over and they would talk for hours. It was strange not to be with him tonight.

She had just started to doze off when she heard the bell above the front door ring as it opened. Mimi must be home early. She closed her eyes again.

She nearly jumped out of her skin when she felt a hand on her shoulder. She knew in an instant that it was Luke. She smiled.

"Isn't it a little early to be in bed," he whispered, sliding under the covers behind her.

"I thought it was good for us to be apart for a night," Cat whispered back, not rolling over to face him.

"I was wrong," he said smoothly into her ear as she scooted further away from him. "So, so wrong."

Cat laughed.

"What do you want, Luke?" she rolled over to him.

The tone in her voice was suggestive; Luke picked up on it and moved away from her.

"I want to give you your birthday present a little early," he smiled. "But you'll have to get up and come with me."

"I'm in my pajamas," Cat raised an eyebrow at him and glanced down at her pajama shorts and tank top.

"I'll go downstairs while you change," Luke kissed her on the cheek and got up.

"How respectful of you," Cat commented.

After throwing on a pair of jeans, a t-shirt, and her Rainbow sandals, she skipped down the stairs.

"Where are we going?" she asked, unable to mask her excitement.

"You'll see," Luke said with a grin.

Cat wasn't used to surprises like this. It felt like butterflies were break-dancing in her stomach. She had no idea what to expect. He helped her into the truck and within fifteen minutes, they had pulled up to a familiar sight. In the light of the moon, Cat could see the barn Luke had taken her to all those weeks before. She looked at him as he took her hand.

"Cat, no one knows about what I'm going to show you," Luke said pointedly.

"And no one will, if that's what you want," she reassured him, squeezing his hand in return.

"Cat, I — I care about you," Luke said.

Cat sighed. She wanted so badly for him to say something else.

"I care about you too, Luke." Cat nodded. "Very much."

Through the dark, up the gravel path, he led her up to the barn. Quietly, he opened the door and motioned her inside — where he kept his deepest secrets. Never before had he shared with a single soul what he was going to share with Cat. He couldn't find the courage to tell her that he loved her. That he loved her more deeply and completely than he knew it was possible to love. This was his way to show her. This was the only way he knew.

CHAPTER TWENTY

CAT TENTATIVELY STEPPED INTO THE OLD BARN. SHE COULDN'T SEE beyond a few feet ahead. Shadows of varying shades of darkness spanned in front of her as Luke led her deeper inside. The smell was of age, not of animals or hay, but of old wood and paint. Unmistakably, the aroma of paint. She stood perfectly still while Luke went around her and began to feel along the wall for the light. Yet, nothing could prepare her for what the light revealed. Cat was the first to admit that she hadn't been in many barns in her lifetime. But in the few weeks she'd been in North Carolina, she'd been in quite a few. When Luke switched on the light, the darkness fled, and all that was left were the most beautiful and colorful murals Cat had ever seen.

"This is what I do when I have time," Luke said quietly, kicking boyishly at the wood flooring with his boot and looking away.

He looked up at Cat. She was standing completely immobile, wide eyed. He wasn't sure what she was thinking. Was it a bad idea to bring her here? Would she make fun of him? Did being an artist not make him manly enough for her? He had been careful to keep this part of his life hidden from everyone. Even his dad didn't know what he did in their old barn. He thought Luke was working on an old car. Luke watched Cat's expression change as she turned to him.

"It's wonderful," she beamed. "Luke, did you do all of this?"

"Umm-hmm," Luke shuffled his feet on the ground.

"Luke," Cat walked forward and took his hands, "it's amazing. Really. I'm so honored that you would choose me to share this with."

Luke looked up at her. There were tears in her eyes. She liked it; no, she loved it. He felt all the anxiety he'd had about sharing this with someone else melt away.

"I don't think this is a talent you should keep hidden, Luke," she went on. "These paintings, your use of color, the movement in the lines, they're like nothing I've ever seen before. Not abstract really, but not impressionistic, either. They're somewhere in between. Just breathtaking"

As Cat spoke, she walked down the center of the barn. Luke had used each stall door as a giant canvas. When he had used all of them, he began painting walls, ceilings, old saddles, pretty much everything. He had even painted a 1961 Ford farm truck that sat at the other end of the barn. It hadn't worked in Luke's lifetime and had been sitting there as long as he could remember. He doubted his dad even remembered that it was there.

"No one else knows about this?" Cat looked at him in disbelief. Many of these works were gallery worthy in her opinion, and she had a critical eye where art was concerned.

Luke shook his head. "Just you," he smiled.

"What about your parents?" Cat couldn't believe even they would be oblivious to their son's talent.

"This barn hasn't been used in ten years," Luke explained. "And since it's down the road a ways from the house, Dad doesn't ever come by. He told me I could use the barn to fix up my old car."

"What old car?" Cat asked, looking around.

"Well, there's not one," Luke shuffled his feet, "I just need an excuse for what I spend all my money on. Good brushes and paints are a bit pricey. So, he thinks I'm buying car parts, when

I'm really doing this." He gestured around him.

Cat still didn't understand the purpose of lying and going through all this trouble to hide something so wonderful.

"Luke, why on earth don't you tell them? You have a talent! I mean, you could seriously sell these," Cat gestured to the large painted doors. "They would be proud of you."

Luke didn't want to talk about it anymore. All he wanted to do was show her. To let her in on his secret. Now, she wanted to expose his 'talent' to the world. She just didn't get it.

"Hold on Cat," Luke's voice got rough, "remember what you said, that no one else would find out about this. I'm holding you to your word."

Cat's voice faltered, "Do you think I am going to take back my promise?"

"I'm not going to tell anyone Luke," she said directly, "but I think that you should. When I say that you have talent, I'm not trying to flatter you. I'm being honest. You shouldn't hide this away. I don't understand why you would want to."

"You wouldn't," Luke shot back at her.

"What the hell does that mean?" Cat yelled at him. Why was he being so defensive? Why was he acting like he was ashamed of something so beautiful?

"It means that your parents probably supported everything you did growing up," Luke snapped. "They probably signed you up for lessons and told you how great you were and encouraged whatever you wanted to pursue."

Cat got quiet, "Your parents didn't?"

"My mom did," Luke looked down. "But my dad thinks 'art is for queers.'" Luke shook his head, "That's a direct quote."

Cat shook her head, "So, why don't you get your mom to talk to him about it?"

"She died at the beginning of my freshman year," Luke kept his eyes down. "Ovarian cancer."

"Oh, Luke," Cat's heart dropped to her stomach as she stepped to him. "I'm so sorry. Why haven't you told me? You let me go on and on about my loss and you've never once shared your own."

Luke shrugged his shoulders, "I guess focusing on your situation and your pain helped me forget a little of my own."

"And it's always good to know someone understands what it feels like to lose someone," Cat stroked his back.

"Yeah," Luke agreed. "Yeah, it is."

He wrapped his arms around her. They stood for a long time like that.

"So," Cat finally broke the silence, "your dad didn't want you doing art anymore after your mother died?"

"Pretty much," Luke sighed. "She used to take me to exhibits in Boone and Asheville. She was the one who would buy art supplies for me. Dad always felt that I should be playing football."

"That sounds so cliché," Cat pursed her lips in disapproval.

"Yeah. Well, my dad is pretty much a walking stereotype. Monday night football is as important as church to him and he celebrates it with a six pack of Bud," he said somberly.

Cat looked at him sympathetically.

"Cat, don't look at me like that," Luke turned away. "It's not like he's some dead-beat drunk who beats me. He's a good guy. We talk, sometimes. He always comes to my cross country meets. It's just that he doesn't like art. It reminds him of Mom. So, I'd rather he never know about it, that's all."

"I still say he'd be proud of you if he knew," Cat urged.

"Cat, let's drop it," Luke said firmly.

"Alright," Cat sighed. "Oh! But what if you showed it under another name? I bet I could think of a good pseudonym for you!"

"Cat," his voice held a mild warning.

"Fine, fine," Cat held up her hands as though to surrender. "I guess it will just be admired by you and me."

"There are a few mice and a tomcat that live here, also," Luke joked.

"Well, then I'm sure they enjoy it, too," Cat laughed.

She looked around at the paintings. They really were a sight to behold. Cat knew with her mother's connections in the art world that she could get them into a gallery. Her mind was starting to whirl with ideas for him. She ignored those thoughts, for now. She knew Luke wouldn't take any more of that encouragement tonight. He had only just revealed it after all. It would be best to work on him slowly.

She walked to him and threw her arms around his neck. Standing on tippy-toe, she kissed him on the lips.

"Thank you," she said, pulling away.

"What for?" Luke asked, confused.

"For this," Cat gestured around her, "it's the best birthday present I could ever have imagined."

"I'm glad you like it," Luke said, kissing her back.

"I don't," Cat beamed up at him, "I love it!"

CHAPTER TWENTY-ONE

RACHEL HELPED CAT CELEBRATE HER BIRTHDAY THAT WEEKEND, since Luke was having his annual end-of-summer camp out. A little girl time ended up suiting Cat wonderfully. They spent the morning on Saturday shopping in Blowing Rock and Boone. Cat was pleasantly surprised to discover two precious boutiques: Copper Penny and Gladiola Girls. Not only were their offerings as fashionable as any cutesy boutique in the West Village, but the prices were enough to make Cat jump up and down — literally. She found a Burberry scarf set from last season that was marked 75% off at Copper Penny. And Gladiola Girls had her favorite James jeans on clearance. She felt that it had to be a sign that she should purchase them as birthday presents to herself. Her parents had sent her a check in the mail for her birthday. One thousand dollars. That was double the typical birthday money she had received in previous years. Cat was certain it was guilt money. Whatever. If they expected to earn their way back into her good graces, they were sorely mistaken. Cat thought about tearing it up as a sign of protest. But then she laughed — like she would really throw away a thousand dollars! Besides, she had an idea of what she really wanted to spend it on anyway.

She had only spent just under two-hundred during their morning of shopping. They were just finishing up eating sandwiches at Macado's when Cat decided to go forward with her plan.

"Hey, Rach?" Cat asked, while taking the last bite of her grilled cheese.

"Hmm?" Rachel responded; her mouth still full.

"Is there an art supply store around here?" Cat asked.

"There's Cheap Joe's," Rachel said. "They have everything. Why?"

"Would you mind taking me by there, after we finish lunch?" Cat inquired nonchalantly.

"Not at all," Rachel smiled. "I didn't realize you were an artist."

Cat couldn't lie to her, "Well, I'm not. But I have a friend who is … I thought I would buy them some supplies, as a little surprise."

"Oh, that's so sweet of you," Rachel looked as though she wanted to hear more on the subject, but the waitress brought their check and distracted her.

Cat was relieved, but she still wasn't sure how she was going to buy eight-hundred dollars' worth of art supplies without Rachel asking any questions. She had promised Luke to keep his secret and she was determined to do so. Now was the one occasion she could see the benefit of having her license.

When they entered Cheap Joe's, Cat saw that Rachel was right. It had everything. The warehouse was quite large and overflowing with every creative tool imaginable. It was like a candy shop for artists. Cat inhaled deeply. She didn't know where to start. Once she started shopping, Rachel would certainly realize how much money she was spending. Dropping nearly a thousand dollars on art supplies was sure to illicit some questions.

Luckily, Cat saw a distraction standing right in front of her: Clarissa.

"Oh, Rachel," Cat whispered. "Look who it is!"

Clarissa's back was to them for the moment, but who knew when she would turn around and spot Cat. It had become common knowledge among their peers, since Cat and Luke's kiss at Watauga Lake, that they were now an item. It was also common knowledge that Clarissa felt towards Cat the same way Cat felt towards squirrels: sheer, unbridled hatred. Clarissa had made that quite clear to the Facebook world moments after leaving the party at Watauga Lake. She had used words to describe Cat that Cat couldn't even bring herself to say. Luke had wanted to attack back, but Cat insisted that they remain aloof and ignore all her jabs. The fact that she had failed to produce a rise out of them had only annoyed Clarissa even further.

"Should I distract her while you shop?" Rachel hissed back.

Perfect, Cat thought.

"Are you sure you don't mind?" Cat smiled.

"Of course not, I don't want her ruining your birthday with her rotten attitude," Rachel patted her on the shoulder and was off to make nice with the enemy.

Cat turned and headed in the opposite direction. What she needed was someone with an expertise in art. She had no idea what brushes or paints were the best to buy. Luckily, she found a middle-aged woman stocking the shelves a few aisles down.

"Excuse me?" Cat approached her.

"Yes? Can I help you?" the woman turned to Cat.

"Yes, I need to purchase some paint, brushes, and canvases," Cat began, "and anything else a painter might need. I really don't know where to start."

The woman smiled. Cat wondered if they worked on commission. If so, today was her lucky day.

"Well, what sort of price range are you looking at?" she asked. "Paints and brushes range from quite cheap to very expensive."

"Why don't you show me the best brands you carry and we'll go from there," Cat responded.

She could tell this wasn't a response they heard very often and certainly not from someone her age. The woman's enthusiasm to help her was contagious. Cat soon found she was overjoyed at her growing stack of acrylics, paint brushes, and easels, too.

Before too long, Cat had added enough items that her money was spent. She examined the mountain of items at checkout with the realization that they probably wouldn't even fit into Rachel's Honda Accord.

"Would you like this delivered?" the saleswoman asked Cat at the checkout counter.

Cat nearly shouted her answer, "Yes! Oh, that's great! I didn't even realize you guys did that."

"Well, we don't advertise it. But we make exceptions here and there," she winked at her. "When would you like it delivered?"

"Could you deliver it tomorrow afternoon?" Cat asked. "I know it's a Sunday."

"No, no" she waved her hand, "that will be fine."

Cat breathed a sigh of relief. This had worked out better than she had imagined. Rachel had led Clarissa outside to chat while she shopped unnoticed. Mimi would be gone tomorrow afternoon to Charlotte for the day with Jim, so she wouldn't be there when the art supplies arrived. It would be perfect.

Cat joyfully forked over $831.42 and left Cheap Joe's. Never before had shopping been so rewarding, and she had had many successful shopping trips in her seventeen years.

Rachel was waiting for her in the car reading the latest *Vogue*.

"Did you get lost?" Rachel joked as Cat slid into the car.

Cat laughed, "No, I just don't know anything about art."

"Well, I'm sorry you didn't find what you were looking for," Rachel said, while backing up her car.

"Huh?" Cat asked before realizing that Rachel was referring

to the fact that Cat didn't have any shopping bags with her. "Oh, yeah. I know. Turns out they just didn't have quite what I had in mind."

"So, how did you manage to get Clarissa outside so quickly?" Cat was anxious to find out.

"Wasn't hard at all," Rachel smiled wickedly. "I just told her I happened to have a note for her from Luke in the car."

"You didn't!" Cat shrieked.

"Yes, and then I rummaged through the mess in the backseat for half an hour until she had to leave!" Rachel giggled. "I told her I'd find it and give it to her later!"

"Classic," Cat nodded.

"She thinks it's an apology note. I told her I hadn't read it," Rachel made a face. "As if he'd apologize to her after the things she's been writing about you."

"Well, now he'll have to write something," Cat mused. "She'll be expecting that note."

"Hmmm, I guess so," Rachel commented.

They drove back through Boone towards Valle Crucis. Cat was having a real high school sleepover at Rachel's house for her birthday. This was something she hadn't done in at least four or five months. A girly sleepover was long overdue.

They picked up Mellow Mushroom and ran by Blockbuster. After much debating, they decided to rent "All the Right Moves," an older 80's flick that was one of Tom Cruise's first films. Cat had never seen it and Rachel assured her she wouldn't be disappointed.

After pizza and the movie, the girls laid giggling on Rachel's bed.

"I told you, you could see it!" Rachel laughed.

"Maybe for half a second!" Cat agreed.

"But still, you saw it." Rachel nodded.

"Only because you played that part in slow motion and paused it!" Cat chuckled.

"Well, I just wanted to make sure you got a good look at it," Rachel blushed. "Consider it your birthday present, from me to you."

"Well, that was mighty generous of you," Cat shook her head at Rachel's silliness. "Now my virgin eyes are scarred forever!"

"Oh, Cat!" Rachel raised an eyebrow. "Are you?"

"Am I what?" her full belly and late hour had Cat's mind working slowly.

"You know," Rachel said suggestively. "A virgin?"

"Oh!" Cat took the last swig from her can of Cheerwine. She had grown quite fond of this Carolina soft drink. It was, in fact, the only soft drink she allowed herself to drink. She was strictly a sparkling water kind-of-girl.

"You don't have to answer that," Rachel added, before Cat had a chance to respond. "That was too personal."

"Rach, we're friends," Cat smiled. "You're my best girlfriend here. I don't mind if you ask me things. But, to answer your question — yes, I am."

"Really?" Rachel looked shocked.

"Why do you look so surprised?" Cat was a little offended by her response, but she wouldn't admit it.

"No, I mean, that's great." Rachel quickly remedied her reaction. "I just thought, you know, being from a place like New York. You would have, you know. You just seem so worldly, compared to people around here."

Cat didn't know how to respond. There seemed to be so many stereotypes she faced being a 'northerner' and a 'city girl' in the rural South. Then again, there had been many stereotypes she'd had about 'them' prior to living here that had been proven mostly false. She shrugged it off.

"Well, I'm no different than you," Cat smiled. "Unless, you have?"

"Lordy, no!" Rachel squealed. "I don't think I'd be so excited about seeing that little bit of one tonight if I had done that."

The girls laughed together until Mrs. McKinney had to tell them to keep it down since the rest of the family was going to sleep.

After the laughter had stopped and Rachel and Cat had settled into their beds, Rachel in the twin bed and Cat in the trundle bed usually occupied by Rachel's younger sister, Rachel leaned over and picked up the conversation where she had left off.

"But, do you think you will?" Rachel whispered, her tone more serious now. "With Luke, I mean?"

Cat paused in thought.

"Maybe someday?" Cat blushed and shrugged. "But he's informed me he's waiting till marriage. So, that will be a while."

"Luke?" Rachel asked.

"That's what he said," Cat nodded, wondering why Rachel looked so surprised.

"Luke is waiting till marriage?"

"Again. Yes." Cat added firmly, "Rachel, is there something I don't know."

"I don't want to upset you Cat, but Clarissa *claims* that they did it," Rachel wrinkled her nose as though disgusted with the thought.

Even though Cat knew this was a blatant lie, she couldn't help the sickening feeling of jealousy that washed over her.

"She's probably lying, Cat" Rachel amended. "It wouldn't be the first time."

Cat just nodded.

"Are you okay?" Rachel's tone asked soothingly.

"Oh, yeah," Cat put on a happy face. "I'm just tired. It's been a long day." She added a fake yawn for emphasis. "Thanks for the great birthday, Rach."

"You're welcome," Rachel said. "Thanks for letting me spend it with you."

"Of course," Cat yawned again. "Night."

"Night," Rachel replied.

Cat lay awake listening as Rachel's breathing grew heavy and even. She knew that Clarissa was lying; but even so, the fact that untold numbers of people thought that she and Luke had slept together made Cat nauseous. She wanted to set the record straight, but how? She knew she would have to get Luke in on whatever she planned to do, whenever she thought of a plan. She wished he was here now for her to talk things over. She had grown accustomed to discussing every thought or question that popped into her head with him. They had only been apart for nearly three days and yet, Cat missed him terribly. That was when it hit her; harder than a train or a piano being dropped from a five-story building (ouch): she loved him. She really loved him; and not puppy love or infatuation, but best friend, would-rather-tell-him-over-anyone-else-all-the-silly-little-things-I-think, crazy jealous, spend-over-$800-dollars on art supplies, *loved* him. She smiled. Cat was in love. It had taken her eight lives to find her true love and she had happened upon him when her life was in the direst of circumstances. One life left and she had found her love.

Cat drifted to sleep with that thought in her mind. Her last life was for love. What else was worth living for anyway?

CHAPTER TWENTY-TWO

THE ART SUPPLIES WERE DELIVERED RIGHT ON TIME THE NEXT DAY, as promised. Cat was grateful that Mimi had left early that morning for a day in Charlotte with Jim, whom she called her beau. Cat smiled as she recalled how excited Mimi had been while waiting for him to pick her up. She hoped that she would always feel that giddy about Luke. Somehow, she knew she would.

Taking another glance out the window to ensure the coast was clear, she bent down to pick up the last box of paints.

"Last trip," she said aloud as she looked up the stairs grudgingly.

Being the only one at home had benefited her in the sense that no one knew of her purchase, but it also left her alone to assume the burden of bringing in all the supplies and carrying them upstairs, box by box. It had ended up being a total of twenty-four boxes and several large canvases.

She was now regretting her six-mile run this morning, climbing the stairs had been exercise enough.

She plopped onto her bed after she placed the last box with all the others, stacked against her wall.

Mimi hadn't been here to see the boxes arrive; but if she came into Cat's room, they were quite in plain sight. Only three boxes had fit into the closet itself.

Cat looked at the time. Four o'clock. If she knew how to drive, she might take Mimi's Jeep for a spin out on the Parkway. It was a beautiful day. She hoped that Mimi had something for her to eat in the fridge because not driving also prevented her from going out for dinner.

Cat looked at the sun streaming through the window. Then, she glanced at her pale skin. She was in serious need of some sun. School started Wednesday and she didn't want to be mistaken for a ghost. In minutes, Cat had pulled off her clothes and found her swimsuit hiding in the bottom of her dresser drawer. She wiggled into it, grabbed an old beach towel out of the linen closet, and dashed out the door.

Delighted by how wonderful the sun felt, she spread out the towel and laid on her back. Just when she was starting to feel a bit too warm on that side, she flipped over to lay on her stomach. Cat didn't even have a base tan, so the last thing she wanted was to get burnt. She figured about half an hour on each side would be perfect. Just perfect — like the way the sun felt on her now. It was so relaxing. Cat sighed.

An untold amount of time later, Cat felt a cooler breeze, making her shiver. Opening her eyes, she knew immediately that she had fallen asleep. It was still light out, but the shadow of the nearby tree, which had been much further away when she'd first laid down, was now stretched across her.

Cat groaned. She prayed that she wasn't completely burnt on her back. Just her luck that she would start the school year looking like a half lobster. She touched the back of her calves. They were slightly tender. Cat pouted as she got up and trudged back into the house.

Approaching the door, she could hear the phone ringing inside. She skipped up the back steps and into the kitchen to pick it up before the machine did.

"Hello?" Cat spoke breathlessly into the receiver.

"Cat? Where in good heavens have you been?" Mimi demanded.

"I was outside," Cat informed. Why was Mimi so snippy all of the sudden?

"I have been calling you for two hours! Since four-thirty! Jim and I were about to come home I was getting so worried," Mimi spoke with a calmer voice now.

"I'm so sorry, Mimi. I was laying out in the sun and I fell asleep," Cat felt bad for making her worry so.

"I thought you might have gone off with Luke without telling me," Mimi said, her tone was suggestive.

"No, no. Besides he's gone camping till tomorrow, remember?" Cat said, realizing just how much she missed him.

"Oh, that's right!" Mimi said brightly, "Well, now that I know that you'll be home safe and sound tonight I wonder ... would you mind if I didn't return till tomorrow?"

"Mimi, you don't have to ask my permission." Cat laughed.

"I know, I know, but I just thought I'd check. Jim has surprised me with tickets to *Mary Poppins*! We'll be getting out late, so we thought it might be better just to get a hotel room. Wouldn't want to fall asleep on the drive home. It gets dangerous driving too late at night, especially at our age," she trailed off.

Cat fought the urge to laugh. It was clear by the way her grandmother was going on that she didn't want Cat to get any other ideas about their overnight trip.

"No, you should stay," Cat agreed. "I wouldn't want you guys driving that late, either."

She could almost feel the happiness in Mimi's voice as she spoke, "Really?"

"Absolutely!" Cat reassured.

"And you won't be too lonely?" Mimi asked again. Cat knew she was just asking again to be polite.

"No, I have my summer reading to do. You guys have fun …
at the show, I mean," Cat added quickly.

"Oh yes, yes. We will." Mimi sounded giddy with excitement.
"We'll be back tomorrow around lunchtime. Bye now."

"Bye-bye," and with that Cat hung up the phone.

She didn't really have any reading to do. She had finished the
book last week at Luke's insistence that she get it over with, so
they could have more time together before school started. But
she had wanted Mimi to feel okay about leaving her by herself
tonight. She knew that Mimi wouldn't have stayed in Charlotte
if she thought her granddaughter would be moping around the
house, lonely, with nothing to do.

She also knew that if Luke was in town, she wouldn't have
stayed, either.

Despite Luke's attempt with his "she's like my sister" comment, Cat had a feeling that Mimi didn't buy it. Luke didn't look
at her like a sister. When he rushed to pull out her chair for her
or to hold open the door, Cat knew Mimi noticed, even though
she didn't say anything.

Though Mimi would be fine with their dating, she also knew
her parents would not. How long would it be before Mimi shared
with her mother what she already suspected? Cat knew her mom.
She was probably insisting on thorough reports on her behavior
and activities. The amount of time she was spending with Luke
would not go unnoticed. She would have to start making other
excuses for where she was going when they were getting together.
Cat was not ready to surrender their unsupervised time.

After a bowl of Kraft macaroni and some Seinfeld reruns, Cat
decided to head to bed and read some past issues of Vogue that
Rachel had been all too happy to supply her with. She had just
finished washing her face when she heard a knock at the door.

She stopped. Who could be visiting at nine o'clock? Cat waited to see if they went away.

After a minute, she peered down the stairs. No one was there. Maybe it was her imagination. She crept down the stairs to make sure.

That's when she heard it. The sound of footsteps — unmistakable. They were on the back porch. She grabbed her grandmother's umbrella from the hat stand by the door, and holding it as a weapon, she walked towards the kitchen. She tightened her grip on the umbrella handle, ready to bludgeon any intruder that might leap out at her. The back door jiggled then creaked open. Someone was in the house. Whomever it was, they were just around the corner from Cat. She could feel her heart pounding loudly through her tank top. She pressed one hand against her chest, as though that would silence it. Closing her eyes, she listened as they walked around the kitchen, and then they stopped. Cat heard a distinct scraping sound and then chewing. The culprit was eating her left-over macaroni. How dare they?

She raised the umbrella over her head and leapt from behind the wall.

"Ahhh!" she screamed towards the trespasser and let the umbrella swing down with a crash.

"Holy shit, Cat!" Luke jumped out of the way just in time.

Cat screamed in shock.

"Oh! Oh my gosh, Luke!" she jumped back. "You scared the crap out of me."

She clutched her chest and leaned against the fridge.

"I scared you?" Luke laughed, picking up the pot of macaroni that had clattered to the floor. "You just attacked me with an umbrella!"

Cat laughed, looking at the other half of the umbrella that

had broken off.

"I thought you were an intruder," she began laughing even harder. "I thought you were an intruder stealing my macaroni."

"You're crazy, you know that?" Luke laughed with her and gathered her up into a bear hug.

"Shoo, you stink!" Cat held her nose.

"I left the campout early and came straight here," Luke smiled. "I wanted to surprise you."

"Well," Cat kissed his nose, "you certainly did."

"Where's Mimi?" Luke asked, looking down the hall towards her room.

"She's in Charlotte with Jim," Cat winked at him, "for the night."

"Really?" Luke nodded in understanding. "So, you're here, all alone?"

"Yep," Cat kissed him again. "But you seriously need a shower before I kiss you again."

"Done," Luke laughed.

Cat sat outside the bathroom door, that Luke had agreed to leave open while he was in the shower, so that she could tell him all about her birthday outing with Rachel.

Cat had wanted to sit inside the door while he showered, only so he could hear her better of course, but Luke thought she would try and peek at him or play a prank. Imagine that.

So, she sat obediently outside the door where she was unable to see anything and tried not to think about the fact that Luke was naked a mere ten feet away. Cat sighed. Weren't guys the ones that were supposed to be like this?

He emerged wrapped in a towel. "Where did you put my clothes?" Luke asked warily, his face aghast as he noticed his missing clothes pile.

"Luke, they smelled as bad as you did," Cat said pointedly. "I put them in the wash."

"Fine," Luke agreed, "I'll just grab something else out of my bag." He walked towards the stairs.

"Luke, they all smelled terrible," Cat insisted.

"Don't tell me all my clothes are in the wash," Luke looked seriously annoyed.

Cat didn't say anything.

"Well?" Luke demanded.

"You said for me not to tell you," Cat tried to hide her grin, "I'm not going to lie to you."

"Cat!" Luke exclaimed. "What am I supposed to wear?"

"I think you look fine in that," Cat approached him.

"I will not wear a bath towel for the next hour," he looked fit to kill.

"Fine," Cat shrugged, "you can take it off."

Luke gave her a look.

"Oh, come on!" Cat laughed. "That was funny and you know it."

"Whatever," Luke stomped around her and walked towards her bedroom.

Cat forgot about the art supplies until she saw Luke freeze in the doorway. When he turned slowly back to her, all she could do was smile and say, "Surprise!"

Luke slowly walked into the room. Cat moved to the doorway, so she could see how excited he was. She had pictured this moment ever since she decided to surprise him.

The look on his face baffled her, but beyond that, she felt deeply wounded. He was frowning, she observed, as he peered into each box — examining the paints, brushes, and canvases. He didn't say a word.

Finally, he put a hand to his forehead and massaged his temple as though he was in deep thought.

"Cat, why did you do this?" he spat the words at her.

The nerve he had, asking her why she would want to do something nice for him. Didn't he know how much she cared?

"Luke, you know why," Cat tried to sound pleasant.

"Because you think I'm too poor to afford it myself," he said acidly.

"What?!" Cat was appalled. "Is that seriously what you think?"

"Cat, there are-," he paused to count, "twenty-one boxes of art supplies here.

"And not just any art supplies. The best quality, the most expensive. I — I — could never afford this on my own. I can't pay you back for this."

"I don't want you to pay me back," Cat nearly shouted. "It's a gift, Luke. A gift. When you love someone, you want to show your love. I just wanted to surprise you."

Well, now Cat just wanted to slap him across the face, to beat on his chest, and maybe even kick him a few times. Instead, she burst into tears. Luke was quiet for a minute.

"What did you say?" he finally asked.

"I said I wanted to surprise you," Cat said through her sniffles.

"No, before that," Luke asked.

Cat looked confused.

"You said 'when you love someone,' that's what you said," Luke stepped towards her.

Cat looked up, "Yeah, I guess I did say that."

Luke held her face with both of his hands, "Cathleen Rhodes, are you telling me that you're in love with me?"

Cat nodded and looked into those beyond-green eyes that made her breathless, "I love you, Luke."

He smiled broadly and then kissed her full on the mouth. She wanted to melt into him. She wrapped her arms around him and locked them in place.

Luke could see the likelihood of things getting out of hand too quickly. Especially, considering his attire or lack thereof.

He pulled away so he could look into her eyes.

"Thank you," he sounded quite sincere. "But it really is too much."

"Nothing's too much for you," Cat tried to go in for another kiss.

Luke stepped back to the boxes, "Cat, there has to be over a thousand dollars of supplies here."

"No, there's not," Cat corrected him, "Not quite that much."

"But, still. Twenty-one boxes of paints and brushes," Luke looked around, counting them again. "It will take me years to use it all."

"There's actually three more boxes in my closet," Cat added sheepishly. "And, I hope it lasts you a while. You will need it to build up your collection so you can show it one day."

Luke gave her a look that told her they were not going to discuss showing his artwork. Cat wondered how long it would take her to change his mind on that point. Someday, he would see what she saw. He would realize what a talented artist he was.

Luke didn't know what to say. Never before had he received such a generous gift. He didn't know how to accept it, but he knew to reject it would hurt Cat tremendously. At the same time, he couldn't help but feel excited. His mind was already churning with ideas of art pieces he could create. He could do something bigger and better than he had previously done. Maybe one of them really could be gallery worthy … someday. Luke pushed that thought to the back of his mind. He could never be an artist. No, for him, it would have to remain a hobby. His father had already lost too much to lose his son to a profession he had little, if any, respect for. Luke had always toyed with the idea of showing his work someday, but ever since Cat had mentioned it, the idea seemed real. Attainable, even. Try as he may, the thought of it had never fully disappeared. It was always there, ever-present, lurking in the shadows of his mind as though waiting for him to let down his guard and attack him once more.

Cat took his hand. "Your work is beautiful. I won't bug you about showing it anymore … at least not tonight. But it's wonderful and I wanted for you to be able to create more … that's why I did this."

Luke turned to her. "Thank you. I mean, not just for this. But, thank you, for everything."

Later, when Luke had dressed and taken the opportunity to go through all of his new supplies, they sat on her bed talking.

Luke had just finished telling Cat another idea for a project he could work on. And, as with his ideas before, she praised his genius and innovation.

"I love it!" she stood up suddenly. "Just think Luke, this is the kind of work that people in New York would be dying to see!"

"Cat," his voice held an all too familiar tone.

"No, Luke, don't 'Cat' me. I'm serious," Cat continued, ignoring the roll of his eyes. "Galleries in the city are always looking for new artists. Your medium and style is something I have never seen before … and not to brag, but I went to a lot of galleries. It would be very marketable."

"Can we talk about something else?" Luke pulled her back onto the bed.

"Fine," Cat sighed, "but only if you promise me, you'll think about it."

"Deal," Luke agreed.

"So," Cat scooted close to him, "do you think you could stay here tonight? I don't want to be in this old house by myself."

"Liar," Luke chided. "You're not a bit scared of this house. You just want to try and attack me in the middle of the night."

They laughed.

"Would not!" Cat giggled. "But I do have to warn you … you know how some people sleep walk or sleep talk?"

"Yeah?" Luke raised an eyebrow.

"Well, I sleep grope," Cat kept a straight face. "Just kidding!" she added when Luke looked genuinely concerned.

"I might just sleep grope you for being such a tease," Luke joked.

"You wouldn't dare," Cat giggled.

"Oh, wouldn't I?" laughing, Luke leapt onto her and began tickling her until she gasped for air.

When he stopped, they both lay on the bed, happy and breathless.

"Cat?" Luke rolled onto his side to face her.

"Hmm?" she turned to face him.

"What you said before …" Luke began, "I didn't really respond, but I meant to."

"Huh?" Cat interrupted.

"You said you love me," Luke smiled at her, "I've never said that to anyone before."

"Not even to Clarissa?" Cat questioned.

"Hell, no!" Luke shouted.

Cat was quietly pleased with his response.

"I'd never said it before tonight, Luke," she touched his hand. "But I don't want you to say it until you want to."

"Cat?" Luke pulled her closer to him, so that their faces were mere centimeters apart. "I love you."

His kiss felt like a fire coursing through her veins. It was as passionate as their short rendezvous in the truck if not more so. She rolled on top of him and returned his kiss as best she could. Pulling her closely with one hand, he rolled so that he was now on top of her. The weight of him made it a little difficult to breathe, but Cat feared that telling him so might cause him to pull away completely, like he had done so many times before. She wrapped her legs around him and locked her feet together. She smiled inwardly at her brilliance — now, he couldn't pull away if he wanted to. And he didn't seem to want to.

He let her pull his t-shirt off. He continued to kiss her as his hand went to the spaghetti straps of her tank. To her surprise and delight, he pulled it down over her shoulder, kissing down her neck as he went. His lips moved across her collarbone. Her shoulder. Cat sighed.

It was that one sigh that seemed to snap Luke back to reality.

He let out a growl of frustration and then pulled away and sat up.

"What did I do?" Cat felt embarrassed, pulling the straps of her tank back into place.

"Nothing," Luke ran his hands through his hair, and he turned to her and smiled. "You didn't do anything. It was me. I let it get out of hand."

Cat looked down at his shirt, crumpled at the foot of her bed, and hastily scooped it up and tossed it to him. Suddenly, she felt self-conscious. Did he think she was some kind of an animal … she hoped not? She hoped he knew that she thought sex was an incredibly special and intimate act. One that she was nowhere near ready to do anytime soon. For now, she just wanted to kiss, and maybe mess around just a little bit. Was that so bad?

"Luke?" Cat bit her lip, as he put his shirt back on. "Do you think I'm awful?"

Luke laughed, "No, I don't think you're awful! Why would you say such a thing?"

"Well," Cat sniffed back a tear, "you're always the one pulling away from me. I'm the girl. Aren't I supposed to be the one saying no? Do you think I'm easy?"

"Cat, come on!" Luke turned to her. "I don't think you're easy at all. I think that I know myself pretty well, and I know the further we go, the harder it gets to stop. I respect you. So, I just want to stop before you have to tell me to."

He kissed her on the mouth and wiped a tear from her cheek, "I don't know if I like being called the girl in that situation." He winked at her.

"I understand. But just so you know, I don't want to do that yet, either. I just like to be close to you," Cat leaned in for another kiss.

"I like to be close to you too," he returned her kiss. "And I'll stay here tonight … if you want me to. So, you won't be scared," he teased.

"I would like that," Cat smiled.

After getting ready for bed, Cat lay in his arms listening to the sound of crickets outside her window. One thing Luke had said bothered her slightly. It reminded her of what Rachel had told her about Clarissa's claim.

"Luke? What you said earlier, about the further you go, the harder it is to stop," Cat began. "Were you speaking from experience … with Clarissa?" Saying her name reminded Cat how much she disliked her. She wrinkled her nose.

Luke closed his eyes. He had been hoping to avoid this conversation as long as possible, hopefully forever. He could see now that that would not be an option.

"Yeah, maybe," he turned to Cat. "I guess I was."

"Well, what did you guys do?" Cat really didn't want to know, but felt compelled to ask.

"Cat, I love you," Luke kissed her hands, "I'm so sorry that I ever even dated her. I really am sorry."

"Luke, you're scaring me," Cat frowned. "Just tell me so I won't imagine anything worse."

"I'm ashamed because I did a lot of things and I didn't even want to be dating her for most of our relationship — if you can even call it that," he rolled away and looked out the window.

"But you said — you said you didn't have sex," Cat felt as though she could cry.

"We didn't!" Luke said quickly. "But,"

Cat breathed a sigh of relief.

"But we pretty much did everything else," Luke was quiet.

Cat was quiet.

"Do you forgive me?" Luke whispered.

"What's to forgive? Luke, you didn't even know me at the time," Cat rubbed his back.

"Doesn't matter," Luke looked angry at himself. "I knew that she wasn't going to be my wife. I knew I didn't love her and I let her do those things to me anyway."

"It's not your fault," Cat soothed.

"Yes, it is, Cat. I was a participant," Luke turned to her.

"More like a victim," Cat tried to make a joke out of the situation. It wasn't successful.

"Cat, I'm serious. You have no idea what I would give to go back and change what I did. I wish I had never experienced any of those things, so I could experience them with my wife for the first time."

Cat was beginning to see where he was coming from.

"It upsets you to think of me with her like that doesn't it?" Luke asked Cat.

Cat made a gagging sound in an effort to be humorous, but in truth, that was exactly how she felt about that thought. Just picturing Luke and Clarissa being intimate in any way made her shake her head to get rid of the disturbing images that popped up.

"Yes," Cat admitted, "it upsets me. But it doesn't change the way I feel about you."

"If you had done the things I did," Luke shook his head. "It'd make me sick to my stomach." He paused, "I would still love you the same, but it would make me sad not to be your first ... everything."

"What made you change?" Cat was confused. If he had done these things with Clarissa, whom he didn't even love, why wouldn't he do them with her?

"I became a Christian," Luke said honestly. "Gah. I sound so typical Bible-Belt, don't I? I had gone to church my entire life, but I don't think I understood the gravity of it all until this past summer. I didn't understand grace."

Cat didn't know what to say. It sounded cliché in her head, yet coming from Luke it sounded so sincere. It was the kind of response she would have laughed at months ago; yet now, in the wake of everything that had happened to her, she wanted to understand it. The assurance, the peace he seemed to have--she couldn't help but want that, too.

"Wow," Cat finally spoke. "That's ... well, that's pretty awesome, Luke."

"So, you won't even do the things with me that you did with Clarissa?" Cat finally asked. "I hate the thought that she saw more of you and touched more of you than me. I know that sounds stupid," she shook her head.

Embarrassed, she retreated under the covers until he pulled her out and onto his lap. It only served to make her feel more ridiculous — like a child. She closed her eyes and buried her head into his shoulder.

"No, it doesn't sound stupid," he lifted her chin and kissed her. "It sounds normal to me."

"But," Cat urged him to answer her.

"But, no. Not yet, anyway," he kissed her cheek. "Someday I want to do all those things and more, but we'll just have to wait."

Cat felt as though she was having an out-of-body experience. Had he just said that they would be married one day?

"Did you just ask me to marry you, Luke?" she felt her heart pounding louder and harder than ever before.

"Not officially," he watched her response carefully.

Cat felt her head swimming. She knew her answer before she would let herself admit it. She swallowed and looked up to see him smiling at her.

Cat smiled back, "Well, I un-officially accept."

His kiss was gentle this time. Sweet, but still with passion underneath it all.

"I really don't know if I can wait ten years or so to be with you," Cat sighed deeply, "but I'll try."

"Ten years!" Luke sat up. "Cat, there's no way I'd want to wait that long. I was thinking more like four years, five at most."

"Luke, I'd be 21 or 22!" Cat exclaimed.

"So?" Luke stared at her. "Oh, that's right, people don't get married that young in New York."

"Uh, no!" Cat couldn't believe what he was suggesting. She could just picture telling her parents, or worse, her friends. They would think she'd completely lost it.

"So, when do New Yorkers get married?" Luke teased.

"I'd guess around thirty-five is average, twenty-seven would be really young," Cat informed.

"Why?" Luke asked pointedly.

"Why what?" Cat shot back.

"Why do they wait so late?" Luke looked genuinely interested.

"Well, because, well they," Cat realized she didn't have an answer. "Honestly, I have no idea," she laughed.

"Well," Luke pulled her to him once more, "I believe in marrying when you've found the person you love and want to spend the rest of your life with."

"In that case, I would be getting married now," Cat watched his response.

Luke smiled, "Me too, but I don't think our parents would be too keen on it."

Cat laughed, "Maybe not."

"That's why being un-officially engaged will have to do for now," Luke said while getting up and walking over to the nearest box of art supplies. He pulled out a bronze colored wire that was wrapped around a group of brushes and began twisting it. His artful eye quickly fashioned it into a rope-like bronze ring.

"Let's see how it fits," Luke took her left hand and slipped it on her ring finger. "Perfect," he commented, lifting her hand to his lips.

Cat's eyes filled with tears.

"Do you like it?" Luke looked up at her hopefully.

"I do," Cat closed her hand in his, never wanting to let go.

CHAPTER TWENTY-THREE

THE NEXT MORNING CAME WITH BIRDSONG AND SUMMER BREEZES flowing through her open window. Cat couldn't recall a time when she felt more content. Gently, she touched her fingers to the twisted wire that rested on the ring finger of her left hand. Luke was sleeping behind her. She could feel the even rhythm of his breath against her neck and she closed her eyes. Contentment.

Like a gentleman, he had insisted on sleeping above the covers. She smiled to herself. Sometimes, she found his old-fashioned charm frustrating, but at this moment it was sweet. Slowly, as not to wake him, she shifted her body and rolled towards him. The goal was to watch him sleeping, but he was already beginning to open his eyes. She smiled.

"Good morning," Cat leaned in to kiss him; and then, thinking suddenly of how terrible her breath must smell, she held the sheet up over her mouth and rolled away.

"What are you doing?" Luke laughed and pulled her back in.

"Don't smell my breath!" Cat giggled uncontrollably as he fought the covers away for a kiss. "Ahh! I haven't brushed my teeth yet." The tousle led to a wrestling match in which Cat was determined to keep her mouth covered. Before she knew it, she had wrapped herself up like a mummy and was somehow dangling head first off the foot of the bed, breathless from laughing and exhausted from playing this game.

She let Luke win, but kept her lips tightly closed when he gave her a "good morning" peck on the lips.

Leaving him sprawled out on the bed, she scurried to go brush her teeth. I hope we will always be like this, Cat thought to herself. Playful. Silly. Fun. That's what I want in a relationship, as she ran through a list in her head of qualities that she valued in a partner. Of course, they had to be intelligent and hold a conversation. Check. Honest, Kind. Check, check. Cat continued down her list as she rinsed with mouthwash.

"How do you like your eggs?" Luke interrupted her thoughts from outside the bathroom door.

She spit in the sink.

"Scrambled, please. Lots of pepper," she suddenly felt so grown up. Is this how you feel when someone makes eggs for you? Of course, they hadn't actually slept together. However, Cat knew this would be as good as it would get for a while and she wanted to soak it all in.

Dressing quickly and running a brush through her hair before plaiting it in a quick braid to the side, she ran down the steps, skipped the last two at the bottom, and bounced into the kitchen where Luke was already busying himself with breakfast.

"What can I do?" she asked. He had bacon frying in one pan, eggs in the other, and had just laid out ingredients from the pantry onto the kitchen table.

"I thought I'd make you biscuits," he smiled up at her. "Surprised that I know how to cook?"

"A little," Cat was embarrassed to admit but pleasantly surprised. "I know how to make Kraft macaroni and cheese and microwave popcorn and that's about it."

"I'll teach you," Luke took one of the vintage aprons off the hook on the wall and tossed it to her. "Put this on. You can be my sous chef."

"You are full of surprises, Luke Presnell," Cat shook her head as she tied her apron and watched as he slipped a bright yellow one over his head.

"Is it my color?" he winked.

"Well, the yellow looks good with your tan ... but I'm not so sure about the daisy print," Cat walked slowly around Luke in mock examination of his ensemble.

"Only real men can pull off flowers," he pulled her in close. "Now, are you ready to learn?"

"I'll let you teach me anything," Cat leaned in suggestively before erupting in laughter.

"Lord, Cat," Luke tossed a handful of flour at her. "That's what you get for being such a tease."

Within an hour, breakfast was on the table and flour covered nearly every surface. Cat and Luke sat opposite each other with their bare-feet touching under the table. Cat's braid had come mostly undone in the flour fight. Luke's hair looked white. The jar of apple butter they had discovered in the pantry made the perfect accompaniment to the buttery biscuits. She felt so grown up, but at the same time, like a child playing house. This moment was perfect. She felt her heart just fluttering out of her body, like she might need a giant butterfly net to catch it and put it back in place. The exhilaration of it all made her positively giddy. It felt so innocent and just a little bit sneaky, all at the same time. Cat rubbed one foot up Luke's leg, until it rested on his chair.

"This is amazing," Cat said with a mouthful of biscuit. "I know I said you should be an artist but I lied ... you should be a chef."

Luke shook his head, "I don't know about that."

"What else can you make?"

"Well, let's see," Luke smeared another spoonful of apple butter on his piece before taking a bite. "I can make biscuits and biscuits. Oh, and I'm also pretty good at making biscuits."

Cat laughed before popping the last bite into her mouth, sliding her plate aside and leaning forward towards Luke.

"If you had a biscuit restaurant and served only biscuits, I still think you would be a success," she joked, half-seriously. "They are just that good. Who taught you how to make them?"

As soon as the words left Cat's mouth, she wished she could take them back. Luke's smile dropped and he started gathering the plates on the table. He moved her foot from where it was resting on his lap and stood from the table.

"My mom," he said quietly. Then, looking up to Cat, he smiled tenderly, "She made the best biscuits."

"And now you do too," Cat smiled back. "I think it's wonderful that she taught you things and supported you, encouraged your art and everything. She sounds like an amazing lady, Luke."

"She was," Luke agreed. He carried their plates to the sink and Cat began to gather the pans on the stove to be washed. "But, didn't your parents teach you things? You lived on the Upper West Side and attended private schools. Didn't you feel supported?"

Cat paused. She had never thought too much about it until this past year. But when she reflected on it all, and really thought about it, she wasn't sure what she had learned from her parents. What a sad reality to recognize. A nanny had been employed throughout her childhood and well into middle school, when Cat and Lilienne could be trusted to come home alone together on the bus and get started on their homework. Her father was a proud, self-proclaimed workaholic. Cat rarely saw him, save a family dinner here and there on the weekends. Her mother, always the socialite, spent so much of her time serving on committees and flitting to and fro, that Cat wasn't sure she really knew her at all. Cooking lessons never happened in their home with a chef to cater meals. She was certain her mom had imparted fashion advice, but other than that, nada. Cat searched her brain for a memory akin to what Luke experienced with his mom.

"They've always provided very well," Cat decided this was an appropriate response, but her eyes didn't meet Luke's.

"That's not what I asked," Luke said knowingly.

"What do you want me to say, Luke?" Cat startled herself with the harshness of her response. She felt this overpowering anger rising up in her. Not towards Luke, but towards the parents who had refused to listen to her, refused to believe her, or even care. The parents who had a plane ticket with her name on it no matter what she wanted. She felt so deceived; and even though things in Boone had turned out better than she could have ever imagined, she was still hurt by their actions.

"They provided everything Lili and I could want," Cat continued, unable to steady herself or lower her voice. "We had every opportunity, activities, over-the-top birthday parties, the latest-greatest-whatever, we had everything a kid could want," she threw her hands up in exasperation.

"What is it you're wanting to say, Cat?" Luke turned off the water in the sink where he was washing dishes and held her shoulders.

"We had everything," Cat took a breath. "Except the things that matter most." A lump rose in her throat. "I don't even know who they are. They are the puppeteers of my life. They have it all planned out. I just — I just." She broke down. "I just hate them for what they did to me."

Luke pulled her close as she cried on his shoulder for longer than Cat had intended. She let the tears go. All of that anger and frustration that had built up inside her broke loose. There was no reeling it back in.

"Now your shirt is gross," she sobbed harder when she pulled away and saw his tear-stained shirt.

"It's not gross," Luke shrugged. "You just needed a good cry."

"It's gross," Cat corrected him. "This part is snot." She pointed to a greenish smear on the shirt.

Luke examined it closer. "Yeah, okay," he stepped back. "That is gross." He pulled the shirt off and tossed it to the floor. "Better?"

"Mmmm," Cat raised an eyebrow, "Much."

"Uh-huh," Luke nodded. "Now I see what you're doing. Let's cry and cover his shirt in snot so he has to take it off."

"Yep," Cat wrapped her arms around his waist and leaned on her tip-toes to kiss him. "You got me."

Luke tilted her chin up with his hand to kiss her again. Cat ran her hands up and down his back. Secretly, she hoped Mimi would make these out of town adventures more regular. She could get used to morning cuddles, homemade biscuits, and a half-dressed Luke in her kitchen.

Still tangled together, Luke managed to sit down in the closest chair so that Cat could sit facing him. This is getting dangerous, her mind told her, but her mouth just said more. More kisses. More of Luke.

She was unaware of everything else except him. His hands in her hair, his lips on her neck, his … oh my God, Mimi! Cat's eyes had shot open to see her grandmother standing at the screen door with her mouth hanging ajar. Her "friend" Jim Buchanan was only a few feet behind her and had his hand over his mouth, eyes wide. He looked to be hiding laughter though, and not the shock that Mimi wore. Cat didn't know which was worse.

Cat bolted off of Luke's lap, landing on the flour covered floor. Luke turned and leapt up so quickly you would've thought he'd been shot out of a cannon.

Mimi, Mr. Buchanan," Luke began, while looking frantically about on the floor for his shirt. "I — I — this isn't what it looks like."

"Oh, isn't it?" Mimi had no laughter in her eyes. In fact, she wasn't looking towards Cat at all. Her daggers were aimed at Luke Presnell whom, ten minutes ago, she would've trusted with her life. Now, this teenage boy had the nerve to ….

"Mimi!" Cat stepped in front of Luke, taking on the full glare of her grandmother. Mimi was intimidating, the epitome of a strong mountain woman, and not afraid to speak her mind. Cat knew she had to intercept, before anything else was said. "Mimi," Cat began again, "I know what this looks like." She glanced around the disaster of a kitchen — the flour-coated floor, the breakfast plates on the table, not to mention the fact that Mimi had just caught them in a full-blown make-out session, with Luke topless at that. Cat glanced at Luke for assistance, but he looked like a helpless puppy with his head down.

Without a word, Mimi stepped into the kitchen, letting the screen door slam behind her. She was formidable. Slowly, she ran her hand along the flour covered table, looked at it, and walked to the sink to rinse it off. She lifted the pan in the sink that the eggs had been scrambled in and glanced at them both with pursed lips.

Cat was certain her heart had stopped. This was it. She was dead. Surely a person cannot be more mortified than in this very moment.

"Did you spend the night here, Luke?" Mimi remained calm.

"Well, what happened …"

"Yes or no," Mimi held up her hand.

"If I could …"

"Yes or no," Mimi's voice raised slightly.

"Yes, ma'am." Luke's face was turning pink.

Mimi swallowed and nodded, "And where exactly did you sleep?"

"In a bed," Luke answered directly this time.

"With Catie?" Mimi added.

"Yes, ma'am."

Cat looked past Mimi to see Jim on the porch, barely able to contain his laughter. She glanced at the kitchen table and wondered if she could duck and roll underneath it, just to be out of sight. That seemed like a good place to hide.

"Cathleen," Mimi's soft voice interrupted Cat's thoughts. "We are going on a drive."

"Oh, um, okay ..." Cat looked nervously towards Luke before moving cautiously towards the door.

"Jim," Mimi called. "Would you mind staying here with Luke? I'd like to speak to him when I return. You boys can clean up this mess."

"Yes, ma'am," Jim saluted her with a wink as she passed.

Cat followed dutifully towards the jeep. She thought she heard Jim's voice teasing Luke in the kitchen, "So, how does she like her eggs?" Cat flushed a new shade of pink.

"Let's take the truck," Mimi motioned towards the farm truck that was parked out back.

Cat climbed into the cab of the truck and searched for the words to begin, but nothing came. She watched as her grandmother put the truck in drive instead of in reverse — meaning they were driving up into the Christmas tree fields and not turning around to go down the driveway, as she had expected. Cat manually rolled down the window. She loved the smell of Fraser Fir trees more than anything else in the world. She could never understand how her mother could have left this place so easily.

"Catie," Mimi said softly. "I know it sounds impossible, but I really do remember being your age. I know what it feels like to be young and in love."

Cat had been wrong. A person could feel more mortified than she had felt in the kitchen. Here she was, riding through a tree field, about to tell her grandmother that she was a virgin … even if she didn't want to be. She would leave that part out, for her grandmother's sake.

"We didn't do it, Mimi," Cat covered her face with her hands. Somehow, this made it easier to say. "We didn't have sex. We didn't do anything other than kiss. He even slept above the covers."

Mimi tapped the brakes until the truck came to a stop, "You didn't have sex?"

Cat still couldn't bring herself to look at her. She was certain her face was red as the cherry tomatoes in Mimi's garden. She simply shook her head in her hands, until she felt her grandmother's light touch on her shoulder. She looked up.

"I'm glad, Catie," Mimi said. "This means I don't have to shoot Luke and bury him in the holler."

Cat playfully swatted her grandmother's hand, "Mimi, that is not even funny."

"Might've happened," Mimi continued driving once more. "I would've been sad to see him go. He's good help … and not bad looking." Mimi grinned at her granddaughter.

Cat shook her head, "You are terrible."

"I really am glad, Catie." Mimi put the truck into four-wheel drive to make it to the steepest part of the ridge. This was the place on the farm that had the best mountain views.

Cat was looking straight across to the profile of Grandfather Mountain. It was breathtaking. She had some faint recollections of coming up to the top of the ridge with Mimi and Pop when she was little. Even though their visits to North Carolina were few, they were memorable.

"This is my thinking spot," Mimi said brightly, as she hopped down from the truck. The news that Cat had not actually "slept" with Luke seemed to cheer her up immensely.

"It's so gorgeous up here, Mimi," Cat said while hopping out to join her grandmother.

They stood shoulder to shoulder taking in the view. The breeze was steady on the ridge. She could see most of the farm from here. All eighty acres of it. Even though Cat was a self-proclaimed "city girl," she thought that this corner of the world must be the most beautiful, peaceful spot on the planet. She breathed it all in.

"I believe you, Catie," Mimi reached over to squeeze her hand. "About what happened last night and what happened in New York."

Hearing those words from an adult that Cat cared about meant so much. She didn't even realize how much they had meant until the words were spoken. She felt her eyes fill with tears.

"But, Mimi," Cat turned to her, "you haven't even heard about everything that happened back home yet."

"Doesn't matter," Mimi squeezed her hand again. "I don't need to. It doesn't change the fact that I believe you. And I believe in you."

The tears were flowing liberally down Cat's cheeks at this point.

"Sometimes, we just need to hear that someone believes in us," Mimi's arm pulled Cat in closer, so that their heads touched.

"I love you, Mimi." Cat leaned into her embrace before pulling back, "You're not going to fire Luke, are you?"

"Well, I thought about it," Mimi looked serious for a moment before laughing. "I've never seen that boy move so quick in his life as when he jumped out of that chair." She whooped, "Moved like his pants were on fire!"

Cat couldn't help but join in the laughter.

"No, I can't fire my best farm hand," Mimi winked. "He's a catch, Catie. And I'm glad to hear that he's as much of a gentleman as I would've expected. I knew his momma well."

"Thank you, Mimi," Cat blushed. "And he was. The perfect gentleman."

"Until you were straddling him in that chair," Mimi interjected, walking back towards the truck. "I'm sure he wasn't thinking gentlemanly thoughts then!"

"Oh my gosh! Mimi! You weren't supposed to see that," once again Cat buried her face in her hands.

"Just promise me one thing," Mimi looked her granddaughter straight in the eye, "take it slow."

"We will," Cat nodded, unsure of what exactly she was promising.

"Things can move quickly at that age, I know." Mimi sighed. "I had your mother just when I turned eighteen."

That fact had never registered with Cat until now. She nodded again to Mimi, "I promise."

"And, Catie," Mimi added before getting back into the truck, "try to keep your clothes on."

CHAPTER TWENTY-FOUR

PANT, PANT, PANT. CAT COULD FEEL THE SWEAT DRIPPING FROM HER face. Her shirt was drenched, her legs were on fire, and her feet had gone numb half a mile back; but at last she could see the finish line. It was the first meet of the season against Wilkes High School and she was in third place. Rachel had crossed first about a hundred yards ahead and the second runner was about ten feet ahead of Cat.

Out of her peripheral vision Cat could see Luke waving his hands like a lunatic, "Take her, Cat! Push it! Come on!"

Cat really just wanted to yell for him to 'shove it,' but that would have taken too much effort. Instead, she pushed her aggravation through her legs and used every last ounce of energy to push herself just a little bit harder. She was gaining on her. With fifty feet to go, Cat could reach out and touch her. The girl had noticed her now and was matching Cat's energy. It was a dead sprint to the finish. Cat loved when races ended like this, except she enjoyed watching them rather than being the one in the action. She loved running, but it was something she'd rather do for pleasure than competitively. She cursed herself for letting Luke talk her into cross-country. She pushed forward once more, with the last ounce of energy she could muster, and launched herself across the finish line, her competitor following by a few feet.

The voices of the crowd, that she had done so well of tuning out during the race, hit her instantly. The men's cross-country team, which was racing next, were whooping and hollering the loudest of all. Cat slowed but kept jogging around for a minute more to get her heart rate down before stopping. She had made that mistake the previous week during practice and had passed out cold. Thankfully, Luke had been close enough to catch her before she collapsed on the cement. Cat tried not to think about how painful that would have been.

She slowed down but continued in a brisk walk to the refreshment table. She needed something to eat. She tended to get slightly hypoglycemic at times and wanted to make sure she didn't have another incident. Though, getting swept off of her feet by Luke certainly wasn't the worst thing that could happen. She smiled to herself and reached for a banana.

"You were awesome!" he exclaimed. A bear hug from behind was Luke's signature greeting now. It didn't catch her off guard anymore.

"Ew!" Cat gasped. "I'm disgusting! Don't touch me!"

"In half an hour I'll be as sweaty as you are, Cat. Probably more," Luke laughed at her and squeezed her tighter.

Cat turned and kissed him gently on the lips, not wanting to drip sweat on him, "Yes, and in half an hour, I won't be hugging on you."

"Is that right?" Luke raised an eyebrow. "Well, what if I come get you?"

"Then, you'll just have to see what happens," Cat chugged Gatorade from a bottle Luke had just given her. "I'm warning you, though. It won't be pretty."

Cat kept a look of seriousness in her eyes until she dissolved into giggles.

"Good luck," she said, giving him a quick peck on the cheek as they called the men to approach the starting line.

"Cheer for me," Luke said as he turned to go.

"I will!" Cat called, mimicking him. "Push it! Come on!"

Luke turned back laughing, "Hey, it worked!"

Cat stuck her tongue out at him and turned to find Rachel. She spotted her at the far booth by the finishing line, waiting for the times to be posted. Since there were still runners out on the field, they hadn't posted the times yet.

"You did great!" Cat called as she approached her.

"Likewise, friend!" Rachel smiled. "You almost gave me a run for my money there."

"Hardly," Cat shook her head. "You finished a full minute ahead of me."

"I really hope I broke the Watauga record," Rachel looked nervously to the computer screen where the results would be posted any minute.

"Who holds it currently?" Cat asked.

"I do," Rachel admitted sheepishly.

"So, you want to beat yourself?" Cat couldn't help but smile as she asked.

"That is correct," Rachel admitted.

"Wow," Cat shook her head. "Is everyone so competitive here?"

"Not *everyone*," Rachel laughed. "But we do take sports rather seriously."

"I'll say," Cat watched as the numbers came across the screen.

Rachel let out a whoop of joy and nonsensical bouncing that strangely reminded Cat of Tigger from *Winnie the Pooh*. Cat found her own number: 19:23. Her best time yet. Cat joined Rachel in her celebratory bouncing, even though her legs did not want her to.

"What was your time?" Cat asked as they held hands and bounced joyfully about.

"My new record — 18:38!" Rachel squealed.

"My record, too!" Cat shrieked. Then, she was squeezed into a hard bear hug by Rachel until she found it a little hard to breathe.

"Can't. Breathe. Rach." Cat gasped.

"Oops!" Rachel quickly let her go. "Sorry. Got a little carried away there."

Cat breathed deeply, "Quite alright."

"Hey! The guys are about to race. Let's go see how your man does," Rachel locked elbows with Cat and led her toward where the boys were lining up.

Cat couldn't help but feel ecstatic. Even for a non-competitor like herself, it still felt great to run her best time. She also couldn't be happier about her relationship with Luke. Every time she thought about him, she got butterflies. She liked how it sounded when Rachel had called him 'her man'. Just about everyone thought they were the perfect couple — except Clarissa and her minions.

The pop of the starting gun shook her from her daydreams and brought her back to reality. She watched as Luke took off at a smooth, steady pace. He was masterful at running, Cat realized as she watched him. She and Rachel walked from point to point on the course to watch him pass and cheer him on. He knew exactly when to make his move, exactly when to increase his speed. Just when the strength of others who had started out strong seemed to be waning, Luke kicked it into gear. He moved up from fifth, to fourth, to third, and now into second. He was rounding the last corner and climbing the last hill of the course.

"TAKE HIM, LUKE!" Cat shouted at the top of her lungs. "Push it! Come on!"

She found that it was much more exciting being on this side of things. She hoped she hadn't thrown him off by yelling, but she desperately wanted him to come in first.

A smirk crossed his face as he breezed by her, along with a look of determination.

"He's got this," Cat leaned over to Rachel.

"I don't know," Rachel breathed.

"No way!" Rachel exclaimed as he began to gain on the leading man.

"Come on! Come on!" Cat called.

Since when has running been so exciting? Luke was neck and neck with his opponent. Fifteen feet to the finish line. Ten.

"Come on baby! I love you!" Cat called out suddenly. She didn't know what had possessed her to yell it.

Luke's step faltered only for an instant, and the other guy crossed the finish line a moment too soon.

"Ohhhh!" Rachel groaned, along with half the crowd. "Cat, I don't think you should go to him just yet."

"Crap ... he'll be mad at me, won't he?" Cat could feel the tears building in her eyes. It was all her fault, she knew it.

"Cat, he can't blame your yelling for his not winning," Rachel patted her on the back. "He should be better at tuning out the crowd by now."

"Maybe," Cat shrugged.

"But, just the same, Luke is very competitive. You won't want to be around him for the rest of the day ... maybe the week, just to be safe," Rachel informed her.

"But he came in second!" Cat was astonished by this revelation.

"That's as good as last place to Lucas Presnell," Rachel grimaced and left Cat alone with her thoughts.

Why did I have to yell that? Cat scolded herself. She looked past the finish line and saw that Luke had jogged on a bit further to cool down. He put his hands behind his head and stretched back. Then he leaned forward with his hands on his knees, panting. Cat approached him cautiously. She was the only one. Everyone else seemed to know that it was better to give him space. She was the only person within fifty feet of him, as he had retreated to the edge of the woods. She could hear him swearing to himself; she stopped short, unsure whether or not to go any closer.

"Jiminy Cricket!" Luke shouted and turning towards her, he was caught by surprise.

Cat stifled a laugh. She had never heard that expression before. Wasn't that the little cricket in Pinocchio?

Luke seemed to realize what she must have been thinking.

"My mom used to say it when she was angry," he said as he stomped past her.

"Whatever works," Cat shrugged her shoulders.

"I need to be alone right now, if you don't mind," Luke said with frustration, as he grabbed water from the nearby refreshment table.

"You did great. Amazing, Luke, honestly," Cat said sincerely. Luke grunted as a response.

"I've never seen anyone run like that before," Cat continued, hopefully. "It was incredible."

"Yeah, well, not incredible enough," Luke spat out, and poured the water over his head after chugging half of it.

"Luke, I'm being honest," Cat responded. She was beginning to get a little aggravated. "You should be proud of yourself. I'm proud of you."

"Of course, *you* are," Luke turned away.

"What the hell is that supposed to mean?" Cat rounded on him.

"Come on baby! I love you!" Luke imitated her in a high-pitched voice. "What were you thinking, Cat? How am I supposed to focus when you're yelling stuff like that?"

Cat could feel the tears about to spill over. She quickly turned away from him and hurried in the other direction before he could see the effect his words had on her.

He didn't come after her.

Cat went and sat on the school bus while the rest of the team finished up, enjoyed the awards ceremony, and changed clothes. Slowly they began to filter back onto the school bus for the half hour journey back to Watauga High. Everyone had returned. Everyone except for Luke, of course. No one had sat beside her. Cat knew they all assumed Luke would be sitting with her for the ride home, just as he had sat by her side for the ride there. She had just decided to look for Rachel and ask her to switch seats with her, when she saw Luke climb the steps onto the bus. He had his cross-country hoodie on with the hood up, though it wasn't really cool enough outside for that. With his iPod in the front pocket and his earbuds in his ears, he made it clear that he had no interest in engaging with anyone. Cat still looked at him hopefully as he sat down beside her. He didn't acknowledge her. Cat was infuriated. She wanted to kick him out of the seat and throw her phony wire engagement ring in his face, but she didn't. Instead, she turned and faced the window so he couldn't see the tears that streamed silently from her eyes. She could hear the prolific lyrics of Lupe Fiasco blaring through his headphones. She leaned her head closer to his so she could listen in.

He didn't speak to her the entire way back. Cat started to wonder how she was getting back to Mimi's. It seemed clear that he would not be giving her a ride as planned.

When they arrived back at the high school, Cat lagged behind getting off the bus so she could ask Rachel for a ride.

"What are you waiting for?" Luke yelled to her from his truck.

Cat felt confused. Did he really expect her to ride back with him after he'd yelled at her after the meet and ignored her the entire way back on the bus? She turned away from him as though she hadn't heard. Rachel was coming down the steps of the bus, and Cat nearly jumped on her.

"Can you give me a ride?" Cat practically shouted.

"Lord, Cat," Rachel clutched her chest in surprise. "You just gave me a heart attack."

"Sorry," Cat apologized and repeated her question. "Would you mind giving me a ride, Rach?"

"No, of course not," Rachel looked past Cat to where Luke had started his truck up and was staring at them. "Why aren't you riding back with Luke? Or should I not ask?"

Cat groaned, "I'm not speaking to him at the moment."

Just then, he pulled up beside them in the truck and Cat turned her back to him.

"Hey, Luke," Rachel acknowledged him, "I think I'm giving Cat a ride."

Luke looked from Cat to Rachel, then back to Cat.

"Cat, get in the truck," Luke sounded exasperated.

Rachel looked from Luke to Cat, who still hadn't acknowledged Luke's presence.

"I really should get back," Rachel said quietly to Cat. "Since you guys are neighbors, it does make more sense for you to ride with Luke."

Cat gave Rachel a look that was supposed to convey just how much she didn't want to ride with Luke. It didn't work. Rachel walked around Cat towards her car.

Rachel leaned over and whispered as she walked past, "Just make up with him, Cat. You know you want to."

Now Rachel was officially on the black list. Cat stared after her feeling utterly deserted, but her feet remained firmly planted.

"Cat," Luke tried to get her attention. "Do I have to physically put you in the truck myself?"

Cat looked around. There were still quite a few people milling about. Cat decided being put into the truck kicking and screaming would be embarrassing, so she begrudgingly walked around the truck and climbed into the passenger seat.

They didn't speak as he drove her home. Suddenly, without warning, he put on his blinker and turned on a side road. Cat knew by now that this was the road that led to Luke's old barn. What she didn't know was why he was taking her there.

"I don't want to go to the barn," Cat glared at him. "Mimi will be expecting me home."

"Cat, Mimi will still be at dinner with Jim," Luke said, though Cat already knew that to be true. "I'm bringing you here because I have something to show you."

Cat felt as though steam could come out of her ears. She never normally turned down an opportunity to go to the barn with Luke. Ever since she'd given him new supplies, he spent every extra minute there, usually with Cat by his side. Cat took every chance she could to encourage Luke to show his work professionally. He still protested, but with much less fervor.

When the truck came to a stop, he came around and opened the door for her, as always. Cat stayed where she was and looked at him complacently.

"I'm sorry," Luke said sincerely, holding out his hand. "I was mad at myself, not you. I was angry that I lost focus so easily when I was so close to winning."

Cat paused. "Apology accepted," she said somewhat reluctantly, taking his hand. She found it impossible to be angry with him for too long.

"I'm sorry, too," Cat admitted sheepishly. "I don't know what possessed me to say something so ridiculous."

"It *was* a little embarrassing," Luke smirked.

"But," Cat paused again, "it was true."

Luke took both of her hands in his and brought them to his lips.

"I love you, Luke," Cat whispered.

"And I love you," Luke smiled. "I see you haven't taken your ring off," he added looking at her ring finger, where the carefully crafted wire ring remained.

"Not since you gave it to me," Cat looked at it, too.

"I thought you might have," Luke paused, "after the way I acted tonight."

"Thought about it," Cat responded honestly. "But then I remembered what a famous artist you are going to be someday, and I decided I'd like to stick around to see it."

"Oh, is that right?" Luke laughed as he led her towards the door.

"Yep," Cat gave him a peck on the cheek.

"Well," Luke began, "speaking of being an artist, professionally, I mean. I have something to show you."

Cat was surprised. She couldn't imagine what he could possibly have to show her. She thought she'd been with him nearly every time he'd come to the barn since he'd shown it to her. What could he have in there that she hadn't seen?

He took her hand and led her into the dark barn. She stood still while he felt for the light. It only took him a second. Flipping on the switch, the light revealed all the beauty Cat already knew existed. She didn't see anything unusual.

Cat smiled at him. She hoped she wasn't supposed to be noticing something.

"What do you think?" Luke smiled.

"Wow! Luke, it's … great," Cat played along. What was she supposed to be seeing?!

Luke began laughing. "Cat, I'm kidding! I haven't showed it to you yet."

Cat breathed a sigh of relief, "I thought I was going crazy! That was a mean trick."

"I know," he laughed and crossed to the other side of the barn. The door creaked as he slid it across and stepped into what used to be the old feed room.

Cat leaned to the side to see if she could peer in.

Luke emerged carrying a large canvas covered partially in old burlap. He sat it up on an easel about ten feet from Cat.

"This was what I wanted to show you," Luke said as he pulled the burlap away and revealed the most intricate and striking painting Cat had ever laid her eyes on.

Luke let her take it in for a minute, then his feet started shifting from side to side. He was dying to know what she was thinking. She had been gawking at it more than a good minute or so now. First, she had taken it in from where she was standing, and then she had walked forward. Slowly. Cautiously. When Cat had begun to examine the detail an inch from her face, Luke had stepped back behind her to give her more room. He couldn't see her face now as she studied the painting. It was killing him. If he could see her face, he knew he'd be able to read exactly what she was thinking. Cat was never good at hiding her expressions, especially from him.

Finally, after what seemed like hours of scrutiny to Luke, Cat backed away. She sighed, and then turned to him at last.

The tears shimmering in Cat's eyes confirmed to him that she liked it, loved it even, perhaps.

Luke smiled relieved, "You like it?"

"No," Cat shook her head. "I love it."

"It's us," Luke looked down at the dusty floor. "I mean it's the way I feel for you. That's what I tried to paint."

"It's our love?" Cat asked. The painting took on new levels of beauty with that understanding sinking in.

"Well ... it sounds really cheesy like that," Luke coughed. "But, yeah. It's our love, Cat."

"It's the most beautiful painting I've ever seen," Cat said quietly. Her voice held such sincerity that Luke knew she was telling the truth.

He walked forward slowly and taking her in his arms, he kissed her. He wished that they could start their lives together now — as husband and wife. He wished that he could be with her, touch her, hold her in all the ways he wanted, but they were high school seniors. If anybody knew of their plans to get married, they would laugh. People would call it puppy love, infatuation, or whatever else they call it when people fall in love this young. But Luke knew this was the real thing: the stuff songs were written about, the stuff in movies, or Shakespearean sonnets, or ... paintings. Love.

Cat was adamant about not getting married until graduating college. Even then, she said, it would be unnaturally young for any New Yorker. Luke thought of waiting five more years, he pulled away from her. At the rate he was going, he'd be lucky to make it five more months. Best to take things slow.

"I'm glad you like it," he smiled and took a step back, under the pretense of examining his own painting.

"It reminds me of a fire, with the way the red melts into the blue," Cat commented.

"That is partially what I had in mind," Luke smiled at how easily she was able to decode his abstract painting. "But can you make out what the flames resemble. The red melting into the blue. I know it's kind of abstract."

Cat gasped, "Are they bodies?"

Luke nodded.

"They're unreal," Cat stepped closer. "I never would have seen it that way if you hadn't said that. I guess that's what makes it abstract. They look like their intertwined and falling at the same time. Where are they falling into?" Cat looked to the darker edges of the painting.

Luke laughed, "You tell me! You're the one who's creating this story with it."

"I'm getting carried away, aren't I?" Cat suddenly felt embarrassed.

"Not at all. You said nearly all the things I was thinking while I was painting it," Luke stepped up behind her with a bear hug.

"Then, where are we falling?" Cat asked again.

Luke caught that the 'they' had changed to 'we.'

"Love, maybe?" Luke smiled.

"We're already in love, silly," Cat reminded him.

"Of course. Well, let's see … deeper into love. An adventure," Luke thought aloud to himself.

"I like the thought of that. An exciting adventure," Cat sighed and turned to him. "You'll always love me." It wasn't a question so much as a statement.

"And you'll always have my heart," Luke confirmed in his own statement.

They kissed once more. Their bodies holding each other tightly together, like the flames in the painting.

Luke pulled the truck around to the back of Mimi's house, turning his headlights off well before they rounded the curve, lest they shine into the windows. Cat was getting back much later than expected.

"Looks like we were worried for nothing," Luke commented. "She's not even home yet."

This had become a common occurrence with Mimi as of late. Cat didn't mind. She actually thought it was quite cute to see her grandmother falling in love again.

"Can you come in?" she looked at Luke hopefully, though she knew he had homework to do.

"Uhhhh ... just for a minute I guess," Luke decided reluctantly.

"Yipee!" Cat hopped out of the car and skipped to the front porch.

"You sure have a lot of energy for all the running you did today," Luke shook his head in amusement.

"I'm happy, that's all," Cat bounced. And she was happy. So happy. For the first time in a long time she felt the happiness that warms you from the inside out. She felt like she could glow. She was so happy.

Luke stayed long enough for Cat to make them a quick Bertolli frozen pasta dinner. Mimi had gotten in the habit of leaving quick fix meals for Cat, since she'd been going out to dinner so often. She also knew that Cat had no real experience in cooking.

"That was great, babe, thanks," he said taking both of their dishes to the sink and washing them for her.

Cat came up beside him with a dish towel to dry them, as had become their routine.

"Luke?" Cat asked thoughtfully. "What is the painting called?"

Luke paused, "I don't know. What do you think it should be called?"

Cat thought for a moment. "How about 'The Last Life of Cat?' My last life will be spent falling into this crazy-love-adventure with you," she said joyfully.

"I like it," Luke smiled. "And when I show it someday, people will just think it has something to do with the whole 'cats have nine lives' thing. It's a good play on words."

"When you show it someday, huh?" Cat couldn't hide the grin that had spread across her face.

"Yeah, well," Luke shrugged. "I guess you've finally convinced me."

Cat embraced him and squeezed him tightly.

"Hey don't squeeze me to death, Cat," Luke laughed.

"Sorry," Cat let go, "I'm just so happy to hear you say that. You will be wonderful. Really."

"I thought," Luke began. "Whenever I'm ready to do my first show, I want 'The Last Life of Cat' to be the center of my collection. Sort of the piece that defines me."

Cat got tears in her eyes.

"Does our relationship define you, Luke?" she leaned her head on his shoulder.

"As much as it defines you, I'm sure," Luke answered in typical male fashion.

"Wow," Cat breathed. "That's a lot."

CHAPTER TWENTY-FIVE

CAT STARED AT HER FINISHED ESSAY. SHE'D HAD JUST ENOUGH TIME to proofread it before the timer on Mrs. Miller's desk went off. She wouldn't mind timed essays so much if she could type it on a computer. At least then she could use spell check. Thank goodness she had an eraser, otherwise her paper would have looked like a war zone from all the scratching and marking out. She gave it another quick once over as Mrs. Miller proceeded around the room to pick up the papers. Luke winked at her when she caught his eye. He was sitting two rows over from her, looking as handsome as ever. She was thankful he wasn't sitting directly in her view, otherwise writing a passing essay would be quite a challenge. He was wearing his cross-country sweatshirt just as Cat was, well, just as the entire team was. State Championships were coming up Saturday, which was tomorrow, Cat realized with some anxiety. The team would leave as soon as the bell rang to make the short journey to Winston-Salem where the championship would be held early in the morning.

The bell rang signaling both the end of the period and, to Cat, the beginning of nauseating anticipation.

"Don't look so worried, Cat," Luke spoke, catching up to her on the way to their lockers.

"I need some Tums or something," Cat responded, digging furiously in her bag.

Luke laughed and shook a travel sized container of Tums

above her head.

Cat jumped up to grab them and laughed, "Since when do you carry Tums?"

"Since I started dating a girl who has more indigestion than a sixty-year-old," he laughed.

"Very funny," Cat smirked, popping a few in her mouth. "But, one of the many reasons I love you."

"Mmmm," Luke smiled as Cat pushed him into the locker and kissed him firmly on the mouth.

"Ugh! Don't make me puke," came the voice of Clarissa passing by.

"Yeah, get a room!" chimed in one of her sidekicks.

Cat rolled her eyes at them and turned back to Luke to kiss him with even more fervor, knowing Clarissa would still be watching. Over the last few months, she had made it quite clear that she would be there to snatch Luke away as soon as she got the chance.

Clarissa had cornered Luke at the Homecoming game several weeks before. She'd obviously started partying before the game had gotten underway, which was not a good thing when you're the cheerleader on top of the pyramid. After a nasty fall and a bruised ego, she was sitting on the sidelines with ice on her knee.

Cat had taken the low road and couldn't help but laugh and mutter the word 'karma' as she passed her by. Clarissa hadn't been pleased, and decided to express her displeasure to Luke by cornering him at the concession stand during half time.

Cat happened to walk up to find half the senior class listening in on Clarissa's rant about what a bitch Cat was.

"How could you date her, Luke?" Clarissa shouted.

"Clarissa, you're embarrassing yourself. Maybe you should go back to the field," Luke said calmly. "Your break is almost up."

"But didn't you just hear what I said about how she treated me?" Clarissa shrieked. "She's hateful. How can you like someone so hateful?"

Cat felt her face go pink. Perhaps she shouldn't have been quite so quick to gloat at Clarissa's misfortune.

"I don't like her, Clarissa," Luke said as Clarissa's face became smug. "I love her."

Cat swallowed hard. She was pretty good at reading body language, and Clarissa's said that Luke should duck before he gets slapped. To Cat's surprise, Clarissa did an about face and made her way back through the crowd, to the field, directly towards where Cat was standing.

She spotted Cat and walked towards her with determination. Cat braced herself for what she was certain was coming. Luke was already a step behind Clarissa. He'd obviously been thinking the same thing. Instead, Clarissa shocked them all, as she smiled at Cat.

"Since Luke cares so much about you, I hope we can be friends from now on," she said with a pseudo-saccharine tone in her voice.

Cat knew that this front was simply for appearance's sake. She glanced to where Luke stood, his expression disgusted.

"That sounds fabulous," Cat didn't even try to hide the sarcasm in her own voice.

Then, Clarissa stepped forward to embrace her. Cat found that her own arms were glued to her side.

"Watch your back, bitch," Clarissa hissed in her ear. "I'm going to take you down when you least expect it." With that, she hobbled back onto the field, leaving Cat and Luke both fuming and speechless.

Cat shook her thoughts from that unfortunate incident with Clarissa from her mind and back to where she stood, still in lip-lock with Luke. She pulled away and smiled at him.

"Wow," Luke said as he composed himself. "Cat, if you put that passion into your running, you'll be unstoppable tomorrow."

"I don't know about that," Cat laughed as she watched Luke gather his things from his locker. He stood facing it much longer than usual. Cat was glad her kisses could produce such a powerful effect on him.

"Ready?" Luke turned to her, throwing his duffle bag over his shoulder.

"Almost. I just need to grab my bag out of the ladies' locker room," Cat replied.

"Want me to come?" Luke took her hand.

"No, just save us good seats on the bus. In the back," she winked.

"Alrighty," Luke gave her a playful smack on the rear, as she turned to scurry down the hall.

Cat was on cloud nine. She and Luke had been together nearly four months and things couldn't be better. She still wore her wire ring, even though it had changed the color of her finger underneath it. Luke kept telling her she should just take it off and let him buy her a real ring. The thought was tempting. But, the thought of what her parents would do if they found out their seventeen-year-old daughter was semi-engaged to a farm boy from North Carolina, whom they had never met, was enough to squelch those ideas. When she was eighteen, she told him, then he could propose. Then it wouldn't matter what her parents said. It would be perfect.

These were the thoughts going through Cat's mind as she began to skip down the stairs, two at a time, towards the ladies' locker room. These blissful thoughts completely distracted her from the sounds of feet scurrying up behind her. It wasn't until she felt the force of something heavy against her back and found herself tumbling head-first down a flight of stairs that she snapped back to reality. Just in time to see a pair of white cheerleading sneakers running around the corner — Clarissa's shoes.

Cat landed on the tiled floor with a thud. She had been too surprised to even scream out. But, seeing her knee turned in an awkward position had caused Cat to scream out more in shock than in pain. Her head was pounding from hitting the floor, but she was thankful that she'd reacted quickly enough to bring her arms up to catch most of her weight.

Whimpering, Cat pulled herself up to a seated position. School had been out for some time now. The buses had left. The halls were empty. What if no one came and found her?

"Help!" Cat called out. "Please, help! Somebody!"

No response.

Finally, Cat heard footsteps and saw Rachel emerge at the top of the stairs.

"Oh, my gracious! Cat, what happened?" Rachel was by her side in an instant. "Luke sent me to get you out of the locker room when you didn't come to the bus. When you weren't in the locker room, I started walking the halls to find you."

Cat winced as Rachel gingerly lifted her knee to elevate it on top of her duffle bag.

"Clarissa," Cat said, clenching her teeth. "It was Clarissa. The bitch pushed me!"

Rachel looked at her with wide eyes, "No way."

"Way," Cat closed her eyes in pain as Rachel looked at her knee.

"She will be in huge trouble for this, Cat," Rachel said with certainty. "We'll make sure of it. You try to relax for a second and I'll go get Coach Foster."

Rachel returned with Coach Foster, Luke, half the cross-country team, and the medic from the football team. After Cat had recounted what happened to them at least twice, Coach Foster got on the phone to call Principal Weaver about the situation. While the medic had re-positioned her knee, Luke held her hand tightly. Cat didn't even know it was possible to dislocate a knee like that. She felt nauseous just thinking about how sickening it had looked before it had been popped back into place. At least everyone else had had the decency to leave them alone while he re-set it. It was embarrassing enough to cry in front of all of them, let alone scream out in pain. Luke had given her two Advil to take right before he did it, but they hadn't begun to work yet, of course.

Coach Foster came over with a furrowed brow, "Principal Weaver just spoke to both Clarissa and her mother over the phone. According to them, they were halfway home by the time your accident occurred. They have three of Clarissa's friends who were with them, as well. All claiming the same thing."

"Of course, they're all *claiming* the same thing," Luke stood up. "They don't want her to get in trouble."

"That's what I told Principal Weaver," Coach Foster nodded in agreement. He turned to Cat, "He's set up a meeting with all of them for first thing Monday morning. You're sure it was Clarissa, Cat?"

"Positive," Cat said definitively. "I know it had to be her."

Cat knew she had said the wrong thing the second it slipped out.

"You know it had to be her? I thought you saw her?" Coach Foster questioned.

"I did. Part of her. Her shoes," Cat knew it sounded lame, but she also knew it had been Clarissa, "I know it was her, Coach Foster."

"I'm afraid we can't expel her with only her shoes as evidence,

Cat," Coach Foster sounded annoyed as well, "I'll call Principal Weaver back and let him know about this new development. Luke, did you get a hold of Cat's grandmother?"

"She's on her way," Luke nodded.

"What?" Cat turned to him confused. "I'm not going home. I'm going to the meet."

"Cat, you know you can't run," Luke soothed.

"Well, duh. But I can still watch you," Cat implored. "This is the State Championship, your senior year. This is important to you … and to me. I don't want to miss it."

"Cat, you dislocated your knee. You're going to be on crutches for a least a couple of weeks. You need to rest," Luke kissed her sweetly on her cheek. "I promise we'll video tape it or something."

"That's not the same," Cat started crying again, this time for a completely different reason.

"I know, but it's better than nothing," Luke took her hand in his. "I'm just glad you're not hurt worse."

"Except that Clarissa's getting off scot free," Cat fumed. "I can't believe she's going to get away with this."

"Just wait," Luke said with a vengeful look crossing his face. "Hell if I'm going to let her get away with this. Just let her think she has. For a little while."

CHAPTER TWENTY-SIX

BEING STUCK ON THE COUCH WITH ICE ON HER KNEE WAS NOT HOW Cat had envisioned spending this weekend. She'd had it planned out perfectly in her head: Luke would come in first at State, he'd be overjoyed, of course, the team would celebrate … maybe they would be able to sneak away and get some time to celebrate on their own, too.

Cat focused back on her grim reality and shifted uncomfortably on the couch; adjusting the ice pack on her knee with a groan that came more from what she was missing than the actual pain. Mimi came in with a tray of piping hot pancakes. Cat tried to look appreciative as she set it down, but all she could think about was the fact that she should be running right now with Luke there to cheer her on.

"She hasn't messaged yet," Mimi answered the question that hadn't been asked. She was referring to Mrs. McKinney, Rachel's mom, who had promised to text Mimi's cell and give them updates throughout the meet.

"Thanks," Cat forced a smile and tucked into the food that sat before her.

The morning dragged on for what seemed like an eternity. She would receive a short update from Mrs. McKinney and then would sit and wait five or ten minutes for the next message to come through.

Rachel had come in 3rd place. She was disappointed, even though

Cat assured her over the phone that 3rd in the entire state was a very respectable position. She would undoubtedly be able to receive a scholarship with that. Rachel called Cat during the men's race. Cat appreciated that Rachel called every two or three minutes — it made the wait a little more bearable.

Cat heard from her as the men were completing the final mile of the race. Luke was in a dead lock with four other guys. Cat reluctantly got off the phone with Rachel, so she could cheer him on during the final stretch of the race. Rachel promised she would call in a matter of minutes so, grudgingly, Cat had said 'goodbye'.

Two minutes passed. Five. Ten. Cat started feeling antsy. If she could have walked, she would have started pacing the room. She had called Rachel back four times already and each time it had gone straight to voicemail. Something had gone wrong — terribly wrong. Cat was sure of it. Otherwise, why hadn't she heard anything yet?

The phone rang, and Cat answered almost immediately, "What the hell is going on? I'm freaking out!"

"Freaking out?" It was Luke's voice that came through the other end. "Well, you should be, because your boyfriend is the State Champion!"

Cat squealed and dropped the phone, but quickly scrambled to recover it, while bouncing up and down as best she could while reclining on the couch. Anyone watching would probably guess she was having a seizure; she was so erratic. Her movements also caused the pancakes that were carefully poised on the tray in her lap to slide onto the floor.

Mimi hurried in and looked at her with disapproval.

"Sorry!" Cat cried, as she tried to lean over and clean it up with her napkin, which only spread the syrup.

"Thank goodness I have hardwood floors," Mimi scolded kindly, as she shooed Cat's hand away and cleaned it up herself.

"Luke. I am so so so proud of you!" Cat exclaimed, once her squealing had subsided.

"Really? You didn't sound the least bit excited," Luke joked. "I wish you could have been here, Cat."

"Me too," Cat responded, a lump caught in her throat. "This meant so much to you. It's such a big deal ... I just feel so bad I couldn't be there."

"I'm glad you're resting," Luke replied. "I want your knee to get better. You'll have other opportunities to support me in the future."

Cat felt a warmth in her cheeks, "Like when you open your gallery?"

"Yeah, maybe," Luke laughed. "I've gotta run, babe. The awards ceremony is about to begin ... which Rachel told me to tell you that she is going to video on her phone and send it to you."

"Perfect," Cat said happily, "Love you!"

"Love you, too," Luke responded.

Cat happily spent the rest of the morning and afternoon with Mimi's cell phone in hand, trading picture messages, text messages, and video messages back and forth with Luke and Rachel.

Cat really hoped that Mimi had unlimited messaging. She would offer to pay a portion of her phone bill if not, Cat decided. If only she could have her own phone back. It was a little embarrassing always having to borrow someone else's. She had asked her parents about it during their last phone conversation a week prior, and they had quickly reminded her why they had taken it in the first place. This had only dissolved into yet another argument; Cat had gotten off the phone feeling frustrated and defeated.

Her parents didn't seem to understand anything that had

taken place in her life over the last year. They knew what had happened, they knew about the events themselves, but they didn't understand them. They still thought the actions she took after Landon's death were suicidal, and they still believed her decision to sneak out to the party to go after Lili was done out of rebellion and not a genuine concern for her sister. She was baffled. She was no longer angry with them for sending her to North Carolina. It was that decision that had helped her put the pieces back together, had helped her to feel like a whole person again. But, the reasons behind that decision still upset her. She still felt betrayed. She didn't know whether or not their relationship could ever be what it had been before. She hadn't seen them in months, and they gave her no signs or hope of seeing them anytime soon.

To be perfectly honest, Cat didn't mind at all. As long as she had Luke and Mimi, she would be just fine. Life is funny that way. Only a few months ago, she couldn't imagine spending the holidays without her family; but now with Thanksgiving just a few weeks away, she couldn't imagine spending them anywhere but here.

Cat looked at her swollen knee and smiled. She'd endured so many injuries this year. Her heart had been wounded the worst of all, and yet, it had healed. A sprained knee was nothing compared to what she'd come through to get to where she was today. Indeed, everything was going to be fine, fine, fine.

Cat let herself doze to sleep, with some old Alanis Morrissette song playing in her head.

CHAPTER TWENTY-SEVEN

THE BELL ON THE FRONT DOOR SOUNDED CHEERFULLY AS LUKE stepped into Mimi's home. He had gotten so used to the sound over the years that he didn't notice it anymore. But Cat, who had spent considerably less time here, had recently made the comment that it was her favorite sound in the morning because it meant that he was there to pick her up. Ever since then, he couldn't help but notice the little bell, too. He smiled as he walked down the hall through to the kitchen.

As always, Cat was sitting at the table with Mimi, but there was something different about today. She didn't jump up to greet him, but that wasn't entirely unusual, considering her sprained knee. It was the look on Cat's face that worried him the most.

Mimi turned to him as he stepped into the kitchen.

"Why don't you sit down, Luke?" Mimi smiled, getting up to offer him her seat. "I made some blueberry muffins. Would you like one?"

"Uh, sure," Luke tried to sound pleasant, but the glower on Cat's face distracted him. He reached automatically for her hand, which she squeezed in turn. Cat looked up from her half-eaten muffin to give him a smile.

At least she's not mad at me, Luke thought to himself. He kept his eyes on Mimi, so he could move his hand away before she turned around. Even though Mimi knew they were a couple, they had been careful to tone things down significantly after the morning make-out session she'd interrupted. As Mimi turned towards them, he tried to slide his hand away, but Cat held it fast as he looked at her in confusion. She had a resolute look on her face. Luke braced himself for whatever might be coming next.

"Mimi," Cat spoke up, "you know what we were talking about before?"

"Um-hmm," Mimi responded with her body half in the fridge. "Do you want butter, Luke?"

"If you can't find it, don't worry about it," Luke answered, his eyes darting back and forth between Cat and Mimi.

"Mimi, it's on the table," Cat said in amusement. "As I was saying …"

"Oh, silly me," Mimi interrupted, and set about to pour herself some coffee.

"Mimi!" Cat nearly shouted in frustration.

"Catie," Mimi turned to her, glancing at their fingers laced together and then to their faces, her eyes softened with a smile. "I'm not going to tell them. I will continue to pretend that I don't know anything and I won't tell them. Okay?"

"Really?" Cat sounded incredibly relieved.

"Now, you better get to school before you're late," Mimi shooed them out, giving Luke his muffin to-go, along with a certain look of motherly concern.

Luke waited till they were out of ear-shoot before turning to Cat.

"She got a call from Principal Weaver about a certain public-display-of-affection," Cat informed him before he could ask. "Principal Weaver suggested that he should maybe call my parents, but Mimi said that she would pass along any information they needed to know."

"Ahh," Luke responded in understanding. Since Cat had

been using crutches the first few days of the week, Luke thought it would be sweet to carry not only her books to class, but to carry Cat to class, as well. They had both received detention for it, unfortunately. They were also supposed to get the detention slips signed by parents, which Luke's father had grudgingly consented to, but Cat had forged hers, instead. Luke could only guess that Principal Weaver had called Mimi in suspicion.

"She played along with him," Cat smiled with gratitude. "I feel so bad that she had to do that."

"What exactly happened?" Luke asked, as he opened the door to the truck so she could hop in.

"Principal Weaver got a 'tip' that I signed my slip instead of Mimi, so he called her to check. When he asked, she just told him that she had given me permission to sign it for her and that she had just forgotten to do it before school. Then, he went on to say how much he liked both you and I, and that he had to be fair and give all couples detention for PDA's."

"What did she do?" Luke asked.

"She asked me this morning if I thought she should tell my parents," Cat frowned, "then you came in."

"Whew," Luke sighed, "saved by the bell."

Cat chuckled and then grew serious once more, "It would be over," she shook her head, "if they knew I was in a relationship … a serious relationship. They just don't think I'm 'stable' enough to be involved with anyone."

Luke frowned, "Cat, you're stable. I think you've always been stable. You were just acting the part. If enough people tell you that you should be messed up by what happened, you will be."

Cat scooted over to give him a quick peck on the cheek before fastening her seat belt.

"So, Mimi's not going to tell?" Luke nodded approvingly.

Cat nodded, "Thank God!"

"But, will she leave us alone as often?" Luke looked at her with a sideways glance.

"That remains to be seen," Cat narrowed her eyes thoughtfully.

They had been enjoying many evenings alone lately. Mimi and Jim spent every weekend together and went out for dinner several times during the week.

"So, I wonder who tipped Principal Weaver off that you signed your slip?" Luke changed the subject.

"Well, I was stupid enough to sign it in front of my locker, and then asked Rachel loudly if it looked real," Cat winced.

"Cathleen Rhodes!" Luke reprimanded.

"I know!" Cat said defensively. "I said I was stupid!"

"Well, as long as you know you are," Luke joked.

Cat punched him playfully in the arm as a response.

"Cat, was Clarissa at her locker?" Luke asked.

"Ugh! I didn't even think to look! I just checked that there weren't any teachers around," Cat replied.

"Her locker is right across from yours," he said thoughtfully, "wouldn't surprise me in the least."

"Evil BITCH!" Cat exclaimed.

"Cat, tone it down baby. We don't *know* it was her," Luke said.

"I know it was her, Luke," Cat was suddenly very certain. As certain as she was that Clarissa had pushed her down the stairs nearly a week ago and hadn't been punished at all. She had to pay.

"You know what I said?" Luke said suddenly, distracting her.

"What?" Cat asked.

"That she would pay for it, for what she did … what do you say to a little covert op tomorrow night?" Luke looked mischievous. It made Cat want him all the more.

"You already have a plan," she smiled eagerly.

"And I already have Rachel in on it," Luke smiled.

"Do I get to push her down any stairs?" Cat laughed.

Luke frowned, "Cat, I only want her to be exposed for who she is and what she did to you … not inflict any harm on her."

"Luke, I was joking!" Cat shook her head. "I thought Christians were supposed to turn the other cheek?"

Luke looked uncomfortable, "Yeah, well, that was Jesus who said that … and I'm not Jesus."

"So, what's this plan?" Cat's voice dropped to a deadly serious tone. She loved a mission.

CHAPTER TWENTY-EIGHT

CAT SAT ON THE BACK BLEACHERS; IT WAS ALMOST HALFTIME AT THE final home football game of the season. She was absolutely freezing. People who claimed New York City was cold should come to Boone, the wind blowing through the stadium was absolutely biting. She had been sipping her hot chocolate slowly and now that had gone cold, too. Cat frowned. As soon as the halftime whistle blew, the plan would be in motion. Clarissa always walked past the back bleachers on her way to the concession stand. Cat heard the distant whistle blow from the field below. She readied herself to get into 'character.' Grabbing a handful of crumbled Kleenex from her coat pocket, she began wiping her eyes and heaving her shoulders with sobs.

She heard footsteps and felt Rachel's hand touch her shoulder, "Here she comes," she whispered.

"Oh, Cat! I'm so sorry! I can't believe he would break up with you like that ... and for HER!" Rachel said loudly, as Cat 'sobbed' into her hands.

Rachel turned around and, as expected, Clarissa was happily watching the scene unfold.

"I hope you're happy now!" Rachel shouted to her. "Luke just broke up with Cat because of you!"

Clarissa looked shocked but could not contain her overcome joy, "Aww, well isn't that too bad. Guess he realized what he was missing."

With that, Clarissa strode past them, but not in the direction of the concession stand as she usually did, but towards the announcer's booth where Luke always sat to read out the half-time announcements. Rachel looked at Cat and smiled, so far everything was going as planned.

Luke had just finished reading the list of team sponsors, when he heard a knock at the door. He clicked off the loud speaker and turned around. He was alone in the booth now that the announcers had left for their break. He took a deep breath. He knew what was coming would require some acting on his part. He didn't think it should be too difficult; he'd pretended to like her half the time they were dating.

"Come in," he said, hoping the trepidation in his voice didn't show through. His teeth were practically chattering from the cold, maybe he could pass the shakiness off as that.

"Luke?" Clarissa peeked her head in the door. "Are you alone?"

"I am," Luke rolled his eyes, before he got up to open the door the rest of the way, "Come in. It's so windy out there." Luke locked the door behind her.

"Oh, thanks," Clarissa's voice became saccharine-sweet. "I just heard … I knew she wasn't the right person for you."

"You did?" Luke knew his best bet was to play along with her for a minute or two, he only hoped he could stand her long enough.

"Of course, how could she be. We always belonged together," she came forward and put her hands on his shoulders. Luke forced himself to allow that.

"I guess I realized it, too," Luke whispered. He felt like gagging, as Clarissa began to run her hands through his hair.

"When did you realize it? This is so sudden," Luke could hear the uncertainty in Clarissa's voice, he knew he would have to try harder.

Luke took her hands in his, "I'm so sorry I hurt you, Clarissa. Cat was a bitch, just like you said."

"Don't forget a Yankee whore," Clarissa piped up happily.

Luke faked a laugh, "Yeah, that too."

"You're just now realizing this?" Clarissa moved in to kiss him.

Luke spoke before she could get the chance, "Yeah, well, ever since she fell and hurt her knee, she's become so whiny and helpless. I can't stand girls like that."

"I'm not like that," Clarissa moved towards him again.

"I know," Luke stepped back towards the sound system until his back was against the table, "you take charge of your life, that's one thing I like about you."

Clarissa smiled and leaned in.

"You see what you want and you get it … no matter what it takes," Luke continued, he reached his hand behind him and started groping for the microphone button.

"Does this mean I'm finally going to 'get' you, Luke?" she asked suggestively, her hands stroking his chest.

"You can 'get' whatever you want Clarissa," Luke said, he felt his stomach churning nervously. "I'm just glad you pushed her down the stairs. It helped me see what a complete loser she really is."

Luke prayed that the next words out of her mouth would be something incriminating, and he pressed his hand down on the loudspeaker button. Clarissa didn't even notice.

"She only got what she deserved," Clarissa purred. "Now, let's get your pants off so I can give you a little bit of what you deserve."

Luke really wished the entire stadium hadn't heard that last part. He took a breath and pressed on, he had to get her to say that she pushed Cat down the stairs. He didn't have much time. Luke was certain that the announcers would be on their way back up to the booth now that the loudspeaker was on, along with Principal Weaver, Vice Principal Clare, and God-knows-who-else.

"I can always count on you to make sure people get what they deserve, Clarissa," Luke chuckled, "I really am glad you pushed Cat down those stairs."

"Me too," Clarissa laughed. "You should have seen the way her feet flipped over her head. It was classic."

Luke joined in her laughter. He had gotten what he needed. He knew he would never be allowed to do the half-time announcements again; good thing it was the last football game of his senior year. It had been completely worth it.

Clarissa jumped at the sudden banging on the door. Luke smiled and clicked off the loudspeaker.

"They're back early," Clarissa frowned, as she watched Luke walk to the door and unlock it.

Principal Weaver walked in, followed by the two regular announcers, and the school resource officer.

"Clarissa," Principal Weaver said tersely, "I believe I have to remove you from school grounds until your expulsion hearing next Monday morning."

"What?!" Clarissa looked at them, then back to Luke who was smiling broadly. "You?! You set me up? They heard me?"

"The entire stadium heard you, Clarissa," Principal Weaver amended. "It was over the loudspeaker. Which means you will also be facing some detention time, Luke, for abusing that privilege."

Luke shrugged, "That's fine. I kind of expected that." He turned to Clarissa, who was seething like some demon-possessed cheerleader. "Clarissa … sucks to be you."

Luke had barely gotten down the stairs from the booth when he felt Clarissa land on his back — screaming, punching, and tearing at his hair. He could see the men scrambling down the stairs to get to her. Luke leaned down and flipped her over his back, so that she landed on the cold, hard ground.

"You're an asshole! ASSHOLE!" she screamed, as the resource officer helped her up and held her back. She continued yelling obscenities at him as she was escorted through the sea of onlookers.

Cat emerged from the crowd and limped over to where Luke stood, straightening his torn shirt.

"I'm guessing both of you are responsible for this," Principal Weaver came up to them.

"We are," Cat said sheepishly. "We get detention, right?"

"You do," he nodded. "But I am glad that the appropriate person is being punished. Maybe only one afternoon of detention is needed."

"Thank you," Cat breathed. For the stunt they had just pulled, she had been expecting more.

As the crowd dispersed, Luke and Cat remained. He took her hand and led her over to a bench by the concession stands. The game had commenced and only a couple of people lingered nearby.

"So," Cat leaned close to him, "she didn't get your pants off, did she?"

"You heard that, did you?" Luke rolled his eyes.

"Luke, the entire stadium heard it," Cat said with a disgusted look on her face, "I almost puked!"

"Me too," Luke laughed.

"I knew you wouldn't let her do that, though," Cat smiled.

"No way," Luke agreed. "The only person taking my pants off is me ... and you, someday."

"Someday," Cat sighed.

"At least now all of our Clarissa-troubles are over," Luke leaned over and kissed her sweetly. "She will be expelled and it will be just you and me."

"I really like the sound of that," Cat kissed him back.

"You and me," he repeated, touching her wire-wrapped ring lightly.

CHAPTER TWENTY-NINE

THE SOUND OF THE BELL ON THE FRONT DOOR HAD CAT JUMPING OUT of bed and hurrying to put her clothes on. She didn't pay attention to what she threw on as she quickly brushed her hair, her teeth, and skipped down the stairs. Lately, her inner fashionista had taken a back seat to Luke's girlfriend. She didn't bother with makeup half the time, as it just took time away from getting to see him.

"Hey, babe," she greeted him with a kiss as she entered the kitchen.

Mimi cleared her throat from where she sat with the newspaper at the kitchen table.

"Sorry, Mimi," Cat blushed, as she sat down beside her. Luke scooted her chair in for her.

"If I am pretending that I don't know anything, you need to make sure that it looks like there is nothing for me to know," Mimi said, as she peered at the two of them from behind her newspaper.

"That's fair," Luke nodded and winked at Cat.

"Luke, that is *my* foot," Mimi informed him with a barely contained laugh turned cough, as she got up to refill her coffee.

Cat laughed and it was Luke's turn to blush, "Footsie at the table is not the best idea, perhaps," Cat chuckled.

"So, what work do you have for us today, Mimi?" Luke asked, changing the subject.

"Well, I don't know how much Cat can help. It might be best if she stays put," Mimi said thoughtfully.

"No! I can help. My knee is almost all better. I can do it! What is it?" Cat sputtered.

"Lifting rocks out of the river bank," Mimi said with a raised eyebrow.

"Yeah, not so much," she sighed dejectedly and sat back down.

"She could keep me company while I load them on," Luke recommended.

"Oh, I can do that!" Cat said happily, that sounded better to her anyway. She really didn't care what she did, as long as she was with Luke.

"Well, I just need enough river rocks to make a raised flower bed at the end of the drive," Mimi informed, "just one load should be enough."

"No problem," Luke nodded.

"You need a whole truck load of rocks?" Cat raised her eyebrows. That seemed like a bit much to her.

"Well, I want to stack them about three or four feet high to make the flower bed, so that does require a lot of rocks," Mimi smiled. Her granddaughter never ceased to amuse her.

"Ready to go, babe?" Luke asked, pushing away from the table. Cat nodded.

"You'll need to get a pair of waders out of the barn, in case you need to walk into the water a bit. Also, grab some extra sweaters and scarves from the hallway closet, the temperature is supposed to start dropping this afternoon. It's going to be in the low teens tonight."

"Is it supposed to snow?" Luke asked.

"Not until tomorrow," Mimi answered, "but you best not take too long, just in case. If it started snowing while you were down at the New River, your truck wouldn't get back up to the highway, four-wheel drive or not."

Luke nodded.

"What's wrong with the road?" Cat asked. She couldn't fathom a road paved or unpaved that Luke's truck couldn't take.

"It's just a bumpy dirt road," Luke shrugged.

"But it's steep, driving from the highway down the five-mile road to the river bank," Mimi said warily. "Luke, maybe you guys should just hang out around here today. The rocks can wait until another day."

"Mimi, we'll be quick," Luke smiled. "Besides, the snow's not due in till tomorrow anyways."

"I'll be fine," Cat reassured, as she walked with her slight limp to the closet for extra layers.

Cat was glad they were getting away for a bit. Even though Mimi pretended that everything was the same as before, she could sense her grandmother was a little bit wary of letting them spend extended periods of time alone together. Recently, their chores had been confined to the area directly around the house. Cat was certain this was so she could keep an eye on them. Maybe she was trying to ascertain the seriousness of their relationship. Or perhaps, she felt guilty for not noticing it earlier and she was trying to catch up on her role as Cat's guardian? Whatever the reason, Cat was relieved that they finally had some time alone together now. Even if it meant Luke doing manual labor while Cat watched on.

She scooted close to him in the truck, as they drove through the winding mountain roads. They passed the small road where they usually turned for Luke's barn, and then about a mile down from there, they turned onto a narrow dirt lane.

"This isn't very steep," Cat remarked as they began to descend.

"Not yet," Luke winked at her.

The truck bounced and bumped through pothole after pothole; Cat thought she might get whiplash from all the jostling about. Finally, the road curved so sharply down that Cat extended her arms and held herself from falling into the glove compartment.

"This is the only way to get to the river?" Cat said wide-eyed.

"No," Luke laughed, "but it's the only access road that Mimi has the right to use. She has some riverfront property and this is the road that leads there. It was probably a logging road 50-some years ago."

"Uh-huh," Cat pressed her back against the seat, "This truck can't fall forward can it?"

"I love you, Cat," Luke laughed, "You amuse me."

Cat blushed. She took a deep breath to make sure her temper didn't rise. Even though she'd spent a considerable amount of time with Luke during the last few months, they still had their little spats. They still could make each other's tempers flare quicker than anyone else they knew. She knew she would always ask 'ridiculous' questions from time to time when it came to rural living, but she was anxious to get him on her turf, where she would be the expert and he would be the novice.

The truck continued down until the ground leveled out, beside a steadily moving river.

"I used to go tubing down this river in the summer," Luke smiled at Cat. "I'll have to take you sometime."

"Not anytime soon," Cat laughed. The water looked absolutely frigid.

"Well, let's get this done before any snow moves in," Luke said, with his eyes on the sky.

"But the weather said the snow wouldn't be moving in till tomorrow," Cat looked up as well.

"Those are snow clouds, Cat" Luke said. "And they will be here before nightfall."

"How could you possibly know that?" Cat asked intrigued.

Luke just smiled, "I'm a mountain boy, remember?"

Cat found it so interesting that he knew little things like that. Things Cat couldn't begin to understand. They had been raised in two completely different cultures. Sometimes, it seemed like they were worlds apart. Yet, she still had never had anyone who understood her so well. Not since Landon. The thought of his name caused her eyes to burn. She hadn't thought of him in a long time. But she knew she wasn't forgetting. Landon would always be a part of her, just as Luke had become.

She and Luke laughed and talked all morning, as Cat watched him pull rocks out of the riverbed. She knew his hands must be frozen solid by now. She watched them plunge into the water and pull out another large, flat, smooth rock.

"So, when Mimi said river rocks, she really meant straight out of the river," Cat commented.

"Sure did," Luke smiled at her.

Cat didn't have to ask what he was thinking. His expression said it all.

"Honey, your hands have to be freezing," Cat said. "Let's take a quick lunch break … I have a surprise."

Luke raised an eyebrow, "Oh really?"

"Not that kind of surprise," Cat giggled. "I made a thermos of hot chocolate for us before we left."

She pulled it out from behind the seat.

"Cat?" Luke asked.

"Yeah, babe," Cat responded, filling up two Styrofoam cups for them.

"Next year," Luke began, "how will we stay together?"

Cat looked up, "What do you mean?"

"We'll be so far apart. I'll be running cross country for App and you'll be up north in some Ivy League ..."

Cat interrupted him, "I'm not going anywhere Luke. I'm staying here ... with you."

"But Yale ..."

"I didn't apply," Cat cut him off. "I mean, my parents think that I applied to all the schools we had discussed, but I didn't apply to any of them."

"What?" Luke looked at her in shock.

"I applied to ASU and one other school," Cat looked up at him, "I didn't want to tell you till I was accepted, but I just got the letter yesterday."

"You're coming to App with me?" Luke looked astonished but excited.

Cat nodded. Luke put down his hot chocolate and wrapped her into a bear hug for a kiss.

Lately, their kisses had been short and sweet. They had been trying so hard to keep things under control. But the knowledge of being together for the next four years, made this moment impossible to resist.

Cat suddenly felt warm, despite the cool air on her face, as Luke leaned her against the seat of the truck. He didn't resist as she pushed down the suspenders that held up his waders. He stepped out of them, with his jeans on underneath. She grabbed his sweater with both of her fists and pulled him to her. Reaching his hands around her waist, he let them slide lower until he could easily lift her legs to wrap around him.

"I think we should move this into the truck," Cat said quietly through chattering teeth.

Luke just nodded.

Cat pulled her sweatshirt off, as she lay down across the seat. Luke did the same. Despite the long-sleeved t-shirts they were both wearing under their layers, it just felt right to be that much closer. His hands moved to her face, he held her cheeks and kissed her fully on the lips, until she felt like she could melt. Then his hand moved lower, across her chest. He lifted her shirt just enough to slide his hand under.

Cat shrieked, "Oh my gosh!"

Luke quickly moved his hand away, "Are you okay?"

"I'm fine," Cat laughed. "Your hand is freezing!"

"Sorry," Luke chuckled. "Maybe I'll just keep it here till I warm up," he said, placing his hand around her waist.

"I could help you warm up," Cat said mischievously, as she slid out from under him and allowed him to take her place, lying down in the seat.

Kissing him forcefully, she straddled him and moved against him. She knew they were taking things too far. The little buzzer in the back of her head was starting to send off warning sirens, but it felt so good. So right.

She could feel him giving in to her efforts. His hands slid under her shirt again. This time, she didn't shriek. She didn't need to — they were warm. She began to kiss down his neck, she lifted his shirt to kiss his chest, his stomach.

"Holy shit!" Luke exclaimed.

Cat thought she must be doing a really good job, as she moved to kiss him again, but Luke jumped up so suddenly it stopped her.

"Holy shit, Cat!" Luke pointed outside, "Look!"

Cat did. The snow was falling thick and fast. There was already a thin layer covering the ground around them. Cat frowned, as she knew that was the end of their make-out session. Now there were other things to worry about.

"Should we go?" Cat looked at him.

Luke paused for a moment, "I only need a dozen more rocks, at most," he said. "Thirty minutes won't make too much of a difference."

Cat bit her lip; she didn't have a good feeling about this.

Luke noticed.

"We'll be fine," he nodded and kissed her quickly, before scooting back out of the truck and sliding back into his waders.

"Thirty minutes?" Cat questioned.

"Not a minute longer," Luke assured her.

She watched him as he quickly set back to work. She could have used a cold shower, but the cold air and heavily falling snow did the trick.

He worked efficiently and before the half hour was up, he had the truck full of rocks.

"With five minutes to spare," he smiled as he hopped into the truck beside her.

"Good. Cause it's really falling now," Cat commented.

"We should be fine. I think," Luke added, as he carefully began to turn the oversized pick-up truck around.

Cat felt her worries subside as they began back up the steep incline. The snow had covered the dirt road and made it slick in spots, but it was no match for Luke's four-wheel-drive. Or so she thought. No sooner had she let herself relax, did the tires start to spin and she felt the truck sliding backwards in the direction that they had come.

Luke took a deep breath, "Let's try this again," he said and he revved the engine to give it another go.

Four tries later and they were no better off. Cat was on the verge of tears and Luke had gone from frustrated to pissed off.

"Luke, you said we would be fine," Cat said, as tears threatened to spill over.

"We are fine, Cat" Luke huffed, "the roads just got slicker than I anticipated and the truck's weighed down with literally a ton of rocks. It's just taking a little while to get up the road. But we'll get there!"

Cat could tell she had annoyed him, so she did the opposite of what she typically did — she said nothing. She said nothing as Luke tried a fourth, fifth, sixth, and seventh time to climb the hill. When the tires began spinning and digging them into a hole they both knew they couldn't get out of, she bit her lip and refused to make a sound. Finally, Luke turned off the truck.

"Damn it!" he shouted, punching the steering wheel.

Cat turned to him. Men could be so silly sometimes.

"You were right," Luke muttered.

"Thank you," Cat responded calmly. "So, what's the plan now?"

"You tell me," Luke smiled at her hopefully.

Cat smiled back, "Well, I think we should start walking to the road. We'll just freeze if we stay here. Then, when you get enough signal on your cell, we can call for help."

Luke nodded, "Yes ma'am."

They started up the steep incline. Cat decided to go first, with Luke behind her so that he could catch her in case she slipped. Several inches of fresh snow were already on the ground now and it showed no signs of stopping. Cat's knee started bothering her before they had been walking for five minutes. She tried to push the pain to the back of her mind and focus on something else, like the cold. Her toes were numb. Her face was burning from the cold. She was grateful for Mimi's suggestion of bringing extra layers along. It would be much worse if it wasn't for that.

They didn't talk as they walked. Cat could hear Luke's heavy breathing as he climbed the mountain behind her. They were almost to the top, Cat realized. This realization should have made Cat feel better than it did. It was followed by the thought that they still would have another couple of miles to get to the road.

Cat felt like someone was driving an ice pick into her knee, but she didn't want to stop walking. She wanted to press on. She wanted to get someplace warm, and quickly.

She picked up her pace only the slightest amount. The snow was falling heavily. Thick beautiful swirling flakes, the kind you see in movies. Cat would have enjoyed watching the snow, if she was watching it from indoors. Preferably in front of a crackling fireplace with a steaming mug of hot chocolate in her hands. She closed her eyes only briefly to picture the scene, as she took another step ahead. Her foot caught on the roots of an over-turned tree. This brief moment was all it took for her misstep. As she put her foot down, she fell forward, right onto her knee.

Cat exclaimed some choice words as she fell forward into the soft cushion of snow. It was almost healed, and to only injure it again seemed so unlikely. But then again, Cat wasn't known for being the most graceful. She cursed at her own clumsiness, and kicked the roots with her other foot as she clutched at her knee.

"Cat," Luke rushed to her side, "are you okay? Do you think you can walk?"

"I'm fine," Cat snapped, wiping tears from her eyes, lest they freeze onto her cheeks.

"I'm sorry," Luke spoke, as he knelt down to hold her. "This is my fault. I let myself get distracted with you. Then, I insisted on finishing the work, even after it started snowing …. I screwed up, and now you're hurt, and it's all my fault. Damnit!"

Cat could see Luke getting more upset as he spoke. She raised her hand to his lips to shush him.

"I will be fine," she said calmly. "We will be fine. Let's just call for help, okay? We're probably close enough to get a signal on your cell now, right?"

Luke didn't seem certain, "Cat, I barely get signal from the barn. And in a snowstorm … it seems unlikely. But I'll try."

"Good," Cat said, trying to stand. The pain was so much that she instantly sat back down. "I don't think I can walk any further, Luke."

Luke looked at her wide eyed as he checked his pockets, a second and third time.

"Don't you dare tell me," Cat shook her head slowly.

"Shit," Luke shouted. "Damn it to hell!"

"Where the hell is your cell phone, Luke?" Cat couldn't hide the frustration in her tone now.

"Your guess is as good as mine," Luke said through gritted teeth. "I had it in my back pocket when we took a break."

"You mean before we started rolling around in the truck?" Cat asked him.

"Exactly," Luke said curtly.

"So, it's probably three miles behind us on the floorboard of your truck," Cat said miserably.

"Probably," Luke sat beside her, the snow falling heavily on both of them.

"This sucks," Cat felt hopeless.

"We can't stay here, Cat," Luke took her hand. "We have two more miles to the road. Hopefully, we can flag a car from there. If not, we'll just go to the barn and stay the night there."

"Luke, I can't walk," Cat felt tears welling up in her eyes. "You'll have to go get help and come back for me."

"Like hell I'm leaving you here alone," Luke practically shouted. "This is my fault. I'll carry you if I have to."

"Well then, you'll have to," Cat said. She was relieved that he wouldn't leave her alone. But if he had to carry her three miles, they would be lucky to get to the barn before nightfall. The sky was already dark from the snow clouds.

Luke lifted her easily and set off. Cat buried her head in his shoulder and shivered against him. Moving had kept her body warm, but now she was absolutely frigid. The parts of her body that weren't numb were so painfully cold that she wished they were. Luke began to slow his steps. Cat could tell he was exhausted, his breath puffed out in short little spasms that reminded Cat of a steam engine.

"Let's stop," Cat said through chattering teeth. "You should rest for a second."

"No," Luke said firmly. "It's getting dark, Cat. I won't stop until we get to the road. We're almost there."

Cat clung on tightly as he continued moving. Cat couldn't help but notice they were going slower and slower. She didn't think she'd weighed that much, but over a few miles, Cat imagined she would be quite a burden to carry.

"I can see the road," Luke spoke finally.

Cat raised her head to see the forest clearing ahead, giving way to a road covered in white.

"There aren't any tire tracks," Cat observed.

"No one's driven on it recently," Luke answered, "but that doesn't mean that someone won't come along."

Cat wasn't so sure. No one in their right mind would drive right now, unless they absolutely had to do so.

"Mimi, will come looking for us," Cat said certainly.

"Her truck wouldn't even make it in this mess," Luke frowned. "Her best bet would be to call the highway patrolmen ... but even they would have to wait until the snow plow clears the roads."

"What should we do?" Cat's voice was rising in pitch, a sure sign that tears were on their way.

"We're going to my barn," Luke said, tightening his grip on her. "We can't wait here for someone who may or may not come by. We'll stay the night at the barn, and in the morning, I will come out to the road to flag someone down."

"How much further?" Cat asked.

"Maybe two miles, at most," Luke's voice sounded worried, though he didn't show it on his face.

Cat could no longer feel her arms that were wrapped around Luke. She hoped her grip wasn't loosening, so she tightened them again.

"I won't drop you," Luke responded to her action by squeezing her tighter.

"I know," Cat whispered, "I'm just making sure I have a hold of you. I can't feel my arms to tell."

Luke glanced at her and picked up his pace. She thought he might pass out at any minute. Cat closed her eyes and whispered a prayer for their safety. She wasn't worried about her knee anymore; she was worried about Luke.

They turned onto the gravel road that led to the barn. Luke had now been carrying her for at least two hours Cat guessed by the darkening sky.

"Let me walk, Luke," Cat said earnestly. "It's not much farther."

"You can't walk on your knee. You'll only make it worse," Luke's teeth were now chattering as well.

"I can put my arm around you and hop," Cat pleaded. "Please, Luke!"

Luke stopped. Cat knew he must be in pain because he nodded and lowered her feet to the ground.

With one arm around Luke's shoulder and his arm around her waist, Cat hopped the remainder of the way to the barn.

When they finally arrived at the door, darkness had fallen.

Cat sighed with relief as they entered the familiar space. Luke flicked on the switch for the light. Nothing happened. He flicked it back and forth several times before letting out a roar of anger. Cat would have jumped back from him if he wasn't supporting half her weight.

"I can't freaking believe this!" he cried.

"At least we have shelter," Cat soothed. "And you have that old lantern in the other room."

"All right. Well, let's get in here," Luke guided her through the dark, into the small former tack room that held most of his art supplies.

In the darkness, Cat could make out the old couch where she had sat a few months ago and told him her whole sad story. That seemed like an eternity ago now. She hopped over to it while Luke fished through drawers to find matches.

The warm glow of the lantern finally greeted them. Luke set it down carefully, far from his paints.

"My space heater is no good to us now with the electricity off," Luke said gloomily.

"Do you have food?" Cat asked.

Luke began scrounging about for any unspoiled snacks he may have inadvertently left there. He returned to the room a few minutes later with two half-full bottles of Gatorade, a pack of crackers, and a small bag of Chex mix.

"Bon appetit," Cat smiled, as he sat in front of her.

Cat was still shivering uncontrollably. She couldn't seem to stop. Even though they were now safe from the snow and the wind, it was still freezing in the barn, and their clothes were still dripping wet.

"We are going to have to get you out of those clothes," Luke noticed her shaking.

"You're shaking too," Cat commented through chattering teeth.

"I don't have anything but blankets for us to wear," Luke said.

"That will probably be better than these wet sweaters," Cat nodded.

Luke left the room once more and returned with two old quilts. When he came in, he stopped short. Cat was standing there shivering, in nothing but her underwear, her wet clothes already in a pile to the side of the room. He walked to her slowly and opened the quilt for her to step inside. Then he wrapped her up tightly.

"Better?" Luke asked.

Cat nodded, "Much."

Luke didn't feel the least bit self-conscious as he stripped down to his boxer briefs, at least, not until Cat whistled at him. He blushed as he looked up at her, and wrapped the quilt tightly around him.

They sat huddled on the couch, wrapped as tightly as mummies, eating their dinner. They talked about what college would be like together, when they would get engaged, and when they would get married. Cat felt like a day that was so disastrous could not have ended more perfectly.

They were still cold and exhausted as the later hour brought with it much cooler temperatures.

Luke noticed Cat was still slightly shivering, though her hair was finally dry.

"Here," he said, "open your blanket."

Cat raised an eyebrow.

"That's not what I'm thinking, Cat," Luke laughed. "We'll both be warmer if we wrap both blankets around us together."

"Ah," Cat nodded, "The old boy scout body heat trick ... so that really works?"

"We'll see," Luke smiled and stood up, so he could unwrap his blanket.

Cat watched him as she unwrapped her own. She stood up and walked into his arms so he could double the blankets and enclose them both.

They laid back down on the couch carefully, so that the blankets would remain tucked snugly around them. Cat felt her breath catching in her throat. Her heart felt like it was pounding through her chest. She was certain Luke could feel it against her own. Being close to him like this was intoxicating, she felt dizzy even.

"Are you sure this is a good idea?" Cat peered into his eyes.

"Are you warmer?" Luke asked as he brushed the hair from her eyes.

Cat nodded.

"Then it was a good idea," Luke smiled. "You're almost impossible to resist, but I'll consider this a test of my willpower."

"Since we failed miserably earlier today," Cat chuckled.

"We won't this time though," Luke looked determined, "I just want to keep you warm."

"I just want you," Cat responded quietly.

"You have me, Cat," Luke kissed her sweetly. "Always."

CHAPTER THIRTY

THE SOUND OF A VEHICLE OUTSIDE WOKE CAT SUDDENLY. IT WAS STILL early. The sun wasn't quite up yet but the sky was lighter; Cat could tell from looking out the window above her head.

Cat nudged Luke. Suddenly, she heard voices outside. Several voices — her heart began to race. Had people been looking for them? She was certain Mimi would be worried sick. What would it look like if they were found like this? In their underwear, wrapped up on a couch; Cat's stomach did a flip at the thought. She nudged Luke even harder.

"Hmmm?" he responded groggily.

"There's someone here!" she hissed in his ear. "Luke, we have to get clothes on. Now!"

What she had said must have registered with him because he was up like a shot and scrambling about the room for their clothes.

"Where are my pants?" Cat spun in her spot, glancing frantically around her.

Cat heard footsteps and voices getting louder. Then, she heard it. The unmistakable creaking of the barn door being opened. They were in the other room. Luke threw her jeans to her as he pulled his own up. Cat was frozen.

When the door to the room swung open, she stood still, paralyzed with her jeans in her hand.

"Oh my!" came Mimi's voice.

"Is this your daughter?" came the voice of the man who was

shining a flashlight in her eyes.

She couldn't see a thing. Had they just said daughter?

"Cathleen Rhodes!" it was her father's voice.

The flashlight turned off so she could see Luke still wrestling with his clothes, two highway patrolmen, Mimi, and to her dismay, her father.

"We'll wait for you two, outside," Mimi said harshly through gritted teeth, looking from Luke to Cat and back again.

The patrolmen followed Mimi without looking back, murmurs and muffled laughter followed them. Her father lingered for a moment before turning on his heel and stomping out. The look was one Cat had never seen and prayed to never see again. She knew this was disastrous.

Luke continued to get dressed. His face was beet red and Cat could hear him swearing under his breath. Real curse words this time, not his usual 'Jiminy Cricket.'

Cat was shaking so hard that she found it difficult to get dressed. In the end, Luke had to help her.

"It'll be okay, Cat," Luke said quietly. "Once they know the story ... I know this looks bad, but ..."

"Looks bad?!" Cat began to cry. "This is bad, Luke. This is the worst thing that could possibly happen. He's going to kill me."

"Why is he here?" Luke asked in a whisper. "Did you know he was coming to town?"

"I don't know," Cat sobbed into her hands. "No, I had no idea."

"They're waiting out there, Cat," Luke took her hand and pulled her off the couch. "We have to go face them."

Cat nodded, though her legs did not want to respond. She felt like she was marching towards the gallows, slow drum beats played in her head.

When they emerged from the barn, she walked beside Luke, not touching him. Her feet faltered and her knee ached from yesterday's fall; Luke gently took her elbow to help her along. His touch steadied tumultuous waves of nausea and nerves Cat was keeping at bay.

"Before you say anything, I feel like I should tell you all what happened," Luke said as Mimi opened her mouth to speak. "The truck got stuck on the river road, so we had to walk to the highway. Cat fell and hurt her knee again so I carried her to the highway. When we got there, I realized I had somehow lost my phone at the river, so we had no way to contact anyone. We came here because there weren't any cars coming along. And we were … like … that … in there … because we were trying to stay warm." Luke took a deep breath in.

Cat had never seen him so unraveled.

None of them looked completely convinced. Her father just looked pissed. He was now shooting daggers at Luke, for even daring to speak.

Mimi cleared her throat, "Thank you, Luke."

The highway patrolman who had held the flashlight spoke, "We're just glad the two of you are alright, regardless of what exactly happened last night." One of them gave Cat a wink; her father caught sight of it as well and Cat noticed his jaw lock into place. She wanted to die right then and there.

"We found the truck on the old river road early this morning," the other highway patrolman said, "and your father just informed us that he owned the barn here. It's a good thing you were able to get here safely."

"Let's get you both to the hospital to be looked over," the first patrolman motioned them towards his SUV.

"I'm fine," Luke spoke up, "But Cat's knee is hurt."

"I'll be okay," Cat found that her voice was barely above a whisper.

"Procedure," the other patrol officer said shortly.

"Cat, your father and I will follow in my truck," Mimi said.

Cat glanced up to her dad. He had not spoken. Cat almost expected to see smoke coming out of his ears. Cat felt tears well up in her eyes. She tried to brace herself for whatever punishment she knew would be coming, as Luke led her to the patrol car.

CHAPTER THIRTY-ONE

"I'M REALLY FINE," CAT REPEATED FOR THE UMPTEENTH TIME AS YET another nurse came in the room to look at her leg.

All she wanted was to see Luke, to see how he was doing. Cat had been ushered to an examining room as soon as they reached Watauga Medical Center. As she left Luke standing in the lobby, she had caught a glimpse of her dad approaching him. She shuddered as she recalled the look in her father's eyes. This couldn't be good. Something inside of her told her that the peace and comfort she had found over the last four months had come to an abrupt halt. So many emotions churned inside of her. She felt like they were playing bumper cars in her brain, her stomach, all over. She literally ached with worry; and of course, she still had no idea what her father was even doing in North Carolina.

"You'll be fine," the nurse smiled as she looked up from Cat's knee. Cat fought the urge to respond with a sarcastic remark and managed a polite smile in return.

"You've just re-sprained it, is all," the nurse continued, as she rewrapped it tightly, "You just sit tight while I go find a doctor to sign your release papers."

"Alright," Cat sighed. She'd been detained long enough. She needed to find Luke and quickly.

Cat watched the nurse leave and she rolled over to face the window. The door opened again.

"Are you sleeping, Cathleen?" her mother's voice said quietly.

Cat jumped at the sound of it.

"Mom?" Cat sat upright to see her mom and Lili coming in.

"What on earth happened, Cat?" Lili asked appraisingly.

"What are you guys doing here?" Cat's emotions overwhelmed her and she felt tears well up in her eyes at the sight of her mother and little sister.

"We wanted to surprise you," her mother smiled. "Thanksgiving is this Thursday and we thought the whole family should be together."

"But we didn't get to Mimi's until two a.m. because of the roads," Lili interrupted, "And there were police there, and you were missing, and well, I guess you know what happened from there."

Cat put her head in her hands. It was too much. Slowly and earnestly, Cat began to tell them what had happened. When she had finished, she looked up but while Lili looked completely convinced, her mother's face bore a look of uncertainty. It was evident her father had spoken to her first.

"That's what Mimi said," Lili said nodding. "I knew it was all a misunderstanding. Told you, Mom"

Cat looked at her mother.

"Cat, you know I love you," her mother began.

"But," Cat interrupted, she could already predict what was coming next.

"But," her mother continued, "Your father is certain about what he saw. And after everything that has happened with you this last year, it is hard to believe you."

Cat felt like she'd been hit with a ton of bricks. Lili stepped back and took a seat in the corner of the room.

"We love you, Cat," she added, "But your father has already decided the next course of action. I'm afraid there's nothing I can do."

"Next course of action?" Cat sat up in her bed. What the hell was she talking about? What was with the formality? She looked at Lili who looked equally confused.

"Lili, will you give us some privacy?" her mom turned to ask.

Lili looked like she was prepared to argue, but something in her mother's face stopped her short.

After the door closed, Cat turned her attention back to her mother.

"We're leaving this afternoon," she said, tears were beginning to form in her eyes.

"I expected you would say that," Cat snapped and crossed her arms. It didn't matter, she would be joining Luke at Appalachian in the fall. They would make it until then, they loved each other.

"You won't be returning to Spence," her mother's voice caught in her throat, "he's, I mean, we are sending you to a boarding school upstate to finish your senior year."

Cat blinked her eyes in disbelief.

"It's Emma Willard," her mother continued, "an excellent school."

Her mother's voice became a mere buzzing sound in the background, while Cat's mind raced through the significance of that statement. She'd heard of Emma Willard and knew it to be a very prestigious school. It was also, to Cat's knowledge, an all girl's school. The chances of having Luke visit her or sneaking away for the weekend to visit him were slim to none. That meant that she wouldn't be seeing her Luke again until they started school at Appalachian in the Fall. A full eight months away.

"Cat?" her mother's voice had become shrill in an effort to get her attention, "Cat? Are you listening to me?"

"Huh?" Cat blinked her eyes as she returned to the pale blue hospital room in which she sat.

"I said your father withdrew your application from Appalachian State University this morning. What were you thinking applying there without consulting with us first, Cathleen?"

"What?!" Cat felt her heart drop to her stomach, "You can't do that! Why would you do that? That's where I want to go to school!"

"Cathleen, I know it's difficult to see now, but following some farm boy to college in North Carolina is not the future you were meant for," her mother's voice had become steely.

"This isn't you talking," Cat sat upright, "I know you don't believe this. Do you know how shallow you sound?"

"You don't speak to your mother that way!" her father's voice boomed from the doorway.

Her mother stepped back into the shadows.

"How could you?" Cat could barely speak. "You can't tell me where to go to school."

"You're right, Cathleen," her father's eyes narrowed. "But I can choose what I pay for. And if you don't go to one of the schools that your mother and I approve of, you won't receive a penny. Not for school, not for anything, ever."

"What are you saying," Cat swallowed hard, "You'll write me out of your will if I don't go to the school you want me to attend?"

Her mom was sniffling quietly.

Her father nodded slowly, "That also includes who you choose to date."

"I don't care what you do," Cat's voice became hoarse in an effort to hold back the tears, "I love him. Do you hear me? LOVE him. Keep your damn money! How dare you think that you can buy me. I'm your daughter."

Cat wasn't even sure at what point her mother ran out of the room in tears. Frankly, she didn't care. She couldn't believe these people were her parents.

Her father held up his hand and Cat was silenced. Old habits die hard. Her brain continued to reel off insults at him while her jaw shut fast.

"I spoke with Luke," her father's voice tinged with amusement. "Nice young man," he added with sarcasm. "I told him I would allow him to tell you goodbye."

With that, her father walked to the door and motioned to someone in the hallway. Luke stepped in quietly. He looked at the floor and barely acknowledged Cat's presence.

"I'll give you two a minute," her father said with an upbeat tone, "Not a second more."

The door closed behind him with an echo.

After a moment of unbearable silence, Luke looked up at her with a sad smile. He slowly walked forward, took her face in his hands, and kissed her in a way that he never had before. It was a good-bye kiss — long, soft, and sweet; it broke Cat's heart. When he stepped back, his eyes were also shining with tears.

"I will always love you, Cathleen Rhodes," he said quietly, before he turned and stepped back to the door.

It took Cathleen's mind a moment before she realized what was happening. "Wait," she called out hoarsely.

Luke's hand stopped on the door handle, but he didn't turn around.

"This isn't over, Luke," her voice pleaded, though she knew his mind was made up. "Whatever my father said to you, it doesn't matter. I love you, Luke. You can't believe this is over."

"It has to be," Luke said in a voice so low Cat could barely make it out.

And then he was gone. Cat's breath held in her throat as the door slammed. She didn't breathe as she heard his footsteps echoing down the hall. When the sound had faded away, with her lungs screaming for air, she began to gasp.

Luke was gone, perhaps indefinitely, and her life would never be the same. Cat folded herself into a ball. That was it — her last life. This — this must be what it feels like to die she thought somberly. All nine lives lost, and in seventeen short years. Well, at least in her last one, she had found love.

About The Author

CHELSEA WILSON THAYER is a writer, theatre educator, wife, and mother of four. She holds her M.A. in Educational Theatre from New York University and works as a writer and theatre practitioner in rural Appalachia. *What Cat Lost* takes place in two very different places: New York City and Boone, NC. Chelsea has been able to call both places her home. She is, at heart, still the city girl her husband met when she moved to the rural Appalachian Mountains. And to this day he is still the country boy who moved to New York City for her so that she could attend graduate school at NYU. Like the characters in her novel, she knows that young love can be intense and confusing. But, most of all, she knows it can be real. Thayer is proud to call the Appalachian Mountains her home. She seeks in her writing to elevate this oft-forgotten and underrepresented corner of the globe. According to her, the Blue Ridge Mountains are certainly the most beautiful place on earth. This is her debut novel.

If you enjoyed *What Cat Lost* be sure to check out **Book 2**

Who Cat Loved

Four years have passed
since Cat and Luke's last pivotal meeting
and the young lovers have gone their separate ways.
With Luke now living and working in New York City,
and Cat now engaged to picture-perfect David,
it would appear that they have moved past
their high-school love affair.
It is only a matter of time before fate
brings them together.
But how will Cat reconcile these unearthed feelings
for Luke with her wedding plans underway
and her parent's expectations higher than ever?

COMING 2021